Moon Vector by Vexteezy.com
Additional cover design feature by CharlVera

Vael El'thyra valdor Asthrae

Molly Chatsworth and the Awakening

S. J. James

MOLLY CHATSWORTH
AND THE
AWAKENING

In the Beginning

In the beginning, the Valdar and their kin, the Valdarie, were both born of the Seraphim, but there were two branches of one sacred lineage: the Valdar, gifted chiefly with the gift of future sight and mind touch; and the Valdarie, who bore within them the deeper spark of sorcery.

These celestial offspring came from the Seraphim (Angels) who abandoned eternity itself. In the sorrowful days following the Great War of Tears, many among the Seraphim laid down their immortality and descended from the shining heights of Seraphinium to live amongst mortals. These were thereafter known as the Halfwings, for when they chose the mortal path, their feathers fell like falling starlight and their wings withered. But the blue fire of their eyes remained, and their ancient wisdom, their strength, and the gifts bound to their blood remained unbroken.

In the first age, in the hallowed reign of Lofiel and Tien, King and Queen of the Seraphim, sovereigns of Seraphinium, came the forbidden children born from a union between Seraphim and Humans. Their children were known as the Nephilim, whose Seraphim fathers sparked the great war. They, the Nephilim, were giants of great might, given to an endless hunger and violence. But, from the Halfwings came children of a gentler nature.

These were the Valdar and the Valdarie, each shaped differently by their celestial heritage. Save for rare exceptions, they were tempered of spirit, humble in heart, and slow to wrath. Their inherited powers changed across the turning of ages, taking new forms. In the Valdar, the gifts unfolded as the sight beyond sight, the touching of minds, and the control of elements; in the Valdarie, the same powers grew sharper still, blooming into the powerful art of sorcery.

But mortal hearts are ever fearful of what they do not understand, casting suspicion upon such gifts. Thus, the Valdarie most skilled in sorcery were branded as witches and warlocks, and blamed for misfortunes that were never theirs to bear. Yet both Valdar and Valdarie endured, walking quietly through the long centuries. In time, they withdrew into silence, carrying their vast lore into hidden places where only whispers could follow until the days of Elithryn.

Though all Valdar bore within them visions of days yet to come, the speaking of mind thoughts, and the grace of profound empathy, it was the Valdarie who mastered the true weaving of sorcery. From their line came the Warlocks and Witches, echoes of the Halfwing's lost glory, carried into the mortal world.

But long ago, before the Halfwings chose mortality, there were others who were forced into exile after the great war, for their crimes against Seraphinium. And while the Halfwings bound themselves to the mortal world, the exiled Seraphims were bound to everlasting shadow. While the Halfwings gave up eternity, they lived an eternity in darkness. They wandered a horror unseen, watching the world through eyes that had forgotten warmth. They began dreaming of a world where the Halfwings and their children were no more. For reasons lost to envy, fear, or wounds so ancient that even memory recoiled from it, they sought the unmaking of all the world, and they waited with a patience colder than winter stone. For one of them believed the fall was not a question of if, but when.

The
The Prophecy

Oceans will rise and lands will fall
If the Five rise up to hear the call
Down below in the earth so deep
A vengeful past in a secret Keep
Hidden from sight and hands to touch
Hidden in the dark from evil's clutch
Suffer you all for the world will weep
If taken from the endless sleep
For vengeance swift will toil and reap

CHAPTERS

Part 1

CHAPTER I

— A DOOR TO DESTINY —

On a lone hilltop before sunrise, a loud noise rang out in the darkness. It crackled and hissed and groaned and rumbled all at once, as curious eyes glistened and glowed in the undergrowth. The strange mixture of sounds invading the hilltop came from the sudden appearance of a cloud. It formed rapidly at the centre of a crumbling stone archway, and probing tentacles of cloud sprouted from its edge, coiling like snakes around the stone of the arch. A busy fox prowling through tall grass nearby stopped at once. This was very strange, she thought, as clouds were normally silent and grew way up in the sky, well away from hills and the business of foxes. This was most definitely not supposed to be here, and she was really rather wishing it would float off and join the rest of the clouds, as clouds could suddenly bring rain, when the cloud opened like a gaping mouth, and four figures jumped out of it.

The first was very short, like a person who had been squashed and then shrivelled like a prune. The other three were most certainly people, two females and a male, much like other people she had seen before, poking about the hill, interfering in a fox's business with their snarling dogs. She sank low amongst the grass and watched these new uninvited visitors closely.

'Arrived we have, at the place you said, while all down there are asleep in bed,' said the short, shrivelled creature.

'Unlike us,' complained a small, skinny, grey-haired woman, brushing white dust and silver speckles from her hair.

The other, taller, plumper woman tutted as she shook her wide-brimmed, blue hat free of the same dust and speckles. 'What is this?' She asked as she watched silver speckles floating to the ground.

'Silver speckles on your hat is all a part of going through that,' said the creature, pointing at the cloud, 'not of concern to one like you, when there's so much more for you to do,' it said, giving her an ugly grin.

'Can't that thing talk normal?' Complained the skinny, grey-haired woman.

'Normal is as normal does, all quite normal to those like us...s,' hissed the creature.

'I believe the house is down that way, madam,' said the man, pointing down the hill.

'Gate Keeper, you will wait as agreed?' Asked the taller woman, addressing the short, shrivelled creature.

'I am bound as we agreed, until you return with the one that's freed. For thirty minutes we can wait, then the laws of time will close that gate,' it replied, flashing a golden timepiece from its pocket. In its other wrinkled hand, it clasped a bunch of golden keys, on a large golden ring, that jingled as it jumped onto a fallen stone block.

'Then we had better not waste any more of that time,' said the taller woman, putting her bright blue hat back on her head. 'You come with me,' she said, turning to the grey-haired woman. 'You wait here, please,' she said to the man. 'That creature is not to be trusted; make sure that it does not close that gate until we get back,' she whispered, as she glanced back at the archway.

'Yes, madam,' replied the man dutifully.

The fox watched curiously as the two women made their way quickly down the hill. This was all very strange, clouds raining people, she had never seen anything like this before, and didn't want to see it again. 'No, not on this hill,' she grumbled, as she kept watch over the two remaining visitors.

A softening of the dark by a slow-rising sun turned the morning's horizon into a deep, rich blue as it crept through the window of a sleepy Molly Chatsworth. Slowly, she opened her eyes. She didn't want to wake up. There was safety and comfort in the sleep she had been pulled from. It had been hard fought for and hard won, and once she had it, she didn't want to let it go. It gave her temporary comfort, a feeling of being somewhere else, much better, and for just a fraction of a second, when she was waking, the horror of yesterday remained at bay.

Yesterday was a Wednesday, and the blustering

afternoon wind and heavy rain brought an urgent knock at the front door. Molly was lying on her bed, busily trying to please her mother by reading a rather boring book by *Arlo Drewsworthy*, called *The Wonderful World of Magical Water Plants.* She was halfway through page thirty-two when she heard the welcome sound of the door knocker wrap hard against the front door. As the sound of the wrapping bounced off the walls and up toward Molly's bedroom, *Arlo Drewsworthy* and his *World of Magical Water Plants* found themselves spinning through the cosmos of her room, to the floor, as she slid off the side of her bed. Her father was expected back today, after a long trip away, and all would be right with her world once more, and maybe, at last, this was him. She hadn't been feeling very well lately; she felt tired, like her body was moving in sludge, and dizziness came with it. Her mother had given her all sorts of nasty-tasting things to drink to help a sickly feeling she had, go away, but it hadn't helped in the slightest. Her mother even seemed to be irritated that she was feeling unwell at all, often dismissing her description of symptoms as her overactive imagination. But what made it all far worse were the strange, unexplainable things that kept happening around her. Seeing things that she couldn't explain, hearing voices she couldn't explain, objects moving on their own, the wild dreams and nightmares. That she hadn't shared. She was beginning to think she had some terrible disease and that madness came with it. But the fear of what she was going through was outweighed by the fear of what might happen to her. She didn't want to be shipped off to a hospital, in the middle of nowhere, to be poked and prodded by a group of unfriendly doctors, just to be declared bonkers. No, it was best kept to herself, wasn't it? The one thing that had kept her going was her father coming back today; he could make her feel better again, maybe she should tell him, and he could make it all go away. She skipped quickly from her room to the top of the stairs. Lucy, the housemaid, scuttled across the hallway to answer the door. Molly held her breath in anticipation, expecting to see a cab driver with her father's bags. Opening the door, Lucy revealed a rain-soaked policeman.

'Afternoon, miss, Constable Ferris,' he said, tipping his hat. 'I've come to see the lady of the house, Mrs Chatsworth.'

'Oh yes, afternoon, sir, please come in,' said Lucy, stepping aside. 'I'll just get her, sir,' she said, closing the door.

Molly stepped halfway down the stairs and sat down with a disappointed thud, because it wasn't who she had hoped for. Rain scattered from the Constable's cape and hat, like a big wet dog, showering the hall rug. Something was obviously wrong, thought Molly. A policeman had never been to the house before. Why now? And where was her father? The Constable shot her a fleeting look. 'Evening, miss,' he said, rubbing and blowing on his hands to warm them up. He didn't smile or even make eye contact, not wanting to give away his reason for being there. His manner made her feel nervous; butterflies fluttered in her stomach, something horrible had arrived with the constable, something floating around unseen, something waiting to pounce. Molly's mother, Virginia, came hurriedly into the hall with Lucy, trailing behind her.

'Hello, Constable, is something wrong?'

'Good afternoon, madam. I'll u.... h, get to the point if I may.'

'Please do, Constable,' said Virginia with a nervous laugh.

'I'm afraid there's been an accident.'

'An accident!' exclaimed Virginia.

'Yes, madam.'

'Really, well, how can we help?'

'U.. h, no madam, I'm afraid you can't, I'm afraid...it involves your husband.'

'My husband,' said Virginia, swallowing hard.

Molly stood up with a gasp.

'Yes, madam, the u...h train, carrying Mr Chatsworth,' the Constable cleared his throat, 'u.. h hum, derailed outside of Bridge Norton. I'm afraid the report we have is that everyone on board has been...lost.'

Molly gripped the bannister. Her mother's eyes watered with tears, closing slowly, as she put a hand to her forehead. 'Constable, I think you had better explain,' said Virginia, half dropping, half sitting down on to the hall chair. 'How do you know my husband was aboard that train?'

'He has been identified, madam, as Edward Chatsworth, that is your husband's name?' replied the Constable.

'Yes,' said Virginia in a disappointed tone.

'He was carrying identification that showed this property as being his home address.'

A lump appeared in Molly's throat she couldn't swallow. 'It must be another Edward Chatsworth, they...they must have made a mistake!' Spouted Molly from the stairs, as a coat rack on the wall in the hall began to tremble.

'I'm afraid there is no mistake, miss,' said the Constable, giving her that fleeting glance again.

'No mother, he's wrong, he's wrong, he has to be, dad's coming home, I know he is.'

'Please, Molly, you're not helping,' said Virginia snappily.

That something horrible that Molly had felt came in with the Constable, had pounced, smothering any and all happiness. The rack full of coats, hats, and umbrellas suddenly leapt from the wall and fell onto Constable Ferris. 'Oh dear, I'm so sorry, Constable,' said Lucy as she tried to untangle him, as he rolled around in the coats and umbrellas on the floor. 'It must have come loose.'

Virginia looked up toward Molly on the stairs with a look of blame. But Molly didn't care. The rack, her mother's hard stares, the Constable, Lucy chattering, it all faded into the background as she turned and climbed the stairs back to her room. Her tears fell harder than the rain outside as she curled up on her bed, wishing for *Arlo Drewsworth's World of Magical Water Plants* to fill her world once more.

But now it was morning, and like a sudden invasion, an army of memories from yesterday had come marching back, bringing with it a horrible, smothering feeling of emptiness. A thrush landed on her bedroom windowsill outside and hopped forward to get a better look at her. Seeing the curious bird, Molly sat up, propping her elbows on the window shelf, and placing her chin on her cupped hands, she whispered. 'Take me away, turn me into a bird, like you, and let's fly away together.' The thrush chirped as if to answer, as if he could understand what she was saying, which he could, of course. Birds are a lot brighter than you think you know, and some more than others. He was just about to explain how it wasn't possible, as he wasn't a magic bird, unlike some, and how he wished he could help, when he was disturbed by something in the garden and flew away. As Molly searched the garden for any sign of the thrush, through the dim morning light, she noticed two mysterious figures crossing the lawn to the rear of the house.

Downstairs, the patio doors to the living room rattled and shook. Loud whispers slipped through the air. Molly pressed her face against the window, glimpsing the two figures once more as they entered the house. Raised but muffled voices rose upward from downstairs. Molly jumped off her bed, eyeing up her wardrobe as a place to hide, but curiosity drove her to open her door a little first. Downstairs, the voices grew louder until there was another noise, a clattering and crunching as if something had been broken, and then, silence. Molly gasped as she heard the sound of the stairs creak from somebody on their way up. She shut the door quietly as the footsteps trod their way down the hall toward her bedroom.

She stepped back from the door as the footsteps stopped outside. There was no time to hide in the wardrobe now as the door handle creaked and turned. As all door handles do, of course, in situations like this. The door swung open, and there, framed in the doorway in a bright blue hat, stood her grandmother, Grand Sally. If there was one face in the world that Molly wanted to see, other than her father, it was her grandmother. There she stood with a big, beaming smile. Molly ran straight into her arms. 'Grandma! That was you I saw from the window. I'm so glad you're here, it's been so long. Everything's a big mess, and I don't know what to do,' she sobbed.

'I know, I know, my poor dear,' said Grand Sally, cupping Molly's face between her hands. 'I know all about it, it's terrible. But how about a nice little holiday? You can come and stay with me for a while. Would you like that?'

'Oh Grandma, I'd love to, but. No, wait! Grandma, Dad's gone. He's dead, they're saying.'

'Yes, I know, they say a lot, don't they!'

'Grandma!' Exclaimed Molly, not understanding

why she wasn't at all upset. 'You do know what's happened, right?'

'Oh yes, but there are a few things you don't know. I'll explain everything on the way. Come along, let's go, there's not much time.'

Molly gathered yesterday's clothes, slipping them on quickly.

'What about mother?' She said, tying up her last shoelace.

'Don't worry about your mother, leave her to me. Quickly now. There's no time to lose.'

Grand Sally grabbed her by the hand and swept her out of the bedroom, back down the hall, and down the stairs. 'Grandma, what's the hurry?'Asked Molly as she was whisked down the next hall and into the living room. 'Mrs P!' You're here as well. But what are you doing to Lucy?'

Mrs P, or Mrs Peabody as she was known, the skinny, grey-haired woman, was sitting on top of a red-faced Lucy, whose hands were now tied behind her back.

'Yes, Mrs Peabody, what are you doing?' demanded Grand Sally.

'It was 'er own fault, she wouldn't stop struggling or be quiet,' answered Mrs Peabody.

'I said to watch her, not tie her up and sit on her,' said Grand Sally, rolling her eyes.

'Help! Yelled Lucy.

'See what I mean,' said Mrs Peabody.

'Never mind her, let's get going, quickly,' ordered Grand Sally.

'Grandma, where are we going? What's the hurry? Asked Molly again as she was pulled through the doorway and out onto the lawn.

'Don't worry, dear, it will all become clear,' answered Grand Sally.

Virginia ran into the living room, tying her dressing gown as she entered. 'Just what is going on? Why are the doors open? And why are you tied up?'

'I'm sorry, Mrs Chatsworth, I tried to stop them, honest I did,' said Lucy, struggling to get up.

'Oh my word. Stop who?' Said Virginia, her voice tightening.

'The other Mrs Chatsworth, Mr Chatsworth's mother, she's taken Molly.'

'She's what!' Exclaimed Virginia, helping Lucy to

her feet and untying the cord around her wrists.

'I'm so sorry, madam,' said Lucy again, rubbing her sore wrists, 'I heard a noise, came to have a look and found the pair of them breaking in. Mrs P, they called her, wrestled me to the floor and tied me up. I'm so sorry, madam, she took me by surprise.'

'It's not your fault, Lucy,' replied Virginia, already shoving her feet into her shoes. 'I'm going after them.'

'I'll call the police, Madam,' said Lucy.

'No, don't! Snapped, Virginia, I'll deal with this.'

Lucy hesitated. 'As you like, madam, then I'll come with you...just to make sure you come to know harm.'

Grand Sally, Mrs Peabody, and Molly had reached the common below the hill in double quick time.

'Gran, I really don't understand where we're going,'

'Just up the hill and we're home free,' said Grand Sally breathlessly.

'Why? People only go up here to get married, why...' Molly saw the cloud, rippling in the stone archway on top of the hill. 'Wow, that's the Door of Destiny, what's happened to it?'

'It's our way home, now let's hurry, and you Mrs Peabody, hurry,' shouted Grand Sally, tugging Molly by the hand behind her.

'Alright, I'm comin', I'm comin',' puffed Mrs Peabody.

Virginia was halfway across the common, with Lucy trying to catch up. 'Molly, stop,' she yelled angrily.

Molly looked back.

'Don't listen, Molly, keep going,' said Grand Sally.

Finally, they reached the top of the hill.

'Harold?' said Molly, breathing heavily, 'you as well.'

'Someone's got to keep an eye on 'er ladyship,' replied Harold, winking.

Molly pulled back on her grandmother's hand with a gasp when she saw the shrivelled creature.

'Don't worry, Molly, he won't do you know harm, just stay by me,' said Grand Sally reassuringly.

Molly stood behind her grandmother, looking

around the side of her coat at this strange thing that stood on a stone block. 'What is it?' She asked, grimacing.

'It's a Sepricorn, something you'll never have the misfortune to meet again, I hope,' replied Grand Sally.

'Almost time, late, late, late, a few more minutes and I'll shut the gate,' said the Sepricorn urgently, hopping off the block and waving his timepiece.

'You two, get yourselves back home now,' ordered Grand Sally to Harold and Mrs Peabody.

'Don't 'ang around Sally, or you'll be stuck 'ere,' warned Mrs Peabody.

'Yes, yes, stop fussing, hurry up, get through, and we'll follow.'

The Gate Keeper jumped into the mouth of the cloud. Then Mrs Peabody stepped in, disappearing into the fog. Molly couldn't believe what she was seeing. Was this all a wild dream again, and just another part of her madness disease?

'Now you, Harold, hurry now,' said Grand Sally.

'Are you sure, Madam? Asked Harold, looking at the Gate Keeper suspiciously.

'We'll be fine, hurry now.'

'Yes, Madam. Right, see you on the other side, folks,' said Harold, disappearing into the cloud.

Virginia was almost at the top of the hill.

'Hold my arm tight, Molly, we're going through now,' said Grand Sally urgently.

Molly let go of her grandmother's arm and stepped back. 'But going through to where? What is this?'

'Late you are, late, late, late, one more minute and I'll shut the gate,' repeated the Sepricorn, jangling his keys.

'Molly! Stay right there, don't move,' yelled Virginia, arriving at the top of the hill. 'Conjuring Sepricorns, Sally, you should know better. Molly, please step away. Step away, or there's no turning back. I know everything is confusing right now, and you're upset. I know you want answers, let's go home and talk about it,' said Virginia, offering her hand.

'So, you've seen one of these things before?' Said Molly, confused, looking from her mother back to her grandmother.

'She's seen it all before,' said Grand Sally, 'And as

for answers, we all know your answers, Virginia.'

'Why couldn't you just leave us alone?' Said Virginia angrily.

'Alone! You've been alone for far too long, hiding down here in the dark,' said Grand Sally, 'time to come into the light.'

'Sally! Molly's father, your son, my husband...'

'My son,' snapped Grand Sally angrily, 'Whatever's going on, Virginia, we will find out.'

'What is going on?' demanded Molly

'I don't know what you mean, Sally, Edwards gone,' said Virginia, taking a step closer toward them.

'Really, Virginia, is he really?' said Grand Sally.

'I don't know what you mean, but please leave Molly out of it.'

'Out of it, she's right in the middle of it,' said Grand Sally, stepping in front of Molly.

'Sally, don't you dare take her,' said Virginia.

'Why, because she might finally know the truth.'

'What truth?' yelled Virginia.

'Yes, what truth?' said Molly.

'The truth you've been denying all her life, Virginia,' said Grand Sally, turning to Molly. 'Feeling sick? Seeing things that you can't explain?'

'Well, yes, but how did you...'

'Because the same thing happened to me when I was your age, and your mother!'

Molly couldn't believe what she was hearing as she looked at her mother, waiting for a reply. 'Mum. You knew why I've been feeling ill? I thought I was going mad.'

'You're not going mad,' said Grand Sally. 'If you want to know more, trust me, and come with me now,' she said, offering her hand.

The Gate Keeper began to count as he looked through his keys. 'Five is for the ones that dally, four is for the few that rally.'

Molly did want answers, answers to everything that she had been going through, and she knew, in her heart, that she wouldn't get them from her mother. 'I'm sorry, mum, I have to know what's going on, I have to know what's happening to me.'

'Three is for the chimes of fate,' said the Gate Keeper.

Molly stood alongside her grandmother, and they both jumped into the swirling cloud together. Lucy arrived breathlessly at the top of the hill as Virginia made a sudden dash towards the arch.

'And two is for the dead that wait, but one is for you, who is far too late,' said the Sepricorn, disappearing into the cloud. The cloud tentacles withdrew as Virginia made a sudden run toward it. As she leapt at the cloud, it gave a rumble like thunder and a loud crack, and the cloud evaporated into thin air. Virginia landed face down in the archway with a thud. There was no trace of the cloud in the arch, leaving her, a bewildered Lucy, and a very confused fox, alone, in silence on the top of Bramblewood Hill.

CHAPTER II

— 10 PLUMBERRY ROAD —

'Gran, it's too dark, where are you?' Said Molly in a loud whisper.

'It's alright, I'm right here, darling,' said her grandmother, 'I'm right next to you. Your eyes will adjust in a second.'

Fumbling about, she found her grandmother's coat and clung to it tightly. She blinked rapidly to get her eyes to focus. As they gradually became accustomed to the darkness, a long, circular tunnel stretched out before her, its surface shimmering like water. 'Where are we? What is this place?'

'The place between, hardly seen, the place forbidden where few have been,' answered the Gate Keeper, creeping up alongside her.

Molly could just make out the twisted look of his ugly, wrinkled face, shrouded beneath a hat, on his fat, neckless head.

'Don't listen, Molly,' said her grandmother, taking her by the arm, 'keep hold of my coat and keep moving.'

Molly's eyes widened as something twinkled in the dark ahead. Something was drifting slowly towards them. Gold and silver coins floating in the air came into view. Then a pair of steel-rimmed glasses, an old shoe, a woman's leather purse, and a silver watch. 'Whose are these?' Muttered Molly beneath her breath as they passed. A gold necklace with a green stone twisted and turned through the darkness like a slithering eel toward her, twirling around above her head. She looked up.

'Ta...ke it, ta...ke it,' whispered the Sepricorn. 'Golden, green, all shiny and bright, left by another who strayed from the light. It's yours, take it.'

Curiosity beckoned as Molly reached for the pendant, when the hand of her grandmother snatched her hand away. 'Don't touch anything! Anything you take requires payment,' she said snappily.'

'No fun,' grumbled the Sepricorn.

'Hurry up, Sally, or the gate will close this end,' echoed Mrs Peabody's voice from the other end of the tunnel.

'Hurry, hurry, time is ticking,' said the Gatekeeper with a sly grin.

Nearing the end, Harold appeared through the gloom, waiting in the mouth of the gate. 'Quickly, madam, quickly.' Grand Sally hurried to the end of the tunnel, pulling Molly with her. Harold took Molly by the arm, swinging her out of the tunnel to Mrs Peabody outside.

'Okay, dearie, I've got you.'

White dust and silver speckles fell from Molly's hair, floating away on the morning breeze. Grand Sally and Harold jumped out of the gate as it began to rumble around them.

'A bargain struck, the deal is done, returned, you have with more than one. Take your gold, I think I will, for returning you safely from the hill.'

'Only just,' said Grand Sally sharply. 'Here's your gold, now be gone with you,' she said, throwing him some gold coins. The Sepricorn took off his hat, leaning out of the gate, using his hat to catch the gold coins as they dropped down through the air in front of him. 'Stand back, Molly,' said Grand Sally, guiding her backwards. They were standing in a dry pool with a huge fountain at the centre. The fountain had been divided in the middle, giving way to the Sepricorn's gate. He gave his ugly smile as tentacles of cloud wrapped around him, and, with a slow wave of his hand, the gate closed, folding in on itself. The fountain clunked and groaned as it folded back to its original form. 'Are you alright, darling?' said Grand Sally, putting a comforting arm around Molly's shoulder.'

'I think so, gran,' said Molly, brushing more white dust from her hair.

Water began trickling down the statues on the fountain. 'Quickly, let's get out of here before we get soaked,' said Harold. 'Up we go,' he said, helping Molly over the step and out of the pond. Just as they all stepped out onto the grass, the water bubbled out of the fountain flutes once more, one after the other, bursting into life and emptying their frothing water into the pool. A man walking his dog stood staring nearby, unable to understand what he had just witnessed.

'Good morning, lovely day,' said Grand Sally. 'Wave everyone, act natural,' she said through a forced smile.

'Natural!' Exclaimed Mrs Peabody. 'It would have been easier to take the car.'

Harold tipped his hat as the man shook his head and walked on quickly, which was much easier than trying to come up with a rational explanation for what he had just seen.

'Let's get indoors before the whole common fills up with nosey dog walkers,' said Grand Sally.

'Where are we, gran?' asked Molly.

'Plumberry Road, darling, my house is over th....'

'You do realise this is 1938, we have cars, trains, and even aeroplanes now?' A man in a white cloak approached quickly across the grass, with two other men following behind.

'Blimey, now we're in trouble,' said Mrs Peabody.

'Oh, Grandmaster, and Baradium, and Mr u...m,' said Grand Sally, unable to recall the other man's name.'

'Mr Parks, Yaddersley Parks, madam,' he said,

irritated at not being remembered.

'What a surprise,' said Grand Sally.

'I imagine it is,' said Baradium, 'you have violated every law we have. Acquiring dangerous spell books and conjuring Sepricorn's, that was hardly going to go unnoticed.'

'Well u...h.'

'Yes, every law broken,' said Yaddersley, echoing Baradium.

'Read the law, Yaddersley, please,' ordered Baradium.

The Grandmaster, in his white cloak, crossed his arms and watched on as Yaddersley produced a thick, heavy book and flipped through the pages.

'Ah ha, here we are, under Valdarie law, page 55, *Objects of Paranormal Interest,* i. e., said Spell Book, section 5, paragraph 3.'

Yadersley took a deep breath.

'No Valdar, shall obtain without special authorisation an *Object of Paranormal Interest.* If obtained by persuasion, by purloining, or by barter, for personnel or private use, with the intention of personal gain, the *Object of Paranormal Interest law,* is deemed broken. *Objects of Paranormal Interest* that are deemed dangerous to the general public, and can alter the natural laws of time, past, present, or future, are listed below in subparagraph 5a.' Yaddersley took another deep breath as he readied himself to read the list in subparagraph 5a. 'Number one...'

'That's enough, Yaddersley, thank you, I think the point has been made,' said the Grandmaster, cutting him off.

'But sir,' protested Yaddersley.

'But sir is right,' said Baradium firmly. 'Laws broken and we've only just started. All the houses will have to be informed and the Council of Twelve.'

'Now she's for it, I did warn her, didn't I, but would she listen, oh no, she knew best, what a mess,' said Mrs Peabody, folding her arms.

'A big mess, a plumberry mess,' said Harold, shaking his head.

'Grandmaster,' said Grand Sally, addressing the man in the white cloak, 'I can explain, of course.'

'I'm sure you can, Sally, but Baradium is right, you have broken many Valdar laws.'

'Expulsion, that's the only course of action,' said Baradium.

Molly stood with Harold and Mrs Peabody, standing back a little way from all the excitement. Yes, this was Plumberry Park alright, right opposite her grandmother's house, a park she had been in many times when she was little.

'Expulsion from the Valdar, there's no other course,' spouted Baradium, a vein pulsating on his forehead.

'Now just one minute,' said Grand Sally, her cheeks flushing an angry red. 'Crossing me would not be wise, Baradium.'

'Yes, one moment, Baradium, please,' said the Grandmaster calmly, 'we will discover the why, and then we'll deal with the what.'

'Grandmaster, I must protest...'

'I'm sure you must, and I'm sure you will, Baradium. But I find it is always more prudent not to shoot. and then ask questions later.'

'The Valdar Council will know about this, Grendellbar, and we will take action,' said Baradium, waving an accusing finger at Grand Sally.

'Well, as I am head of the Valdar Council, and I am the Grandmaster, with the authority over all twelve of you, I look forward to hearing what you and the council conclude, putting your personal preference aside, that is,' said Grendellbar. 'Now, perhaps we should remove ourselves from this park, and retire to your house, Sally, to less exposed surroundings.'

'You Chatsworths, you're more trouble than you're worth,' hissed Baradium. 'Come along, Yaddersley, we have work to do; let's leave them to their plotting. Mark my words, Grendellbar, the Council will rule on this.'

'Mark his words,' said Yaddersley parrot fashion.

Baradium trounced off toward the park gate with Yaddersley in pursuit.

'He will do what he says,' said Grendellbar, shaking his head.

Grand Sally responded with a big sigh.

'Harold, how is this possible? What have we just done? What was that thing in the tunnel? And who are those men?' Asked Molly.

'Excellent questions, miss,' said Harold nervously,

scratching his head. 'Questions I would normally do my best to answer, but, under the circumstances, I fink they're best answered by 'er ladyship.'

'Perfect answer, Harold,' said Mrs Peabody, smirking.

'Molly, I'm so glad you are safe and sound,' said the Grandmaster, his white cloak twirling as he turned and walked toward Molly. 'I'm so very pleased to meet you once again, and all grown up, I see. I'm Grandmaster Grendellbar.'

'So, we've met before then?' asked Molly, raising a confused eyebrow.

'We did, but that was when you were a baby and, a very cute one, I might add.'

She looked Grendellbar up and down. Striking handsome in his appearance, he had long white hair, tied in a ponytail, and a long white beard draped over the front of his cloak.

'Well, Sally, let's move this conversation inside, shall we? I have a few questions of my own.

'Of course, Grandmaster,' said Grand Sally, rolling her eyes as she glanced at Molly.

As they passed through the big iron gate of the

park, there stood Grand Sally's house, standing in a long line of tall, white, terraced Kensington houses. Molly had a warm feeling as she walked up the steps to the front door. She had fond memories of this house, even though they were foggy. She was four years old when they left. Why had it been so long?

'Alright, me darlin,' said Mrs Peabody, affectionately stroking Molly's face, as they stepped into the hall.

'Stop fussing over the poor girl,' said Grand Sally snappily as she dumped her hat and coat on Mrs Peabody.

'Oh, thank you, madam. Anything else, madam?' replied Mrs Peabody sarcastically. 'I'm your 'ousekeeper, not a coat stand.'

'Don't be impertinent, woman! Run along and do some housekeeping then, make tea or something,' said Grand Sally, marching off down the hall.

'Better do as I'm told then, there's no dealing with 'er when she gets like this,' said Mrs Peabody, rolling her eyes.

'Yes, I fink the hedge needs trimming,' better off out of it,' said Harold, winking at Molly.

'That will be a feat, 'said the Grandmaster, smirking at Molly, 'considering there are no hedges.'

Mrs Peabody and Harold headed for the kitchen. Molly and Grendellbar followed Grand Sally down the long hallway, into a large living room at the rear of the house. A sumptuous room, it had long, heavy green velvet curtains at the windows, a big red sofa and two armchairs to match. Pictures of people and places, hung on the walls, all around the room, but the largest of all hung over the fireplace, it was of Alfred Chatsworth, Molly's grandfather. Grendelbar pushed his white cloak aside and sat down on the sofa. Molly stood next to her grandmother as she sat down in one of the armchairs. Grendellbar cleared his throat. 'And how did Virginia feel about what amounts to a...kidnap?'

Grand Sally tutted. 'Kidnap indeed. She wasn't very happy.'

'I should think not, replied Grendellbar, raising his eyebrows. 'And when I said to Molly, all safe and sound, I was referring to your engagement of the Sepricorn, who are mischievous and untrustworthy. You and Molly could have been stuck, neither in this world nor the next. And to conjure it, you acquired a book of spells and a very rare one at that.'

'Really, Grandmaster, I don't think...'

'I said rare,' he said, interrupting her, 'but I should have said it was dangerous. You went to see Mr Athelmaze and tricked your way into his library. You used my name to gain favour and then stole one of his books, a feat in itself. I admire and commend your ingenuity,' continued Grendellbar.

'O...h thank you, Grandmaster,' said Grand Sally pompously.

'That wasn't a compliment,' said Grendellbar sternly.

Funny, thought Molly, it certainly did sound like one and she was eager to hear more, now seeing her grandmother as a criminal mastermind. Her grandmother's popularity with Molly, which was already high, was now going through the roof.

'But of course, he eventually discovered the book was missing and contacted me. I don't mind my name being used, but when it's used to steal something immeasurably problematic as this book...'

'I believed Molly to be in extreme danger,' said

Grand Sally, interrupting him.

Molly stiffened, looking at her grandmother.

'I'm sure you did, but creating more wasn't a very good move.'

'I've dealt with more than Sepricorn's, as you very well know,' said Grand Sally, giving Grendellbar a knowing look. 'It was.... it was the quickest way.'

'A Keeper's feelings of danger can mean many things, Sally, and not necessarily as you have interpreted them.'

'Spells, Keepers,' what did all this mean, thought Molly?

'Whatever the situation, it does not excuse you from conjuring a Sepricorn.'

'Grendellbar, with the risk of repeating myself, I've been a Valdar a very long time, I'm an old hand, you could say, I was aware of the risks when I conjured it, but as you can see, we're all here, safe and sound, as you so delicately put it.'

There was another word Molly hadn't heard before, Valdar, and her grandmother said that she was one, what was it?

'The fact remains you broke the rules when

you...'

'Grandmaster!' Said Grand Sally loudly, interrupting Grendellbar. 'My son Edward is very much alive, I...'

'I know,' replied Grendellbar firmly.

'You do!'

'He is!' said Molly excitedly.

'What do you think we do all day Sally, sit around drinking tea.'

Grendellbar stood up and walked over to the fireplace, looking up at the portrait of Alfred, Molly's grandfather. 'My dear old friend, if only you were here now.'

Grand Sally slumped back into her chair, lowering her head. 'Part of me is glad he's not; he would have been horrified.'

'My father's alive,' said Molly, standing on her tiptoes with excitement.

'Edward had left the train before it derailed,' said the Grandmaster, smiling reassuringly at Molly. 'The dead man, identified as Edward, had some papers on him, planted deliberately, to persuade the authorities of who he was.'

'Left the train, I don't understand,' said Molly, 'but why?'

'How do you know all of this? Asked Grand Sally in a frustrated tone.

'Because I was having him followed. Crystalian was watching him. He was there one minute and gone the next. Crystalian had to jump from the train before it derailed.'

Grand Sally's eyes widened in surprise.

'How is that possible? He vanished?

'Anything is possible, we just have to work out how,' replied Grendellbar. 'May I ask, how did you know he was alive?'

'If my son were dead, I would know. That's the downside of having these abilities. I would have felt his death. I can feel him now, he's alive and when I get my hands on him.'

Grendellbar continued to study Grandpa Alfred's portrait. 'Molly, do you know what your grandmother does, I mean, besides being your grandmother, of course?'

Molly looked at her grandmother, confused by the question.

‘Of course not, she doesn’t know anything. Virginia and Edward would never hear of it,’ replied Grand Sally.

Molly looked at her grandmother and then back at Grendellbar.

‘Wouldn’t hear of what?’ She asked curiously.

‘Allow me to explain,’ said Grendellbar, turning around to face Molly. ‘Your grandmother is, what is known as, a Time Keeper and as a Time Keeper that also makes her a Valdar.’

Molly raised a questioning eyebrow. ‘What is a Valdar?’

‘Valdar work within the light, for good and the benefit of others. They also come in many forms, with special abilities. Your grandmother, as a Time Keeper, can see fragments in time, of a person’s past, or forward into a possible future, and they are a link, a bridge, to a place where time does not exist, also known as the afterlife.’

Molly looked at her grandmother in amazement.

‘Then there are Intuitives,’ continued Grendellbar, ‘who are extremely sensitive to the vibrations around them and the information they provide. White Witches who have mastery of spells and ancient knowledge of healing and natural medicines. Empaths who can feel and read other people's emotions. Telepaths, who can move objects with the power of their mind. That's just some of the talent that dwells within the Valdar.'

'Wow,' said Molly.

'Wow indeed. But we were once scattered. Keeping our talents hidden as a secret, but to the privy few, hiding in the shadows. A man named Elithryn sought to give us all a home, a beacon, to bring as many Valdar and their abilities under one banner, bringing them all out of the shadows and creating an invincible force for good in the world. And so Elithryn created the Hall of Valdar, a vast building of knowledge and wonder. Elithryn had a passionate belief in Astrology, the stars, the planets, their alignment in the cosmos and the Zodiac calendar.'

'What is the Zodiac calendar?' said Molly, raising her hand, like she was in school.

'The Zodiac calendar was started many thousands of years ago. Each month of the year is represented by a sign, taken from the stars and the shapes derived from them, from January through to December. Headed by a council of twelve, the Lords of Valdar. Each Valdar Lord represents a sign of the zodiac, and as Grandmaster, and I oversee them. In creating the Valdar, Elithryn formed a huge network of people, a brilliance of light against the dark, even in other countries. All can be recognised by the Valdarie symbol, like this one.'

Grendellbar turned to show her a silver star pinned to his cloak. Molly moved closer to get a better look. 'Its called the Valdenium star.'

'Wow,' said Molly as she studied its intricate markings.

'You may be suffering from what you think are hallucinations, hearing things you can't explain, nausea, dizziness?'

'Yes, I am, it's been awful. I thought I was going mad,' said Molly with a sigh.

'You are a Valdar, and you're certainly not going mad,' said Grendellbar reassuringly.

'So, I'm different then,' said Molly with a feeling of disappointment.

'No, darling, you're not different, you're special,' said Grand Sally, taking Molly's hand. 'We are all special, talented, like an artist, like a painter, or a sculptor. You have a unique gift.'

'So, I'm definitely not going mad,' said Molly, wanting extra reassurance.

'Absolutely, most definitely not,' said Grand Sally firmly.'

'It's what is referred to as the *Awakening*,' continued Grendellbar. 'The mental barriers of the mind are held up for most, but for people like us, they drop. You will see, hear, and experience things you don't understand, but it's nothing to be afraid of. And your mother did not help?'

'She knew I didn't feel well, but I didn't tell her the rest, I didn't want to be taken away,' replied Molly, looking at her grandmother.

'She knew,' said Grand Sally with a disapproving frown.

Grendellbar closed his eyes, removing his glasses and rubbing the bridge of his nose in frustration at Virginia's lack of compassion. 'There is a whole history out there for you to embrace, Molly.'

'Poor dear,' said Grand Sally, stroking Molly's hair. 'What you must have been going through.'

'The Awakening is something we all went through at your age, Molly. It is easier for some than others, but with a little help, you'll be fine,' said Grendellbar.

'Awakening to what? What does that mean exactly? What's going to happen?' Said Molly anxiously.

Grendellbar scratched his white beard. 'Well, now, how to explain it a little better? U.. m. You may grow another head, or maybe even a leg or two, but..'

'I'll what!' said Molly with a gasp, as Grand Sally laughed into her hand. 'Oh yes, very funny. Hà, ha,' she said as the joke suddenly became obvious. 'No, really, what will happen?'

'Waking from one way of being, to another,' answered Grendellbar. 'Abilities that will awaken within you, like the ones I have described and others have within the Valdar. Any unfortunate symptoms you may have, like nausea or dizziness, can be relieved. Your grandmother can acquire a remedy for it.'

'As long as I don't get any nasty things like mum

gave me.'

'I expect she was trying to cure you, not help you,' said Grand Sally with a disapproving puff from her lips.

'Ar...e mum and dad a part of this, are they, Valdar as well?' Asked, Molly intrigued.

'U.. m they are but...' replied Grendellbar, quickly interrupted by Grand Sally.

She sat up, moving forward on her chair, giving Grendellbar a discreet shake of her head. 'Ahem! Molly, would you go and find Mrs Peabody for me and see what's happening to the tea?'

'Tea! Now!' said Molly.

'Yes, tea, that's what I said, and now please.'

'But gran, I want to know more, I want to...'

'Now!' Said Grand Sally firmly, 'and make sure she is not on her way to India to pick it, please, the tea that is.'

'Al...right,' said Molly, stomping off to the door, annoyed at being prevented from hearing anymore. This was her mother and father, after all, not just anybody. Tea wasn't important, and this was. Turning around, she shot Grendellbar a frustrated look.

'We will talk again,' said Grendellbar reassuringly, 'there's a whole new world for you to embrace now.'

'Close the door properly,' said Grand Sally after her.

The door clicked shut.

'She is bursting with questions, Sally; you can't keep it all from her.'

'I'm not going to, but she's not ready for all of it yet; she didn't know anything a few hours ago,' said Grand Sally, lowering her voice. 'Her father's complete betrayal, her mother's abandonment of all that she is, learning she's different, I think that's more than enough. The rest can wait for another day.'

'Bringing her back to London could put her in more danger.'

'Which is more dangerous,' snapped Grand Sally, 'to leave her to go quietly mad down there in Bramblewood, with a mother that refuses to accept what she is and an unreachable father?

'Virginia is not going to just let this go, you know that.'

'Don't you worry, I'm ready for her, whatever she comes with.'

'Very well. But keep her close, keep her safe.'

CHAPTER III

— SMELL MEMORIES —

Molly stomped into the hall, closing the living room door firmly behind her, very unhappy at being shut out of the conversation. She looked back down the hall when she heard a knock at the front door. Mrs Peabody came from the kitchen quickly to answer it. Opening the door, a tall blonde man with a blonde beard stepped in.

'Good evening, madam. I believe the Grandmaster is here?'

'U...h, yes, sir, in the living room,' said Mrs Peabody, appearing to know who he was.

'Thank you, I'll see myself there,' he replied.

Two more men stepped in behind him, introducing themselves to Mrs Peabody as Mr Browelowe and Mr Whatley.

'Who is this?' Thought Molly? As the tall blonde man strode confidently down the hall toward her.

'Good afternoon, my name is Avindor. You must be Edward's daughter; I can see the likeness.'

'Uh, yes,' said Molly, shaking his offered hand and a little in awe at this new man's striking appearance.

Browelowe and Whatley caught up, giving Molly hard, unfriendly frowns as they passed by, shutting the living room door firmly behind them.

'Is that Edward's daughter?' said Whatley in alarm, on the other side of the door.

'What of it?' said Grand Sally defensively.

Watching Mrs Peabody return to the kitchen, Molly moved closer to the living room door. Bending down, she looked through the keyhole. Voices coming from the other side of the door quickly became loud and disgruntled.

'With all due respect, Grandmaster, this is all getting out of control,' said Mr Whatley.

'Out of control, you're a master at the understatement,' said Browelowe, shaking his head.

'What have you managed to find out, Avindor?'

asked Grendellbar, ignoring them both.

Molly could just see the edge of Avindor as he stood with his back to the fireplace.

'I'm afraid there is no doubt. Edward is in the employ of Lord Skeldrin.'

'What did you say?' Said Grand Sally, putting her hands to her face.

'I'm afraid so,' said Avindor, 'I know how hard that must be for you to hear.'

'What's the use of being a Time Keeper when you can't see what your own son is up to. Said Grand Sally, shaking her head. 'What did I do to deserve a son like this?'

'It is nothing you did or didn't do, Sally. I know Edward of old, and remember, Lord Skeldrin is an evil unlike any we have ever encountered,' said Grendellbar.

Silence fell in the room.

'He can beguile all but the strongest to his will. He is a master of the dark arts, ruthless and brilliant, and be in no doubt, he will use any means at his disposal to get what he wants. Edward has been unfortunate enough to be caught in his web.'

Grand Sally's eyes drifted up to Alfred's picture.

'We've been out all night with Crystalian looking for Edward,' said Browelowe nervously. 'We can't find him anywhere. No word, no rumour, no trace, nothing.'

Molly strained to see what was going on through the keyhole. Whatley and Browelowe moved about the room nervously.

'Some more information has come to light, Grandmaster, which is also somewhat disturbing,' continued Avindor.

'Continue,' said Grendellbar, cleaning his half-moon spectacles.

'It would seem that Skeldrin has recruited another one of our own.'

'Edward, Rankfirth, Zim, now who?' Said Mr Whatley angrily.

'Grumblewit,' replied Avindor.

'Grumblewit, small fellow, walks with a limp, works in the library sometimes?' said Browelowe.

'Yes, that's him,' replied Avindor.

'But he is...'

'Unremarkable, no one in particular,' said

Avindor, 'that's as maybe, but I might remind you, he does currently have access to the most extensive library in the country and some very sensitive material.'

'Well, yes of course,' said Browelowe humbly.

'As you ordered, Grandmaster, anyone acting suspiciously was to be watched. Some suspicious discrepancies in the Valdar library were identified, which were traced back to Grumblewit. These discrepancies led to the discovery that some items had gone missing.'

'Things?' Said Grendellbar.

'Historical literature mainly, but not the type available to the public. So, he was followed,' continued Avindor. 'He has been frequenting so very unusual places of late, with some questionable characters. He was also seen meeting with Edward before the recent incident. Grumblewit has been looking for something. Something that may have pointed him in the right direction. Something, for Lord Skeldrin.'

'In the direction of what?' Asked Grendellbar.

'Everything he's been gathering would appear to

be on the subject of Belegnoth.'

The air in the room seemed to turn cold suddenly.

'Belegnoth, my word, why?' Said Browelowe, his eyes widening.

'Good heavens,' said Whatley, swallowing hard.

'Specifically, the Skull of Belegnoth,' said Avindor.

'If he's looking for that,' spouted a panicked Mr Whatley.

'We don't know that yet,' said Grendellbar firmly.

'It's hardly going to be a college study, is it,' said Browelowe in a high voice.

'Mr Browelowe, please get a grip on yourself. Running around in a panic isn't going to help anyone, other than Lord Skeldrin,' said Grendellbar firmly.

'I believe he is getting ready to meet Skeldrin,' suggested Avindor cautiously. 'To tell him what he knows.'

'Very well,' said Grendellbar decisively, 'everything that has been discussed in this room stays in this room. If Edward and Lord Skeldrin want us to think he's dead, who are we to dissuade them otherwise? If they think they have the upper hand, that may work in our favour. We'll see in due course what the endgame is. I'll put Crystalian on to Grumblewit. Grumblewit doesn't know him, so he can follow him and see where it leads. Leave him his access to the library, we don't want to make him suspicious.'

Everyone began to talk at once and Molly found it impossible to follow. She slumped back on her heels, propping her forehead on the door thoughtfully. Who was this Lord Skeldrin that everyone was so afraid of? And why would her father have anything to do with him?

'Listening at key 'oles, are we?' said Mrs Peabody, rattling up behind her with her tea trolley, 'you know what curiosity did for the cat, don't you?'

Molly stepped back quickly. 'A lot better than me, I think,' she replied in a loud whisper. 'They're talking a lot about dad in there, Mrs P.'

'I bet they are.'

'He's alive, did you know?'

'We all suspected as much, dear.'

'But why, Mrs P, why is he doing this?"

'Don't ask me, dearie, I just work 'ere.'

'Mrs P, you're always here, you know everything,' said Molly impatiently.

'Not this time, dearie. But..'

'Yes.'

'I do know...'

'Yes,' said Molly eagerly.

'Well now...'

Just as Mrs Peabody was about to spill the beans, the living room door cracked open, and gave her an escape route. 'Coming through,' she said, ploughing through the open doorway with her tea trolley, almost running down a surprised Mr Whatley. Mrs Peabody went in, and Mr Whatley came out.

'Not for young one's ears, I'm afraid,' he said, frowning at Molly disapprovingly again, as he closed the door behind him. Molly gave him a deep frown back as Harold peered out from the kitchen doorway. 'Ah, the bathroom, my dear man,' said Mr Whatley, spotting him.

'Down that way, sir,' said Harold, pointing. 'Oh, miss,' said Harold, catching Molly's attention. Molly walked down to Harold, her mind racing all over the place. 'Like something to eat, miss? I was just about to make myself a sandwich. It's been a bit of a day so far, I'm sure you'd agree. I'll make us a nice cuppa as well.'

Molly gave a big sigh of resignation. 'Oh well, I suppose so, thank you.' Familiar smells filled her nostrils as she walked in. Kitchen smells. She couldn't say what they all were exactly, smell memories, steamed out of pots, wonderful dream smells that had bubbled out of pans. Smell memories that hung like invisible clouds, ready to rain at a moment's notice. But one thing she could say was that they brought a comfort, a feeling of being safe and warm. She took a big inhale through her nose. 'It's good to be back, Harold,' she said, as the smell memories filled up her mind.

'Let's hope it stays that way, miss,' said Harold, with a sigh. 'It's not goin' your way, is it, shut out in the hall I mean,' he said, interrupting her smell memories while cutting a slice of bread from a loaf on the kitchen side.

'No, Harold, it's not,' replied Molly. 'Gran

promised to tell me everything, and just as we're getting to the juicy parts, she sends me out.'

'Listen. I've known your gran a long time, she keeps to 'er word. She'll fill you in on the juice later.' Harold picked up a large brown teapot and poured out two mugs of steaming hot tea.

'Do you think so, Harold?' Said Molly, looking for some extra reassurance.

'I know so. I mean, you'll have to have a little patience, sweetness, she's had a rough week, you know, what with your dad turning up and then what followed,' said Harold, putting the mugs of tea on the kitchen table.

'I suppose. No, wait a minute, turning up! You mean Dad was here?'

'Yep, bold as brass, on the front doorstep, several nights back.'

'What happened?' Said Molly eagerly, sitting down at the kitchen table.

'Well,' said Harold, sitting opposite her. 'He didn't come in, they just had words on the doorstep,' said Harold, recounting what he had heard.

'"Edward, listen."'

'"'I'm done listening, mother.'"'

'"'What is it, you're so involved with, that you can put it above all else?'"'

'"'There's something I have to do.'"'

'"'What?'"'

'"'Now that, you wouldn't understand.'"'

'"'Whatever it is, whoever it is, just leave it.'"'

'"'It's too late, mother. I'm in far too deep. Look after Molly for me, she won't understand, keep her safe for me.'"'

'That's your job, Edward!'

'No, it's yours now.'

'Then your grandmother fell silent, and your dad walked off into the night. You know the rest. Your grandmother became obsessed, she was organising getting you, way before we heard anything more.'

'You're better than a carrier pigeon, you with all your gossip,' said Mrs Peabody, rattling back into the kitchen with her tea trolley.

'The poor lass, she's desperate to know stuff, and who can blame her,' said Harold, winking at Molly.

'That stuff might come back to haunt you when 'er ladyship finds out.'

'She's too preoccupied to be worrying' about stuff like that.'

Molly stopped listening as she stared at the table, the never-ending revelations racing through her mind.

'What's goin' on in that head of yours,' said Mrs Peabody, putting a comforting arm around Molly.

'I need to find my dad, Mrs P. If I can just see him, talk to him, I know I can persuade him to come home.'

'I think we're a bit past that point, dearie,' replied Mrs P, glancing at Harold and rolling her eyes.

'Okay, well, who is this Lord Skeldrin they're all going on about?

Harold coughed and fidgeted uncomfortably in his chair.

'That's a name you've said twice now, but it's not a name we like to mention in this house, dear,' said Mrs Peabody, sitting on the chair next to her.

'Why, what did he do?'

Mrs Peabody gave a big sigh. 'Do you remember when your grandfather died?' Probably not, you were too young, I think.'

‘Sort of,’ said Molly, as the kitchen became a moving canvas of the past. Memories of people filled the room. ‘I remember sitting here in the kitchen.’ Mourners in black filled each room, and the house simmered with quiet voices and gentle sobbing. ‘There were lots of people standing around, coming and going, but I don’t know who,’ said Molly as their faces were blurred and unclear. ‘I was sitting on dad’s knee, right here in this chair. Gran sat opposite Dad. She was very upset, and she was crying. Dad was talking to her, trying to comfort her. She wasn’t just sad, she was angry, angry, with...dad.’

The memories stopped and melted away like candle wax, and the kitchen returned to normal. ‘It's gone, I can’t see anymore.’

‘Yep, you’ve got Time Keeper in you alright,’ said Mrs Peabody. ‘I was one of those people in the kitchen ’ere. Your grandfather was a very powerful man, within the Valdar, very well respected and very well-liked.’

‘Who’s the pigeon now,’ said Harold, taking his plate over to the sink. He looked out of the kitchen window to the roses growing in the garden, which

Alfred had shown such care and dedication. 'He was a lovely man, your grandfather; we all miss him.'

'I was always told that grandad died of a heart attack,' said Molly, waiting for confirmation.

'That's what you were told, sweetness, but...,' said Harold.

'Nothing was ever proven,' said Mrs Peabody, 'but everyone knew that man had something to do with your grandfather's passing.

'But that's terrible,' said Molly, as an uncomfortable feeling rose in her chest. 'I could hear through the door; Dad has got himself involved with this man.' Mrs Peabody and Harold exchanged glances. Molly's frustration with her father began to grow. First, he was dead, and then he wasn't. And now he was involved with a man who had been involved with her grandfather's death. She began to think that her madness disease, which she thought she had, was something her father actually did have. Why else would he do this? And why was Gran angry with Dad on the day of Grandad's funeral? She had to get to the bottom of it. She had to find out just what was going on and stop him from doing any more of these terrible things.

'Mrs P. I heard them in the other room mention someone called Crystalian. Who is he? And how can I find him?'

CHAPTER IV

— A PRINCE IN A CAGE —

The kitchen door swung open, and Grand Sally swept in.

'Thank Elithhryn that's over,' she said with a heavy sigh.

'We'll talk some more later,' whispered Mrs Peabody. 'All gone are they now?' She asked, getting up from her chair.

'All gone,' answered Grand Sally. 'I'll have to wait and see what trouble Baradium tries to bring.'

'Well, you know my opinion, you can't say I didn't warn you,' said Mrs Peabody.

'I'm well aware of your opinion, Mrs P, thank you,' replied Grand Sally, mouthing at Mrs Peabody to stop before the conversation escalated in front of Molly. 'What a day,' she said with a big exhale and a roll of her eyes. 'But more importantly, how is my precious girl?' she said, sitting next to Molly.

'I'm okay, gran,' said Molly, giving her a half smile.

'Are you sure, dear,' she said, stroking her long, dark hair, 'the way I brought you here, all these new people, I expect it's all rather a lot to take in, and there's no shame in that. It's hard for me to take in, and I've been a part of it since the year dot.'

'Its 'ard for any of us,' mumbled Mrs Peabody.

'I beg your pardon?' said Grand Sally, scowling.

'I was just saying, and so say all of us,' replied Mrs Peabody quickly.

'She's doing amazingly well, considering,' said Harold as an added distraction.

'Well, yes, of course, I mean she's a Chatsworth and a Chatsworth always...' Grand Sally stopped talking and stood up. 'Can anyone hear that?' she said with her ear toward the door.

A squawking noise drifted into the kitchen, and Molly heard it straight away. 'Something's squawking,' she said, struggling to think what it might be.

'Oh my word,' said Grand Sally with alarm.

'You've forgotten my princey wincey,' she said, flashing Mrs Peabody a look of disgust.

''He's your flippin' bird, not mine,' said Mrs Peabody defensively.

'What bird?' Asked Molly.

'Quick darling, come with me,' said Grand Sally, heading to the kitchen door.

'What now?' said Molly, the thought of another surprise making her feel a little nervous.

Harold began to laugh.

'Go on, hurry up, go and meet his royal highness,' said Mrs Peabody, rolling her eyes with her eyebrows.

Molly followed her grandmother quickly down the hall to a room at the front of the house with a window that looked out onto the road and the park beyond. In the corner stood a covered cage on a stand.

'I told her to remove his cover before we left,' said Grand Sally, pulling back a red silk cloth.

In the cage perched a black bird. 'Orrible, 'orrible,' squawked the bird.

'Gran, what on earth, it's a crow,' said Molly

cocking an unamused eyebrow.

'What!' Said Grand Sally. 'Cover your ears, my princey wincey. He's not a common crow; he's a raven, my prince of ravens. Oh yes, my princey wincey,' said Grand Sally, opening the door on the cage, 'Tell me all about it,' she said, reaching in and tickling him under his chin. 'Y...es, what a horrible woman she is.'

'Wah, 'orrible woman, 'orrible woman. Wah! Wah!'

'He can actually talk?' laughed Molly.

The raven hopped out of the cage door and onto Grand Sally's arm. 'Oh yes, he always talks to his mumsy, don't you, my princey wincey. Come over here and say hello,' said Grand Sally, gesturing to Molly.

'Wah, wah. Molly Chatsworth, Molly Chatsworth,' said the raven with a squawk.

'He knows my name!'

'Of course, he does, and he knows a great many other things. He's a magic raven,' said Grand Sally, stroking the raven's head. 'There, there, my little princey wincey. That silly woman went and forgot your cover, my little coochy coo.' The raven nuzzled against her finger.

'Grandma, how can a bird be magic? And where did you get him from anyway?'

'We found him one morning, a baby, a little chickee, wickee, shivering on the lawn, common nasty crows hovering nearby, ready to swoop on him. We brought him in, nursed him back to health, and raised him to what you see now. I bet you're hungry, my prince?' said Grand Sally, opening a cabinet and removing a half-used bag of birdseed. Reaching into the bag, she took out a handful and held it up to the bird's beak. The raven began pecking at the seed immediately. 'There you are, my hungry, wungry, birdy, wordy.'

'Grandma,' said Molly, laughing at all the names.

'You've got to have a birdy voice and birdy names, darling,' said Grand Sally, laughing along. 'Molly,' said Grand Sally in a serious tone. 'The Awakening can be a hard thing to bear. You must tell me what's happening if it gets too much. The veil is lifting, and things you don't understand will happen.'

'I will,' replied Molly, 'I'm more worried about

Dad than anything else.'

'I know,' said Grand Sally with her head down, 'But we will get him back somehow and then face the music together, that's what we Chatsworths do.'

'I hope so, gran, I really, really, hope so,' replied Molly.

'Anyway,' said Grand Sally, shrugging off the melancholy feeling creeping over her. 'I have a few things to attend to, you talk to my princey wincey,' I'll just be a moment,' she said, putting the raven back on the perch in his cage. 'Ask him a question if you like, my princey wincey will give you the answer, remember, he's magic.'

Grand Sally swept out of the room.

Molly chuckled some more at Grand Sally's endearing names as she disappeared into the hall. What a day this was turning out to be, she thought, as she stared into the cage at the raven. 'I wonder,' she said to herself out loud, and then stepped back, annoyed for even considering it. How could a bird possibly be magic and answer questions? But there again, she had just experienced something extraordinary, travelling from Bramblewood Hill to

Kensington in a matter of minutes, that would have seemed impossible yesterday. Perhaps one question wouldn't hurt, after all, she would lose nothing by trying, and there was one question that was foremost in her mind. Molly turned around and stepped away from the cage. She closed her eyes. Took a deep breath. 'Okay, princey wincey, I have a question for you. What is going on with my father? When will I see him again?' She held her breath in anticipation.

'That's actually two questions,' said a clear voice to her right.

Molly jerked away as the raven was now perched on the back of a chair right next to her. Her heart pounded in her chest. 'Sorry, but d..d.. did you just say something?'

'Yes, I did,' said the raven clearly. 'Thank the stars above, something told me you would hear me, I could feel it,' he said, hopping up and down on the chair with excitement. 'I am, Prince Balthazar, the true Raven King and Lord of the eastern skies. My royal family was traveling to the Rim of Scarth, where I would be confirmed as the true heir to the throne, the King in the Hall of Ravens. But we were attacked by crows, sent by the evil crow Rark with his false claim to the throne. I do not remember much of the attack; it was so quick, so sudden, and I was so young. But I awoke in the hands of a raven angel. Were it not for your Grandmother finding me that day, I would not be here at all.'

'R...ght,' said Molly, blinking at the bird in disbelief. She gave herself a quick pinch, just to make sure she was awake and not dreaming. 'O...kay. I'm sorry, this is unbelievable,' she said, shaking her head. 'A talking bird, I mean,' Molly gave a big exhale, 'and your voice, it's different from earlier.'

'Why is it so hard for humans to believe that we can speak?' Said the raven, his head tilting to one side. 'All animals can speak; you are just unable to hear or understand us.'

'Okay,' said Molly, feeling a little scolded.

'Your Grandmother can not hear me as you do, nor the woman or the man; they only hear a squawking bird. Can you imagine what that's like? Your Grandmother can feel my thoughts sometimes, but alas, she cannot hear,' said the raven lowering his head. But, you hear my voice as it should be heard, which means, you are special, Molly Chatsworth,' he said with excitement.

'So why did I not hear you earlier?' Said Molly, still questioning if she maybe dreaming.

'Because I did not speak, I just played the game. You know, did my little tricks; I can squawk out some words that keep everyone happy, but if I speak properly, no one understands. Until now!'

'You said I was in danger, what did you mean, what sort of danger?'

'Tread your next path carefully, Molly Chatsworth, the path to your father is filled with dangers you cannot imagine, you....'

Mrs Peabody suddenly arrived with a tea towel. 'Squawking bird, get in your cage,' she said, flicking the air with the towel around the raven.

'Mrs P, I was...'

'Talking to a bird, wastin' your time there, love. Your grandmother keeps sayin', he's special, but just a scruffy old bird, I'm afraid.'

Balthazar flew back to his cage and settled on the perch. 'Beware the Black Serpent, Molly Chatsworth, beware the Black Serpent,' he said urgently.

'See, just a squawking bird, who knows what he's going on about,' said Mrs Peabody, ushering Molly toward the door.

'But Mrs P, he can...'

'Come along my darling, we're going for a drive. No time to lose,' called the voice of her grandmother.

'There you go, your grans squawking now, another royal command, let's be off with you, or we'll all be in hot water,' said Mrs Peabody sarcastically.

'Where are we going?' Said Molly, still staring at the raven, as Mrs Peabody shoved her out of the room.

'Hoggs Hill, by the sounds of it.

'Hoggs Hill,' exclaimed Molly. And that is,' she said cocking an eyebrow.

'There's a market there, you'll see, 'urry along now.'

Grand Sally was already waiting in the car, as Molly snatched up her coat, slamming the front door behind her. A talking bird, a real talking bird, a prince, said Molly in her head. And beware the

Black Serpent, what did that mean?

Grand Sally's Royal Blue Plymouth rumbled its way through the streets of Kensington as Molly became lost in her thoughts. Thirty minutes had passed when Harold drew to a halt in a cobbled street. The houses looked dingy and grey and gave no clue to a market; in fact, it looked as if the sky might rain on this road deliberately at any moment, to add to its greyness.

'Don't judge a book by its cover,' said Grand Sally as she saw the look on Molly's face.

Harold stepped out of the car and opened the rear door for Grand Sally to get out. As she stepped out onto the pavement, she began immediately giving Harold instructions. Molly slid along the seat and stepped out of the car. The car was parked next to an alleyway, which looked equally grey as it stepped its way downward. 'Let's get going, we're going to see a lady who will have something for your troubles, and we will have you feeling much better very soon. We will be no more than an hour, Harold,' bellowed Grand Sally as she walked into the alley.

Molly looked at Harold.

'Run along, miss, there's nothing down there that's goin' to hurt you,' said Harold, giving her a reassuring wink.

Molly took a deep breath as Balthazar's warning played over in her mind. She stepped cautiously into the passage, looking back at Harold once more.

'Go on, it's alright,' said Harold, a little confused at her caution.

'Hurry along, darling,' echoed Grand Sally's voice from below.

Molly caught up with her grandmother as the noise of the market rose to greet them. Descending the last few steps, they stepped out of the alleyway, and a busy market burst into life. Stalls as far as the eye could see. Market traders all shouting over one another to advertise their wares, pots, pans, clothes, vegetables, fruits, breads, chickens, goats, rabbits, boys pushing carts, musicians playing for coins. Grand Sally kept Molly in front of her, steering her in the right direction. The market was heaving with people, all pushing and shoving one another to get where they were going. Grand Sally pushed her way through, further and further into the market, finally stopping at a stall, decorated in bright red cloth. Glass jars adorned the stall, all full of herbs, leaves, and different coloured powders. A lady sat behind the stall on a stool, puffing on a hand-rolled cigarette. Grand Sally leaned over to speak to the woman, her eyes darting back and forth to Molly. Molly stood to one side, looking up and down the market, people watching and waiting for her grandmother to finish. But Grand Sally showed no signs of finishing as she chatted away to the woman behind the red stall.

After a while of moving from one foot to another and more people watching, Molly noticed, through the moving sea of people, a Chinese man staring at her from the other side of the market. Feeling uncomfortable, she moved out of his gaze, behind a large, rotund man, who had stopped momentarily as he shuffled bags from one arm to another. The man moved on, and when Molly looked, the Chinese man had also moved on. But once again, as she looked up and down the stalls, she spotted him a few stalls down, still watching her closely. 'Gran,' said Molly, tapping her arm but still keeping an eye on the oriental man.

'Just a minute, dear,' said Grand Sally, continuing to natter to the other woman.

'Gran,' she said a little louder, turning to get her attention.

'Yes, dear, just one moment,' said Grand Sally impatiently.

Molly turned back. The oriental man had vanished once again. She couldn't see him anywhere. Now she went from feeling uncomfortable to feeling intrigued. Where had he gone? Was he real? Or was it just her mad head? Which wasn't really mad at all. She had to know. She stepped away from her grandmother to take a closer look. She stood on her tiptoes, straining to see further. But a passer-by shoved her from behind, and she fell forward into the bustling crowd, a sea of people sweeping her away down the market like a small twig on the ocean. 'Excuse me, excuse me,' she yelled as she was buffeted further away from the red stall. Her cries went unnoticed; she felt like she was going to suffocate as she was pushed and shoved on and on down the market and further and further away from her grandmother. For what seemed like an age, she was pushed along in a sea of coats. Just as he felt that she might drown in it all, a gap opened in the crowd and she squeezed her way out of the throng of people, popping out like a cork from a bottle onto a corner and a shop doorway. Catching her breath, she noticed a discarded wooden crate sitting on the pavement. Moving it nearer to the curb, she stepped up on the crate to see where she was. Nothing looked familiar. There was no sign of the red stall or the Chinese man or, more importantly, her grandmother. Where was the red stall, and where was her grandmother? She stepped up and down on the crate repeatedly, trying to find something like the top of her grandmother's blue hat, something to help her get back to where she was.

The loud raucous noise of people on the opposite corner added to the cacophony of noise in the market. It was coming from a tavern. Above the tavern door hung a large square sign showing the face of a laughing, wrinkly pig. Below, perched on the back of a wooden bench, sat a scruffy, dark-skinned boy with wiry hair. 'What's up wiv you, then?' he called, slipping off the bench to get a better look at her. 'What you jumpin' up and down for, you lookin' for someone?'

'Yes, my grandmother, or maybe a Chinese man,' she said, stepping off the crate. 'I was looking for him, but he's disappeared, and now I'm lost.'

'Well, make up your mind,' said the boy. 'Which one, your grandmother or a chinaman, you don't strike me as being related to any Chinese.'

'I'm not, it's my gran I want, my fathers disappeared, I don't want the same happening to me, my gran will have heart failure.

'I know what you mean, love, my dad did a runner and my mum, she's always goin' spare and 'aving heart failure.'

'Did you find him?' Asked Molly.

'No, not yet,' said the boy, 'goin' to the pub, he said, and never been seen since.'

'Well, it's not quite the same, is it,' said Molly impatiently, as if she had cornered the market on disappearing fathers.

'Disappearin' is disappearin' love, no matter 'ow it is.'

'Did your father vanish on a train and then

pretend to be dead? Magic taking birds, sepricorns, grand wizards, Chinese men, you have no idea what a day I've had and furthermore...'

'Alright, keep your hair on, love, I was just saying,' said the boy, interrupting. 'I'm awfully honoured, I'm sure,' he said, putting on a posh accent.

Molly's face broke into a smile.

'See, it's not all that bad, is it?' he said, putting out his hand. 'Let me introduce me-self. Me name's Charlie. Charlie Babcock, pleased to me you.'

'My name's Molly Chatsworth,' she said, shaking his hand

'You're a right one, you are. Disappearin' dads, magic birds, chinaman, what next, giraffes probably. Have you run away from a circus or something?'

'Certainly not,' replied Molly.

'So, where are you from then? Cos you're not from these parts, are you?'

'I'm staying with my grandmother at the moment, in Kensington. It's u... h,' Molly waved her hand about, as if she had the slightest clue which way Kensington was.

'Yeah, I know. Where all the toffs live.'

'The toffs?'

'Yeah, y'know, the lah-di-dahs. The plumbs. The to...ffs.'

'I'm sorry, I really don't know what you're talking about.'

'The people wiv money,' said Charlie loudly, as if she was deaf.

'O...h, r... ight,' said Molly. 'Well, nice talking to you, but I have to find my grandmother,' she said, stepping back up on the crate again.

'Well, where did you see her last?' Asked Charlie.

'I can only tell you that the stall was bright red,' said Molly, looking up and down the market.

'Bright red, I know that one.'

'You do!' Exclaimed Molly.

'Yeah, that's Aunt Flossy's stall, way down that way. Well, she's not me aunt, but that's what we all call 'er. She sells all sorts of weird stuff. That's way off, 'ow you've ended up down 'ere 'eaven only knows, lucky you found me.'

'Well, can you get me back there or not?' Said Molly, jumping off the crate again.

'O'course I can.'

'Well, come on then, what are we waiting for, gran will be going spare by now.'

'Alright, alright, don't get your knickers in a twist, it's this way.'

They were both about to step off the pavement and back into the crowd when someone grabbed them both from behind. A large African man took them both by their collars and pulled them back across the pavement and into a nearby alley. He was huge, as wide as he was tall, he had hands like shovels, and a sparkling gold tooth. 'You're supposed to be somewhere else, boy,' he growled at Charlie.

'Well, I was on my way, Albert, honest but...'

'No buts, boy, you're a look-out, not a chatter box.'

'Who are you and just what do you think you're doing?' said Molly struggling.

'Mol, meet Albert,' said Charlie, 'Albert, meet Mol.'

'Begging your pardon, miss,' said Albert letting her go and tipping his hat, 'where are my manners, what was I tinkin?'

'I should think so,' said Molly, readjusting her coat.

'Is there anything I can do to 'elp miss?'

'I was trying to get back to my grandmother, and Charlie was about to help me.'

'Was he now,' sneered Albert. 'Where do you come from?'

'Uh, Kensington, perhaps you can help to?'

'Interesting. Well, praps I can,' said Albert thoughtfully, 'after we have seen Mr Bill, now come with me.'

CHAPTER V

—THE BLACK SERPENT—

Albert pushed them along, holding them both tightly by their collars. Weaving his way through alley after alley. Molly protested, and Charlie pleaded, the noise from the busy market slowly dying away behind them. Back doors, rear gates, and windows closed as they passed, as all new Albert, his large frame casting the shadow of fear wherever he walked.

Arriving at their destination, Molly and Charlie were shoved into a large open courtyard with high walls. The sun hid behind the clouds, giving an unwelcome chill in the air. Two men stood guard at an archway at the far end of the courtyard. 'Get me the Butcher,' demanded Albert as they approached. One of the men on guard gestured to the other, who disappeared through the archway. Molly watched as

Charlie continued to plead.

'What's he done this time?' Said the guard with a grin.

'Mind your business,' growled Albert.

'Okay, just asking,' said the guard, walking back to the archway quickly.

'Come on, Albert, it's not too late, let us go, I promise I won't do it again,' said Charlie in a loud whisper.

'That's what you said last time and the time before dat. The Butcher don't be likin' slackers, boy, you're supposed to be workin' off your father's debt, not running up a bigger one.'

'Yeah but...'

'No buts. But, but, but, but, is all I 'ear from you.'

His shovel-like hand closed quickly around Charlie's neck. His sleeve drew back at the same time, revealing the inside of his wrist and a black snake tattoo. Molly gasped. 'Beware the Black Serpent,' she said out loud.

'What?' said Albert, letting Charlie go.

'Th...e picture on your wrist, a black serpent?' Said Molly, giving him a false grin.

'We all have dem,' growled Albert, pulling his sleeve back up.

'And very nice it is to,' spluttered Charlie, nursing his throat. 'It's still not too late, Albert, I mean...'

'Not too late for what?' Said a cold voice from the dark of the arch.

Molly saw Charlie's face drop. She strained to see who was talking in the dark of the arch. 'Who is this, Butcher?' She whispered.

'Bill the Butcher they call him, he runs the Black Serpents, criminals, you name it, if it's illegal, he's at the other end of it, nobody crosses the Butcher, not even the law,' whispered Charlie.

Molly rolled her eyes and sighed heavily. How had she gotten into this, and how was she going to get out? Her nausea that had remained at bay began creeping back, and her head began to swim. She took two big gulps of air in an effort to fight off the feelings, longing for the red stall and a magic potion to make all this go away.

William Grim, also known as Bill the Butcher, stepped out of the shadow of the arch. A black hat crowned a stubbled, acne-scarred face. A faded white shirt hugged his shoulders, and a set of red braces held up his baggy brown trousers. A large dog followed behind. The dog's fur was dirty and matted, and like his owner, his face carried scars. Slimy drool hung from the dog's mouth as he waddled along on a big, bulky body. Molly felt an uncomfortable chill run down her back as Grim walked menacingly slowly toward them. 'He was not at his post again, boss,' said Albert, shaking his head in disapproval. Grim remained silent.

'I'm sorry, boss, really I am, but I met this girl 'ere and...'

'Look,' said Molly sharply, 'I don't know who any of you are, but whatever is going on here, it has nothing to do with me. I'm just trying to find my grandmother, so if you wouldn't mind letting me go.'

'She's right, boss, it really has nothin'...'

Albert clumped Charlie around the back of the head. 'Slacking again, boss, instead of watching for the pickpockets.'

'I wasn't honest, boss, I was just...'

'So, Albert is lying then?' Replied Grim, breaking his silence. 'What do you think, Bruiser?' Grim looked down at his dog. Bruiser looked at Charlie.

'Well, I wouldn't say lying, no,' said Charlie, watching Bruiser closely.

Grim pulled a cigar from his pocket and put it in his mouth. Cigars made Grim feel more important; they gave him status, unlike his employees, who, by their lower ranking, were resigned to rolling their own cigarettes.

Molly's eyes began to widen as she spotted a large black serpent tattoo through his open shirt, spreading up across his chest as Bruiser the dog started to circle them both, sniffing the air around them as he walked.

'You said you don't know who I am,' said Grim, giving Molly a cold, hard stare. 'Well, let me enlighten you.' Grim took a box of matches from his pocket and, striking one, he lit his cigar. 'My name's William, Bill for short. But locally, I'm known as Bill the Butcher. I'll let your imagination fill in the blanks as to why,' he said, blowing cigar smoke in Molly's face. 'And in this part of town, I run things. Nothing happens 'ere without me knowing about it. Young Charlie, 'ere is one of my employees. A little serpent in the makin'. Quite handy in a tight spot, our young Charles. And you had the bad luck to run into him,' he said, finishing with a chuckle. Molly gave Charlie an angry sideways glance. Grim stepped closer to Charlie, his cigar breath filling Charlie's nostrils. Pinching the top of Charlie's right ear between two fingers, he began twisting it. 'I don't care about girls and their grannies, I don't care about any of it, but what I do care about is when my employees don't do what they're asked to do.' Bruisier looked at Charlie and began to growl. 'Even Bruiser doesn't like it when people don't do as they're told. Isn't that right, Bruiser?' Latching on with his front teeth, Bruiser began tugging at Charlie's trouser leg.

'I'm sorry, boss, honest, I won't do it again, I promise,' pleaded Charlie as the pain of Grim twisting his ear became unbearable.

'Reggie!' Yelled Grim, letting go of Charlie's ear.

'Yes, boss,' said one of the guards by the archway.

'Take Bruiser and give him some dinner, before he eats Charlie, even though I'm tempted to let him.'

'Sorry, boss?' Enquired Reggie, hoping he hadn't heard correctly.

'Get over 'ere and take Bruiser for some dinner,' said Grim impatiently.

'Yes, boss, sorry, boss,' replied Reggie nervously, running forward to try and pull Bruiser away by his collar. Charlie held his throbbing ear, sighing with relief as Bruiser turned on Reggie, chasing him around the courtyard and back through the archway.

'Kensington, boss, that's where the girl be from,' said Albert.

'My word, Kensington. Then it's my good luck, isn't it,' said Grim with another chuckle. 'Your old dear might pay a tidy penny to get you back, I shouldn't wonder. Well, done, Charlie. There's hope for you yet.'

'What does he mean?' Said Molly, looking at Charlie.

'He means your gran might pay to get you back,' replied Charlie, wincing in embarrassment.

'That's a boy, Charlie. You can interpret. These posh folk speak different to us, know what I mean,' said Grim in Charlie's ear.

'I'm sorry, but you can't do this. Let me go immediately,' protested Molly, struggling.

'I'm afraid I can, in fact, I very often do. And if your gran or whoever is responsible for you decides not to pay, well, that will be very disappointing. But then of course you'll be of no further use and...disposable.'

Molly's instinct was to run, but Albert held her collar tightly from behind, making it impossible.

'So, you see...' Grim stopped abruptly. 'Albert!'

'Yes, boss.'

'Someone is standing in my courtyard that I don't know,' said Grim, his eyes fixed on someone behind Albert. Grim backed away as Albert felt the cold of a steel barrel on the back of his head.

'Let the girl and the boy go,' said a voice behind him. Behind Albert stood a man with dark hair and a long coat, holding a long-barrelled gun to Albert's head. Albert let go of Molly and Charlie, as more of Bill's men, alerted to an intruder, filed out from the archway. 'Molly, get behind me,' said the man. Charlie took hold of Molly's arm, pulling her away, quickly moving behind the stranger. 'My name is Crystalian, Molly, a friend of your grandmother. On your knees, please, big man,' said Crystalian to

Albert. Albert sank to his knees. Crystalian pulled some rope from his coat pocket. 'Here, boy, tie his hands behind his back,' he said, passing Charlie the rope. Now he pointed his gun at Bill the Butcher.

'Sorry about this, Albert,' said Charlie sarcastically as he tied Albert's hands.

'I'll be seeing you again, boy, don't you worry about dat,' growled Albert.

Once Albert's hands were tied, Crystalian pushed him over with his foot, and Albert rolled over like an upturned turtle.

'The family negotiator, I presume, the middle man?' Said Grim. 'A little ahead of time, don't you think?'

'There will be no negotiating.'

'Whoever you are, just how far do you think you're going to get? Just as he had finished talking, there was the sound of flapping wings. Everyone looked up as a large black bird swooped down on Grim, scratching at his face with its talons. Grim yelled out in pain, covering his left eye, as he swiped wildly at the bird.

'We are leaving,' said Crystalian firmly, 'both of

you, run, now, back to the road.'

Grim fell to his knees. 'What are you waiting for? Get them,' he yelled at his men, as trickles of blood ran down his cheek.

Crystalian fired his gun at advancing men. A fine white powder and white pellets filled the air, knocking several men off their feet, while others dove for cover. He fired another shot before turning about quickly, running after Molly and Charlie, who were now running down the passage toward the road. As they reached the end and turned the corner, their path was blocked by a Chinese man. 'That's him, that's the man that was watching me in the market,' cried Molly.

'Blimey O'Reilly, what next?' Exclaimed Charlie.

Crystalian caught up. 'Molly, meet Milee, he's with us.'

'He's what?' Said Molly.

'Pleased to meet you,' said Milee, bowing his head.

'There are more coming after us, Milee,' said Crystalian, looking back down the passage.

'I deal with them, get these two to car, it is at end

of road,' said Milee, unconcerned.

Crystalian, Molly, and Charlie ran down the road toward the car. Eight men ran out of the passage, and more were coming, as Milee took on a fighting pose.

'I would leave now while you still can,' he warned with a smile.

'Your mate had a gun with nothing but rock salt in it,' said one of the men stepping forward, 'can't see you 'aving much more to offer.'

The man made a fist with his right hand and then started punching the palm of his left.

'Very well,' said Milee, beckoning the man with his finger.

The man rushed at Milee, and with a spinning kick, Milee sent him crashing to the ground. The other men sprang into action, but each one was dispatched one by one as they came.

Grand Sally's Blue Plymouth sat rumbling at the end of the road, ready to go. Arriving at the car, there was a flapping of wings again, and a black raven landed on the car's roof. 'Balthazar, it was you back there,' said Molly.

'I told you, beware the black serpent,' said the

raven, winking a black eye.

'Quick, get in,' said Crystalian, opening the back door.

'I told you my prince was magic,' said Grand Sally as Molly climbed in. 'I was going out of my mind looking for you. Are you alright?'

'I am now,' said Molly, falling back into the car seat.

'I don't know you, lady,' said Charlie, squeezing in next to Molly, 'but I'm much obliged for the lift.'

'Passengers,' said Grand Sally in alarm.

'Gran, this is Charlie,' said Molly, introducing him.

Crystalian jumped into the front passenger seat, slamming the car door behind him.

'Harold, get us out of here, quickly.'

CHAPTER VI

— THE DREAM WELL —

Slamming into a wall, Molly gasped for breath. She pressed her back hard against the ice-cold bricks. Perhaps it would pass by without seeing her. She couldn't run anymore; her lungs were aching from that last sprint. How long would it continue to hunt her?

She peeped around the edge of the wall. The rain was teeming down like a waterfall out of the night sky, soaking her through. 'We can't wait here,' we'll freeze to d..d.. death,' said Balthazar, shaking the rain from his wings.

'Quiet,' whispered Molly, looking up, 'It's coming.' The shadow of the beast floated overhead in the night sky. Molly held her breath as it drifted silently past. 'What is it?' She whispered.

'It's called a Sla. A demon of the old world,

neither dead nor alive. They were human once, like you, in their old life. That's what they craved, the beauty of life itself, something they could never have again. Jealously, rage, and an eternal hunger for that life drove them to destroy the very lives they craved. But they were all supposed to have been destroyed in the great war.'

'It's gone now,' whispered Molly.

'Yes, but look where it's going,' said Balthazar.

'Oh no,' said Molly as she looked beyond the park. She watched as it floated down and then clung to the chimney pot of her grandmother's house. Slowly, it slithered from one side of the stack to the other, its black skeletal face and its black smoky body highlighted in the moonlight. But what could she do? Her hands and feet were numb from the cold, and her legs wanted to give way. Then it came. Another noise above the sound of the rain. The last thing she wanted to hear. The slow creak of a door opening; a yellow, glowing light from a hallway. The Sla, alerted by the sound, began to hiss.

'Molly, are you there?' came the unmistakable voice of her grandmother, peering out through the doorway into the street.

A terrified whisper flew from Molly's lips. 'No! No! What are you doing? Get inside! Get inside!'

'Quick, quick, do something,' cried Balthazar, jumping up and down.

The Sla was on the move, making its way down the roof towards the gutter. Molly moved out of the shadow of the wall. 'Grandma, get in, get in!' She cried.

'Hurry, Molly Chatsworth, hurry,' cried Balthazar.

The Sla slipped silently over the gutter. Molly made a run towards her grandmother's front door. Flexing its razor-sharp talons, it floated down towards her. But the faster Molly ran, the wider the road became. 'Get in!' She screamed, running as hard as she could to get to the other side. 'What's happening?' the other side of the road just kept moving further and further away.

'Hurry, hurry,' cried Balthazar.

The Sla hung just a few feet above grandmother's head. It stretched out its hand. Closer, closer, closer it came. 'N...o!' Cried Molly, reaching out toward her grandmother as she ran.

Suddenly, Molly awoke with a start, breathless and sweating. She wasn't outside at all, but in bed, safe and sound at number Ten Plumberry Road. It was all just a bad dream. The sun was slowly rising outside and was beginning to peep through the curtains. A sparrow twittered noisily on the window ledge. The small clock on the cabinet beside her bed read six-twenty-five. Taking a deep breath to calm herself, she got out of bed, feeling damp and clammy from the nightmare. Patting herself down with a towel, she sat on the stool in front of the dressing table. 'What was that dream? What did it mean? It was so real, like I was really there,' she said quietly to her reflection in the mirror. The Awakening was showing her things she didn't understand. 'A Sla, a monster, destroyed in the old war said Balthazar. What war?' Molly closed her eyes, taking a breath again to steady her nerves. Then, with a sudden recollection. 'Charlie!' She said, opening her eyes, remembering he was just down the hall. Shutting the door behind her, she crept down the landing to the next bedroom to look in on him. To her surprise, he was awake, dressed, and tying his bootlaces.

'Morning, Mol.'

'Charlie, are you going somewhere?' She said, closing the bedroom door.

Charlie sat down on the bed with hunched shoulders. 'It was nice of your gran to put me up, but I think we all know I have to be off.'

'Off?' Said Molly.

'Yeah, off, adios, au revoir, see you later, off.'

'What for, where?'

'Look, princess, William Grim, or Bill the Butcher, as they like to call him, didn't come by that nickname by chance, he'll 'ave people out looking, mark my words. And I don't want to end up like a Sunday dinner. Like I said last night, I can't go home; that's the first place they'll look, heaven knows how me mother will fare. And your friends, they might ave been a great help to you yesterday, but there'll be consequences, mark my words, it's only a matter of time before they trace us both back to 'ere. No, got to keep movin', that's my only hope.'

'Why did you have to work for that man in the first place?' Said Molly in an exasperated tone.

'I told you why, I told all of you last night. To pay

off my dad's debt to Grim. No, there's nothing else for it, got to move on, leave town,' said Charlie, slipping on his jacket. 'And another thing, princess, maybe you haven't noticed but there is a difference in shade between you and me, you know, our colour. I don't expect the likes of me 'as been seen around here much. Sooner I'm gone, the better for all concerned.'

'Don't be ridiculous,' answered Molly snappily. 'I really think something's wrong with your eyesight,' she said, snatching a photo frame from the top of a chest of drawers.

'Wake me up, I've gone to Mars,' said Charlie, raising his hands.

'Maybe you have,' said Molly, thrusting the photo under his nose.

'What's this?'

'A picture of my father,'

'But he's...'

'A different shade,' said Molly in a sarcastic tone. The black and white photo of Molly's father showed a dark-skinned man. Molly sat down on the bed. 'It's okay, Charlie, I understand,' she said, putting her arm around his shoulders. 'I'm a different shade too, you know, but, aren't we all? She said, looking at her father's photo affectionately. 'And no, you don't have to go. Gran will have you here for as long as you need to be.'

'Well, I don't think...'

'Let's go and see if Mrs P's up yet, shall we and get you some breakfast,' said Molly, slipping off the bed, 'before you get...off.'

'Breakfast!' Said Charlie, the corners of his mouth turning up into a smile. 'Well, maybe I could slip in an egg before I leave.'

Sure enough, Mrs Peabody was in the kitchen, boiling water for tea and toasting bread, and she had company. 'Cor blimey, you're up early, me dears. Never mind, you can join the rest of us. Sit yourselves down. The tea will be ready in a minute.'

'Good morning,' said Crystalian, sat at the kitchen table. 'How did you sleep?'

'Like a stone,' said Charlie.

'Not too bad,' said Molly, yawning.

'Good morning,' said Milee, stepping out of the pantry, holding a butter dish.

'Hey, you're the fella we left behind,' remarked Charlie.

'Are you alright? What happened?' Enquired Molly.

'Yes, very well, thank you. Men dispatched, then I lost rest in alleys, no problem, all good now,' said Milee. 'I am sorry if I frightened you yesterday. But Grandmaster asks me to watch you.'

'That's okay, it all worked out in the end, sort of,' said Molly, glancing at Charlie.

Mrs Peabody placed a big plate of wobbling, hot, thick toast on the table, Milee put the butter dish in the middle, and Mrs P returned with a bowl of bright red, homemade strawberry jam. Charlie's eyes bulged with delight. 'Dig in all of you,' said Mrs Peabody, 'the tea and porridge are on their way.'

'Grim knows you're from Kensington,' said Crystalian. '. I don't think he will venture this far, at least not yet anyway. But, I will be staying here for a few days, just to be on the safe side, just until we know how the land lies.'

'You don't know Grim like I do,' warned Charlie. 'He won't just leave it, and he has spies everywhere, and they'll be lookin'.'

'Grand Sally has something up her sleeve to help take care of that,' said Mrs Peabody, ladling out a bowl of porridge.

'Well, she better 'ave big sleeves, that's all I can say,' said Charlie, sinking his spoon into the porridge.

'Yesterday was good luck for you,' said Milee, nodding his head.

'Good luck. I'm on the run from one of the biggest gangs in London, I don't think lucky is the right word. How d'you figure that one?'

'Because you run into Molly.'

'Me,' said Molly, chomping on some thick buttered toast.

'Yes. This has started a chain of events in your life, both your lives. Things will not be the same from now on, for either of you.'

'R...ght,' said Charlie, rolling his eyes, suspicious of what this Chinese man was saying.

'Where you sleep night before?'

'In me mum's armchair,' replied Charlie. 'But that was only because...'

'What you eat yesterday?'

'Uh, a bit of soup, I think,' replied Charlie, trying to remember.

'Today you wake up in comfortable bed and now eat toast and porridge. I need say no more.'

'He's right, you know,' said Molly, chuckling.

'Yep, you can't argue with that son,' said Mrs Peabody.

The back door opened, and in walked Harold. 'Morning peeps,' he said, removing his hat.

'There he is,' said Charlie, 'the getaway driver.'

'Aye, cheeky,' replied Harold, 'if Mrs Harold knew what I was up to, well, I'd rather face Grim and his men again than that.'

'Peggy's not that bad,' laughed Mrs Peabody.

'You're not married to her,' replied Harold, shaking his head.

'Talking of Grim,' said Crystalian. 'Anything on the grapevine, Harold?'

'It's as quiet as a morgue out there at the moment, just the usual chatter, 'haven't heard a thing about Grim or yesterday yet,' replied Harold, his eyes widening at the porridge steaming in a saucepan on the stove.

After breakfast, Molly took Charlie to the living room. Overwhelmed by the big, sumptuous room with its large red sofas and velvet curtains, he looked up at Grandpa Alfred's picture above the fireplace.

'That was my grandfather,' said Molly, moving alongside him.

'But he's...,' began Charlie, wide-eyed and pointing at the picture.

'Charlie, if you're going to point and say something stupid every time you see someone that's a different colour, you'll spend forever doing it in this family. We're all different colours.'

'So, where is he?' Asked Charlie.

'He's dead now,' answered Molly in a melancholy tone. ''I only knew him when I was very young.'

'Bit sudden, was it?'

'I'm beginning to find out, it was complicated.'

'Life can be that way,' replied Charlie with a sigh.

'Come with me, Charlie, I want to show you something else.'

'Right you are, princess. Lead on.'

Molly led Charlie to the room at the front of the

house. 'Morning, Balthazar,' said Molly as she walked in.

'Good morning, Molly Chatsworth,' said Balthazar, hopping forward to the open door of his cage.

Charlie stopped halfway across the room.

'What's the matter?' Molly asked, seeing his expression.

'Is it my imagination or did that bird just speak?' He said, looking for someone else in the room.

'You heard that?' Said Molly in surprise.

'He can hear me?' Said Balthazar, giving a little flap of his wings.

'No, no, birds don't speak, that's impossible,' said Charlie, still looking for someone else.

'Here we go again,' said Balthazar.

'The...the, bird, can speak,' said Charlie, pointing at the cage.

Molly walked quickly to the doorway, peering into the hall to see if anyone else was around and closed the door quietly. 'Yes, this one does,' she said quietly, pushing Charlie's arm down. 'Well, they all do really. Charlie, this is so exciting. We can both talk to him now. Balthazar, say something else.'

'What like, who's a pretty boy then, give us a kiss,' said Balthazar, mimicking a parrot.

'N...o, you know what I mean.'

'The b...bird can speak?' Said Charlie, still in shock.

'Is he going to keep saying that?' Asked Balthazar.

'I've got to sit down,' said Charlie, reaching for a chair.

'It's not that he speaks, it's that you can hear him.'

'I've never heard a bird speak before.'

'That's because you weren't listening, but this house can have a strange effect on people sometimes; it has heightened your senses, so now you're hearing,' said Balthazar.

'Come and say hello,' said Molly, taking Charlie by the hand.

Charlie got up hesitantly and then stepped closer to the cage. 'You're the bird that swooped in on Bill the Butcher yesterday?' He said, with a flashback to the courtyard.

'Yes, it was. Got a little bit of his own medicine,' replied Balthazar.

'I owe you one,' said Charlie. 'I still don't believe I'm talking to a bird, though.'

'And I don't believe I'm talking to another human, two in two days, but hey, we both better wake up because we are. It's like Grand Sally's radiogram, you have to tune in to the right frequency to hear something.'

'Oh, and one thing more,' said Molly, 'Gran can't hear him. I think it's best we don't say anything right now, and before she comes down, Balthazar, I have a question,' said Molly.

'Slas, the great war,' said Balthazar.

'But that was my dream, how did you know what I was going to say?'

'Because I was there.'

'No, I know you were there, but not there, there. I just dreamt you were there, didn't I?'

'No, you didn't just dream it. Well, technically you did, but I was there, there, really there, in your dream, with you.'

'What are you two goin' on about?' Asked Charlie, scratching his head in confusion.

'Quiet!' Said Balthazar and Molly both at once.

'Your Awakening is in the early stages, boundaries are blurred, you are very powerful, Molly Chatsworth, but you haven't learnt to control your power, and when you dream...'

'Excuse me, dream?' Said Charlie, who was still trying to work out what they were talking about.

'Quiet! They both said at once again.

'As I was saying, when you dream, you can create a Dream Well, and if you're not careful, you can pull others in, into your dream, while they are sleeping. I was there in your dream, and it was pretty terrifying, I can tell you.'

'A Dream Well,' said Molly, shaking her head in disbelief

'Uh...k, I know, it's complicated,' replied Balthazar.

'How d'you think I feel?' Said Charlie.

The front room door swung open, and in swept Grand Sally.

'A...h, there you are, both of you. I see you've met my princey wincey, Charles?'

'You're what?' Said Charlie, frowning.

'Just go with it,' said Balthazar as Grand Sally

launched into every endearing name of hers that came to mind.

'Yes, my princey wincey, hungry wungry, chickee deeky, mumsy wumsies, birdie wordy.'

Molly covered her mouth to cover the laughter. Charlie closed his eyes and squirmed on the spot.

'So how did you sleep, Charles?' Asked Grand Sally.

'Like a stone, Mrs G, like a stone,' answered Charlie. 'Just a bit worried about Grim's lot turning up at the front door.'

'First of all, that won't happen. I will be putting a spell on this house shortly that will keep all evil doers away and not just William Grim.'

'A spell?' Said Charlie, glancing in Molly's direction.

Molly's expression didn't change, as this didn't sound like anything unusual after the experiences of yesterday. 'And what does that involve, gran?' She asked.

'No naked dances in the moonlight, I hope,' laughed Charlie.

'Heaven forbid,' answered Grand Sally, 'I don't

think the moon wants to see all my bits and pieces. No, in the daytime, I'm sure the sun won't mind, although I'm sure the neighbours might have something to say.'

'What?' Said Charlie in alarm.

Molly laughed while Charlie just shook his head.

'Nothing quite so dramatic as dancing in the moonlight, I'm afraid, Charles,' continued Grand Sally. 'A jar of nails and a few special words is all it will take. And when I've finished, you'll both carry one of those nails each in your pocket, and it will protect you when you're out of the house. This might seem a little far-fetched to you, Charles...'

'A little,' said Charlie, raising his eyebrows.

'But you've fallen into an entirely new world, and a new way of doing things. Molly is new to it as well.'

'I think Milee was trying to tell me the same thing.'

'A very wise man,' said Grand Sally, nodding in approval.

'A very wise man indeed,' agreed Balthazar.

'You see, even Balthazar agrees,' said Grand Sally, hearing him squawk. Grand Sally carried on with her coochy coos and princey winceys, as Molly's senses pricked up. She could hear the low droll of voices outside by the front door, and something told her to pay attention. Looking out of the window, she could see that Milee and Crystalian were talking outside on the doorstep. She turned her head and moved closer to the window.

'I go back to Gwandmaster now. I will let him know what happened.'

'Very well, Milee, thank you. I have to track Grumblewit tomorrow night, see where he goes and where it leads. I'll take Sally's Plymouth.'

'Be careful,' said Milee.

'What are you listening to?' Whispered Charlie, moving up alongside Molly.

'Charlie, I don't know how,' whispered Molly, 'but I have to be in gran's car with that man tomorrow night, it may just lead to my father.

CHAPTER VII

— BANSHEE BOG —

Grumblewit pushed open the door of the Twisted Knot. The cool night air rushed in behind him, and the warm air of the tavern rushed toward the door, slamming it shut.

Heads turned to look at him as he tilted his hat downward and pulled his coat collar up around his neck to hide his face. He had not been to this tavern before and knew no one in it, and that's how he wanted it to stay. Spying a free table by the far wall, he hurried over to sit down under the watchful eye of the landlord. He had only sat for a moment when the grubby man arrived in front of him. 'You'll 'ave a drink if you're going to sit there.'

'No thank you, I'm just waiting for someone,' mumbled Grumblewit from under his hat.

'Meet whoever you like pal, but you'll be buying a

drink while you're 'ere, or wait somewhere else. And what is that disgusting smell?' Putting a glass of watery ale down on the table, the landlord stuck out his hand. Grumblewit fumbled around in his pocket for coins and dropped some in his grubby palm and pushed a sack with his foot, which he'd brought with him, the source of the smell, further under the table. He sat for a while watching the clock above the fireplace, feeling more and more uncomfortable by the minute, when the tavern door creaked open once more, and a tall, thick-necked man walked in. Grumblewit recognised him as Lord Skedlrins' chauffeur, Kraine, and raised his hand to wave him over. The landlord watched as the man weaved through the tables, getting ready to charge someone else for unpleasant ales. But he didn't sit down.

'Lord Skeldrin awaits you,' said the chauffeur.

The chair scraped noisily on the stone floor as Grumblewit stood up, pushing it backwards, causing unwanted stares from disgruntled faces. 'Let's go,' he said, eager to get out. Outside, Grumblewit walked to the car and the chauffeur opened the rear door.

'Good evening, Grumblewit,' said a cold voice,

'Do you have something for me?'

'I do, sir,' said Grumblewit keenly as he climbed into the car.

Another car sat further back, down the street in the shadow of a wall, with Crystalian behind the wheel, watching closely.

'Ouch! Get your foot out of my ear,' said a voice in the back.

'My foot, you're lucky it's just my foot,' replied another in a loud whisper.

'Stop moaning and move over, will you?'

'Moaning! Now listen 'ere princess...'

The boot of the car cracked open, and the cold night air rushed in.

'How, when, what, are you doing in here?' said Crystalian in a surprised whisper. 'Do you realise who I'm following and what danger you're putting yourselves in?'

'Sorry, boss, I was just following orders,' replied Charlie, disentangling himself from Molly.

'I'm not sorry,' said Molly, firmly as she climbed out of the boot. 'I have to find out what's going on with my father, and this Grumblewit might just know something, if I can just talk to him, persuade him...'

'I don't know how you know this,' said Crystalian, 'but you could get us all into a lot of trouble.'

'We won't get in your way, I promise,' pleaded Molly.

'I'm not happy about this,' said Crystalian, 'but I can't go back now, so you do exactly as I say, when I say it, understand?'

'We understand, don't we?' said Molly, looking at Charlie.

'Of course, you're the boss,' he replied.

Lord Skeldrin's car started up and pulled away.

'Quick, both of you, get in the car,' ordered Crystalian.

Crystalian kept a safe distance, so as not to be seen, as they weaved their way through London streets, until Lord Skeldrin's car finally came to a halt in a road with a lone house at the end.

'You know where we are, right?' Whispered Charlie, looking around. 'Banshee Bog, a bad place to be. I've heard of this place, people come down 'ere and don't come out.'

'Don't be stupid,' said Molly in a loud whisper.

'Years ago, they used to hang people here, hundreds of them, they say, and now they haunt the marsh.'

'Well, if you see any ghosts, let me know,' said Crystalian as he pulled off the road, hiding the car beneath a tree.

Getting out of the Plymouth, they all watched from behind the tree as Lord Skeldrin's car pulled away, leaving Skeldrin and Grumblewit standing in front of the house. Grumblewit stood behind Lord Skeldrin, looking him up and down. He was an imposing figure, tall and handsome, seductive, everything Grumblewit wasn't. His sleek black hair glistened beneath the moonlight, and by his side, he carried a long black cane that held a blue glow from a crystal at the top.

The house stood above the road with steps running up to a front porch. 'Well, Grumblewit, you've brought me all this way, with that disgusting smelling sack,' said Lord Skeldrin impatiently.

'Yes, sir, sorry, sir,' replied Grumblewit, lowering his head like a submissive dog, 'follow me, sir.' They climbed the steps to the front door. Grumblewit knocked hard three times. The door creaked open, revealing a hunchback with a jagged scar down the right side of his face. Bent over at the middle, he stood swinging a lamp in front of him, eyeing them both up and down. 'W...we have come for an audience with the Hedrin,' squeaked Grumblewit nervously.

The hunchback leaned out of the doorway, looking around suspiciously for any sign of anyone else. Satisfied they were alone, the hunchback waved them both in and closed the door behind them. 'Come with me,' he said, leading them with his lamp down the hallway.

Crystalian, Molly, and Charlie weaved their way cautiously down the road until they reached the house.

'You're not thinking of going in there, are you?' Asked Charlie.

'Follow me,' said Crystalian. Passing the main steps, leading them around to the side of the house. Molly and Charlie kept a tight walk against the edge of the house as they passed crumbling outbuildings, with ominous dark doorways, with unimaginable things lurking inside. As they neared the corner of the house, Crystalian slowed to a stop, peering cautiously around the edge of the house. He could see Skeldrin and Grumblewit talking to the hunchback at the end of a long backyard.

'What can you see?' Asked Molly.

'I don't care,' said Charlie,' we shouldn't be 'ere.'

'Not much they're talking.' Then, as he watched, Skeldrin, Grumblewit, and the hunchback stepped down into the ground and vanished from sight. 'They've gone,' he said, puzzled.

'What do you mean, they've gone?' Said Molly, looking around the corner.

'I don't care, let's go 'ome,' moaned Charlie.

Crystalian stepped out from the corner and began walking across the yard. Molly followed quickly behind. Reluctantly, Charlie followed behind. As they approached the spot where Skeldrin had disappeared, a low, rounded stone wall appeared through the gloom. On the other side, a shaft sank into the ground, a faint glow shining up from somewhere below. 'Where do you think it goes?' whispered Molly as she stepped over the crumbling wall.

'Down into hell, most likely, let's go now before it's too late,' said Charlie.

'Look,' whispered Molly, looking down into the hole. 'The light is fading.'

Stone steps circled their way down, fading into the darkness as the light diminished.

'Quick, follow me, before the light completely goes,' said Crystalian, stepping cautiously into the dark shaft.

'He's not going in, surely?' Said Charlie.

'Get in quickly,' whispered Molly, shoving him toward the first step. Treading their way down as carefully as they could, the bottom of the shaft revealed a tunnel. Crystalian paused at its entrance. He could see the silhouettes of Skeldrin and Grumblewit ahead, as the hunchback's lamp swayed through the dark of the tunnel. 'There they are,' whispered Molly.

'Yes, we will wait for a moment until their light fades a little more. We don't want to be seen.' They watched as the light grew fainter until it was hard to see anything at all. 'Molly, hold on to my jacket.

Charlie, you hold hers and do not let go.'

'I hope there are no spiders in there, I ruddy hate spiders,' whispered Charlie as they crept inside.

The tunnel was long, the walls were wet and slimy, and several times they tripped and stumbled on big stones that lay scattered on the tunnel floor. Rusty cage doors lined the sides of the tunnel. 'You see these doorways, they're the cells they held the prisoners in for execution,' whispered Charlie, 'and you thought I was 'aving you on.'

Molly could feel the misery left behind, which hung in the air of the tunnel like a bad odour, and picked up the pace.

After what seemed like an age, they reached the end. The opening peered out through an overgrown embankment, looking out onto a marsh, covered with a heavy mist. 'Where are we now?' asked Molly.

'This is the marsh, where the dead walk. Can't yer smell it, that rotten stink? It's the stench of death, that's what it is.'

'Heavens, Charlie,' snapped Molly.

'Look 'ere, Mol, remember earlier when I said we were in a place where people go in and don't come out? Well, I'm changing it. People don't go in 'ere at all.'

'Grumblewit and Lord Skeldrin have, and I intend to find out why,' said Crystalian. 'Follow me and follow my steps, bogs are treacherous places, so we must tread carefully.'

Grumblewit was feeling more than unnerved as he followed the hunchback. An unnatural atmosphere hung over the marsh, and the rotten smell of unmentionable things drifted through the air. Out of the mist loomed two large pillars holding a set of rusty and twisted gates. Upon the top of each pillar sat an ugly stone gargoyle, and beyond, steps ran down into a graveyard. The hunchback pushed open the gates, which let out a rusty screech. 'We go there,' he said, pointing.

At the centre of the graveyard, rising out of the mist, stood the remains of an old church. The roof had long since gone, and the walls had fallen to rubble, but its new occupants were not interested in its appearance or what comforts it might have to offer. Around a small fire stood three horrible hags. Dressed in ragged, hooded cloaks, two of them were eyeless, and skin covered the place where their eye sockets should be. One of the two had a pair of sharply pointed ears, while the other had a large hooked nose. The third had one large eye that sat in the middle of her forehead. They remained close to one another, constantly touching, and they could all see, hear, and smell as one.

The hunchback led Lord Skeldrin and Grumblewit in through a gap in the rubble. 'The Hedrin,' he said, stopping and bowing his head.

'I hear footsteps,' said the Ears.

'I smell trouble,' said the Nose.

'And I see Lord Skeldrin,' said the Eye.

'The Dark One,' they all said in unison.

Pawing at each other, they stepped forward, and Grumblewit shrank back behind Lord Skeldrin.

'You, we did not expect to see,' said the Eye.

'Nor I you, for I do not wish to look upon your hideous faces a moment longer than is necessary,' replied Lord Skeldrin.

The Hedrin hissed like cats at his remark.

'Payment before we say anymore,' snapped the Ears.

'Give them the sack, Grumblewit,' sighed Lord Skeldrin impatiently.

Grumblewit threw the sack at the feet of the Hedrin. An ooze ran from the sack as it landed with a splat. Grumblewit gagged at the smell. Pawing and sniffing, the Nose emptied the sack and cackled in pleasure at the smell of rotting fish, as it slopped out onto the ground. Grumblewit turned away, heaving in disgust as the Hedrin crammed the slimy mess into their toothless mouths.

Crystalian, Molly, and Charlie had found their way through the bog to the gateway and the graveyard. Charlie kept his eye on the gruesome gargoyles perched on top of the pillars as he slipped through the gates, as if they might leap down at any moment. Quietly, they crept through the graves towards the church. Hearing voices coming from inside, Crystalian led them along its edge to a part of the wall that was high enough for cover but low enough to see over. Molly watched Lord Skeldrin, the man she had heard so much about, the one who had enchanted her father and taken him away. She felt angry. She wanted to jump the wall and demand that he bring him back. 'What are they?' She whispered, watching the three hags gorging on the rotten fish.

'I believe they are called the Hedrin,' whispered Crystalian. 'Dark witches, this is not good, not good at all,' he said, removing his gun from under his coat.

'Not good?' whispered Charlie hysterically. 'You can say that again.'

'When you have quite finished, ladies, I have a pressing matter I wish to discuss,' said Lord Skeldrin impatiently. The Eye spat out some fish bones at Skeldrin's feet, and a fishy mess splattered against his boot. An evil look came over his face as he raised his cane. The crystal at its tip glowed brightly, and he pointed it at the Eye. A blue bolt shot out, enveloping the hag in crackling light. She screamed and dropped to the floor in agony, while the Ears and the Nose shrieked alongside her. The hunchback ran off into the graveyard in panic, howling as he ran. 'I think you are forgetting who I am,' said Skeldrin angrily.

'Please, please, do not hurt her, do not damage our Eye,' begged the Ears and the Nose, grovelling on the ground.

'Well, ladies, if we have all realised our place in the order of things, perhaps we could continue.'

'What is it you want of us?' whimpered the Ears.

Skeldrin stepped forward, standing over them, like a bird examining its prey.

'Am I right in assuming you're aware of Anatana Mutara?'

'Yes, my Lord,' replied the Hedrin together.

'I want to know more.'

'You expect much, My Lord,' hissed the Eye.

Lord Skeldrin raised his cane again, its tip glowing brightly.

'We do not have that knowledge,' said the Nose desperately, 'we are not the keepers of that secret.'

'Nothing mortal does,' said the Ears.

'No, but we know of one who might,' said the Eye, grovelling at Lord Skeldrin's feet. 'The demon Menocropolis, yes. One who is old beyond years and sees all, yes. He will know.'

'Then summon him,' snapped Lord Skeldrin.

'Ye...s, my Lord, yessss,' hissed the witches.

The Hedrin got to their feet and moved to a bare

patch of ground. The Eye took a short, crooked stick from her cloak and scraped a large circle in the dirt. The Nose took a small clay bottle from under her ragged robe and gave it to the Eye. 'Do not step inside the circle once we are completed,' warned the Eye, as she poured the contents of the bottle in the middle of the circle onto the ground. A thick, dark, slimy, green ooze, slopped out of the bottle, bubbling and fizzing as it sank into the earth. She stepped out of the drawn circle quickly. The Hedrin now stood equally apart around the s edge and began to chant.

'Devils and Demons in the depths so cold,
Bring forth your knowledge,
Like snakes that unfold.
Slithering, slathering teeth that bite,
Only Menocropolis has the gift of sight.
Open the way that we may see,
Come forth, Menocropolis, and show it to me.'

Again and again, they spoke their spell, waving their arms in a circular motion and swaying as they chanted, until the ground beneath the circle began to shake. Then suddenly, the green ooze spouted out of the ground, rippling and building outward and upward, as the Hedrin continued to chant. It grew taller and wider, and arms rippled out from its side. A large head grew out from the top, taking the shape of a bull with horns, its body expanding to form a torso like that of a man, and its fingers grew long, pointy, and sharp. A hush fell all around, not even a toad croaked in the bog. The Hedrin moved away quickly, clinging to each other in fear of the demon. Grumblewit and the hunchback hid behind a tree stump in terror. Lord Skeldrin did not; it held no fear for him, although he was careful not to step too close to the edge of the circle, for breaking it by stepping inside would release the demon out into the world.

The hairs on the back of Molly's neck stood up, her eyes almost popping from her head. 'What is it?' She whispered.

'It is an ancient and demon, a keeper of knowledge with something that Skeldrin wants,' whispered Crystalian.

'I am Menocropolis, who has dared to call me?' Said the Demon.

'It is I Menocropolis,' replied Lord Skeldrin.

'Lord Skeldrin, the Dark One. What knowledge can I impart to one as diabolical as you?'

'What do you know of Anatana Mutara?' replied Skeldrin.

'Anatana Mutara, the way to merge the dead with the living,' replied the demon, snorting. 'I know that the way was hidden from mortal eyes.'

'Do you know where?'

'I do,' said Demon with a cunning smile. It watched Lord Skeldrin carefully as he walked the circle, for it was always looking to leave the circle if the opportunity arose. 'Come closer, Lord Skeldrin, so that I may whisper the secret to your ear.' Lord Skeldrin laughed at the mere suggestion and shot the Demon an impatient look. 'Very well, listen carefully,' said the Demon. 'Hidden forever in a devil's tail, guarded by claws to make grown men wail, the way is...'

The Hedrin huddled nearby, while Skeldrin listened to the demon. 'We are not alone,' hissed the

Ears to her sisters.

'I smell them too,' said the Nose.

The Eye began scanning the ruins of the old church. Molly was pushing herself up against the crumbling wall in front of her to get a better look when the wall suddenly gave way, falling into the church ruins with a loud crash. Crystalian leapt in front of Molly through a cloud of dust, pointing his shotgun at Menocropolis. He fired. The cartridge of salt erupted, penetrating the demon. Its skin bubbled and fizzled, and its body expanded, and then, with a loud cry, it exploded. The Hedrin screamed and hissed as they were splattered with green ooze from the demon. Crystalian turned about and fired at them. The cartridges exploded, splattering them with stinging salt, but all it did was to anger the witches more. With a scream, the Eye ran towards him. But snatching a burning log from the fire, Crystalian struck her with it, knocking her backwards into her sisters. Her cloak caught fire from the burning log, which spread to the Ears and the Nose as they clung to her. Then, in a sudden burst of wild flames, they vanished into thin air, leaving nothing but smoke and raining ash. In the commotion, Lord Skeldrin had slipped away. Grumblewit had not been so quick-thinking. Knocked off his feet by the exploding demon, he squealed and rolled around in the green ooze. Crystalian planted his boot on his chest. 'You are discovered, Grumblewit, and you will answer for what you have done,' he said, taking a piece of rope from his pocket. Turning Grumblewit over where he lay whimpering, Crystalian bound his hands. 'Now get up and move,' he barked, hauling Grumblewit to his feet. 'Charlie, Molly, take hold of his arms and bring him with us.' Crystalian ran for the church entrance. He could see Lord Skeldrin running through the graveyard and took off after him.

'Please, miss, don't let him hurt me, I did not mean any harm,' snivelled Grumblewit.

'Don't bother yourself, matey, you're done for,' said Charlie.

Grumblewit shrieked, barging through the pair of them, and tried to run, but Charlie was too quick and tripped him up. He hit the floor with a crunch and rolled onto his back, yelping and yelling. 'You must let me go, please.'

'You know something about my father, don't you?' Yelled Molly.

'Tell her,' said Charlie, kicking Grumblewit in the rear.

'Y... you're the Chatsworth girl, Edwards's daughter, a... aren't you?'

'So, you do know him!'

'Yes, I do. I liked Edward; he was kind to me, but I cannot tell you anything. Lord Skeldrin will kill me if I talk.'

'Please,' pleaded Molly, 'tell me what you know. Tell me!'

Grumblewit rolled about in the mud, snivelling and muttering incoherently.

'He won't tell you, Mol, I've met his type before,' said Charlie, trying to pull Grumblewit to his feet.

'But he's my only hope!' Said Molly with frustration.

Lord Skeldrin stopped running when he reached the gateway to the graveyard. From his pocket, he removed a small pouch and poured out a red powder into the palm of his hand. He stood calmly at the top of the stairway, silhouetted by the moon against the mist as Crystalian reached the bottom of the steps. 'You should have stayed at home this evening, tucked in bed,' said Lord Skeldrin. 'Oh dear, I am sorry, I forgot, you don't have a home. You're living off the charity of your Grandmaster.'

'You know nothing of me, Skeldrin,' said Crystalian, drawing his gun.

'Really? Are you sure?'

Raising his palm upward, Lord Skeldrin blew his red powder left and right, up towards the gargoyles that sat upon the pillars. The powder swirled and twisted around them, and they began to move. Their heads turned down to face Lord Skeldrin. 'Kill them, kill them all, now!' He yelled. Skeldrin turned about and disappeared into the mist of the marsh.

'What devilry is this?' said Crystalian, staring in disbelief at the moving gargoyles.

Molly and Charlie were catching up fast, shoving a distressed and uncooperative Grumblewit along in front of them. The gargoyles leapt from their perch, landing on the steps below them with a great thud. They were apelike in body with lashing tails, short stubby wings, lizard-like heads and enormous teeth.

Crystalian turned towards Molly, Charlie, and Grumblewit. 'Run!' he yelled, grabbing Grumblewit by the arm on the way past.

'I told you this was a bad place,' said Charlie, spotting the snarling gargoyles. 'We'll be lucky to get out of 'ere alive.'

Crystalian ran on with Grumblewit, as Molly and Charlie sped off in another direction. The stone creatures came bounding through the graveyard, snapping and snarling as they ran. One gargoyle bound after Crystalian, while the other bound after Molly and Charlie. Crystalian spied an open grave and pushed a squealing Grumblewit into the hole. 'You can wait in there,' he said, as the gargoyle snapped and snarled somewhere behind. Crystalian ran on, weaving his way through the graves until he spotted a huge stone tomb with a large statue at its head. The gargoyle leapt in great bounds, heading straight for him. He climbed onto the tomb and pushed with his shoulder against the statue. The creature reached the tomb, and with one final push, Crystalian tipped the statue over. It crashed down on top of the gargoyle, smashing it in two and a red mist rose from its lifeless body.

The graveyard fell silent as Molly and Charlie hid behind a large headstone. 'What can you see?' whispered Molly.

'Nuffing and I 'ope it stays that way,' replied Charlie, peeping round the gravestone.

Somewhere in the mist they could hear a thudding noise upon the ground, heading their way. The gargoyle was coming.

'Where's that noise coming from?' Asked Molly.

'I think it's behind us. No wait, it might be in front,' said Charlie, looking one way, then looking another.

'It's getting closer,' said Molly nervously, as she looked in every direction. The thudding stopped, and silence fell once again. They both listed carefully. Then, with a sudden loud crunch, the gargoyle appeared above them, perched on the gravestone. Snarling and snapping, it was ready to pounce. They both yelled as the stone creature was about to jump, but, with a loud crack, the headstone broke beneath its weight. Falling backward, a hole opened up as the gargoyle and the headstone hit the earth, and the stone creature disappeared inside an old grave. 'Come on, let's run for it,' yelled Molly.

Sprinting through the mist, they ran straight into Crystalian, who was dragging Grumblewit behind him.

'Blimey O'Reilly, you frightened the life out of me,' yelled Charlie angrily.

'Where's the other one?' Demanded Crystalian.

'It's back there somewhere, in a hole,' replied Molly.

'Yeah, but it won't be in there for long,' said Charlie looking back.

'Then we must move quickly and get to the bog. We can lose it there.' They all ran as fast as they could, weaving through the graves, back up the steps, through the gates, and back into the bog. 'Now we do as before and hold on to each other. And you will go first,' said Crystalian, pushing Grumblewit forward, who squealed in fright as they moved quickly into the bog.

They wound their way through the mist, struggling to find their way out, until Crystalian stopped them. 'Wait, does anybody hear that? Just stand where you are, don't move and listen.'

'It's that thing,' whispered Charlie.

Everyone froze, waiting for any sound of a thud. A light breeze picked up and the mist began to shift. Suddenly, the gargoyle swooped down, snatching Molly by her coat, pulling her upward and away. Molly screamed as she tried to wriggle free of its grip, but the gargoyle flapped its wings hard, trying to get higher. But its stone body was too heavy. Tumbling back down through the air, it crashed down into the bog water, pulling Molly down with it, vanishing from sight. 'Molly!' cried Crystalian.

Silence fell.

Charlie and Crystalian looked helplessly into the water, while Grumblewit quivered helplessly on the soggy ground.

Suddenly, Molly burst to the surface, coughing and spluttering. Crystalian waded into the bog and pulled her out, as the gargoyle sank silently to the bottom.

'Crikey, Mol, we were supposed to lose it, not swim with it,' said Charlie with relief.

'Are you alright, Molly?' said Crystalian, taking off

his coat and wrapping it around her

'Y...es, j... just, f ...freezing.'

'Let's get you out of here,' said Crystalian.

Back at the car, Crystalian squashed a squealing Grumblewit into the boot.

'What happened to Lord Skedldrin?' Asked Molly.

'I do not know, vanished it would seem,' replied Crysalian, looking about the marsh.

'What are you going to do with Grumblewit?'

'I will take him back to the Hall of Valdar,' replied Crystalian. 'We have places to keep him there, and then the Grandmaster and the Council of Twelve will decide his fate. If he knows anything, they will find out. It's what I am to do with you two, that is more important right now.'

'You won't tell gran, will you?' asked Molly, concerned.

'I will not tell her, but Grendellbar will have to know what's happened here tonight, and I cannot speak for him. Now, let's get you both home.'

CHAPTER VIII

—THE CRYSTAL NETWORK—

Molly spent the next couple of days trying to hide her smelly, wet clothes, finally triumphing when Mrs Peabody started the washing machine on Saturday morning, and sneaked them in the top when Mrs Peabody left the kitchen.

Her feelings about herself and her new world had changed now. No longer did she feel the fear of the unknown; she now felt stronger and wiser than she once did. Of course, her father had apparently still tried to fake his own death, her mother it seemed had known all along what her mysterious illness was and her grandmother, well, that was a story that just kept on giving with each day that passed. She went upstairs, leaving Charlie talking to Harold in the garden. She passed the jar of nails by the front door, which her grandmother was using to protect the house, as she climbed the stairs to her room. She took her time getting ready, as she wondered when the dreaded moment would arrive when her mother would come to take her home. That just wasn't going to happen, not without her father anyway.

It was around ten-thirty when she finally came downstairs, and as she walked through the hallway, she could hear voices. Following the sound, she came to an open doorway in the hall, and, peering inside, she saw her grandmother wearing a rather startling purple robe, sitting with another woman at a round table. 'Thank you so much, Grand Sally, I feel so much lighter now,' said the woman.

'Not at all, my dear. I am here anytime you need me.' The woman got up with a beaming smile on her face, which became even bigger when she saw Molly. 'If you would like to pay Mr Abebi by the door on your way out, he would be most grateful, Mrs Browning,' said Grand Sally. Mr Abebi was a carving of a man, holding a golden bowl. It had taken Grand Sally many years to charge for what she did, thinking her gift was something to share with others rather than profit herself and Mr Abebi was a way of alleviating her guilty feelings. Almost as if he was taking the money and not her.

'No need to get up. I'll see myself out, Sally,' said Mrs Browning, brightly.

'Very well, dear. See you again soon.' Grand Sally spotted Molly standing by the door. 'Oh, Molly, perfect timing. Come in, come in.' In the centre of the room, on the round table, sat a large glass ball on a stand. The light in the room was supplied by large white candles placed on shelves, giving a magical glow to the room. Tapestries with peculiar-looking writing hung upon the walls, and strange coloured rocks with a glassy look to them sat on display. On one of the shelves sat a small brass bowl on a stand; a candle burned beneath it, heating an oil inside that gave an unfamiliar but pleasant aroma.

'What is this room? I don't remember it?' asked Molly, fascinated by all the different things on display.

'This is my spiritual room,' said Grand Sally, standing up and pulling out a chair for Molly to sit on. 'You spent a lot of time in here, as a baby, crawling around on the floor. You don't remember?'

'No, I don't,' said Molly, a little frustrated.

Grand Sally got up from the table and opened a wooden trunk behind her. She pulled a large leather-bound book from the trunk and set it on the table. 'I know things have been a little difficult lately.'

'That's putting it mildly,' said Balthazar, flapping into the room and landing on Molly's shoulder.

'Oh, look, it's my princey wincey,' said Grand Sally.

'Here we go,' said Balthazar.

Molly did her best not to laugh.

'My little chicky wicky. Looks like you have a friend there.'

'So, what's the book gran?' Asked Molly, still trying to stifle her laughter as she shuffled her chair a bit nearer.

'The family bible,' said Balthzar.

'It's a little history, and this may help explain a few things. Time to meet the family,' she said, turning back the cover to reveal a large photo. 'This is the only photo of the family together,' she said with a mix of joy and sadness.

'Oh well. I'll leave you to it,' said Balthazar, fluttering off again.

'W...ow,' said Molly, 'I've never seen this before.' The photo was fading, turning brown in colour with tattered edges, but brightly lit by the sun on the day of the photo. Three rows deep, people stood alongside each other, all grinning from ear to ear, and there stood her mother and father, in the front row, standing proudly, her mother cradling Molly as a baby in her arms.

'Look at me, squashed into that dress,' said Grand Sally, chuckling.

'Look at me, so small,' said Molly. 'So, who are all these people?'

'Your family, of course!'

'But I don't recall any of them.'

'Well, everyone came to see you. They were all here in this house, all at once, and the photo was taken in the garden.'

'Really!'

'Yes, really.'

Molly looked in fascination at all the family in their fine suits and smart dresses, smiling for the camera.

'So, from left to right, starting with this lady here, this is Diana, she's my cousin, excellent Homoeopath, you name it, she has a concoction to cure it. Next to her is Donald, her husband, always very quiet, a bit of a mystery. Cousins Janet, Jane, Henry, George, Margaret, and then there's Bert, Harry, Ranold, Betty, Sue, Maud, Jessica. Next is your auntie Maisy and her husband, your uncle Joe, one of my brothers.'

'Yes, I do remember him,' said Molly excitedly, 'I don't know why, but I remember that smile.'

'A...w yes, that's when you know you're in trouble,' said Grand Sally, laughing. 'He's an Intuitive, he can read you and size you up from fifty paces, and now of course, he's a very wealthy man and aunty Murele, his wife, she's an amazing Telepath. Next to him is my sister, your auntie Judy, and her husband, your uncle John, another one of my brothers. He's a Time Keeper like me. We will have to pay them a visit, they're not that far away, I know they would love to see you.'

'A...w, yes, can we,' replied Molly enthusiastically.

'And then there's Auntie Blanche, one of my sisters.' Grand Sally fidgeted uncomfortably in her seat. 'We don't see much of Blanche, in fact, we never see Blanche.'

'Why?' Asked Molly curiously.

'Blanche was, or is, I should say, a Witch.'

'She is!' said Molly, startled as she thought back to the Hedrin at Banshee Bog.

'Yes, but it's not the sinister kind, you're thinking of the kind in fairy tales and story books, although,' said Grand Sally, pausing thoughtfully, 'I have met a few in my time that could definitely fit into that category.'

'You have!' said Molly in surprise.

'Blanche was sent away.' Grand Sally's eyes widened, glistening with salty tears that clung to the corners of her eyes. 'It was awful, we came home from school one day and she was gone. Gone to live somewhere else, we told.' Grand Sally dabbed her eyes with a hanky.

'But, why, what happened, Gran? Molly asked, eager to know more.

'Another time, dear, another time,' said Grand

Sally, shutting the book like the closing of an old wound that had unexpectedly reopened.

'Grandma. I love it here, and you, but something tells me that things won't be the same again; not unless we get Dad back.'

Grand Sally let out a big sigh. 'I know it's hard, dear. I really don't know what to think about Edward. All those years I tried, and now look. The shame of it all.' She shook her head and sighed again, as more tears collected at the bottom of her eyes. 'As a boy, he had amazing potential. Grendellbar himself took him under his wing, then one day it was like he woke up and changed his mind. That's why you were never told. I think your father knew you had a gift as soon as you were born. Being an Intuitive, he would, and before you showed any signs of it, they whisked you away from me.'

'Don't worry, Grandma, we'll find a way to get him back,' said Molly, clutching her grandmother's hand.

Grand Sally wiped her eyes with a handkerchief. 'Now then, there's something else I wanted to show you, and this is most important.' Pulling the big glass ball on the table nearer to her, she clasped it tightly with both hands and closed her eyes. 'Marjorie? Marjorie Maddocks, are you there?'

'Grandma, what are you doing?' asked Molly, intrigued.

'This is the Crystal Network, a marvellous wonder. I can speak to all my friends on here, and anyone else with a crystal ball.'

'Hello?' said a voice. 'Who's that?'

Grand Sally took her hands away, and there, as clear as day, was a woman's face. Molly moved closer, her eyes bulging in disbelief.

'Oh, Grand Sally, it's you.'

'You mean she can see you?' said Molly, leaning forward and touching the glass.

'Of course, she can dear. Yes, Marjorie, it's me. Who else?'

'There's somebody there with you. Who is it?' asked Marjorie, her face distorting in the roundness of the ball as she moved closer to her own.

'This is my granddaughter, Molly. Just showing her the ropes and the Crystal Network.'

'Oh, jolly good. How are you doing with it all?'

Molly gaped, completely flabbergasted by the face in the glass ball.

'She's talking to you, dear,' whispered Grand Sally, nudging Molly with her arm.

'Oh, sorry. Well, yes, okay, I suppose.'

'I expect it's all a bit strange, dear, but you'll get used to it.'

'We'll say goodbye for now, Marjorie,' said Grand Sally. 'It was just a quick call.'

'Okay, my dear. See you at the Festival of Light. Goodbye.'

With that, Marjorie's face faded from sight.

'Well, what do you think?' asked Grand Sally.

But before Molly could answer, another voice sprang from the crystal ball. 'Hello, hello, Sally, is that you?' Another woman's face appeared in the ball.

'Oh, Finella Fudgecombe, and how are you?'

'You know how it is. That husband of mine, he's up to no good again, and that's what I wanted to talk to you about...'

'Finella,' said Grand Sally, hastily, 'I have my granddaughter with me. It's not really a good time to speak to you now.'

'Yes, but...' Grand Sally threw a silk cloth over the ball, muffling a distressed Finella Fudgecombe.

'That's the trouble. The moment they know you're on the line, they're queuing up to tell you all their problems.' All of a sudden, a commotion could be heard coming from the living room. 'Whatever is going on now?' said Grand Sally.

They found Mrs Peabody clapping and laughing, and Charlie grinning from ear to ear. Grand Sally and Molly both ducked as Balthazar came flapping around their heads and swooped about the living room. Charlie made a whistle with his fingers, and the raven flew down and landed on his shoulder. 'Wah, wah! Clever boy. Clever boy. Wah! Just playing the part,' whispered Balthazar in Charlie's ear.

'A clever boy indeed,' said Mrs Peabody.

'My word, Charles, what are you doing with my princey wincey?' Said Grand Sally.

'Now don't go getting all upset. It was my fault,' said Mrs Peabody, one hand on her hip as she stood branding a wet tea towel.

'Don't be ridiculous, woman, I'm not a complete ogre.'

'Well, maybe not complete, no,' said Mrs Peabody with a sly grin.

'Impertinent woman!' Bellowed Grand Sally.

'Wah, wah, imper... tinent! Imper... tinent!' squawked Balthazar, as he took off and flew around the chandelier once more.

CHAPTER IX

—THE CHAMBER OF FIRE—

When the evening arrived, 10 Plumberry Road became busy preparing for the Valdar annual Festival of Light. Grand Sally had bought Molly a new dress, especially for the occasion, and Mrs Peabody had laid it out neatly on her bed as a surprise. Molly was overjoyed, she had never had a dress like It was long, flowing, and golden in colour, pulled in at the waist with short billowing sleeves, and open at the neck. Next to the dress were some gold shoes to match, stitched by hand with a little bow of black ribbon on each one. Grand Sally was busy putting on her ceremonial robe in the hall with Mrs Peabody's help. The robe was black with gold braiding at its edges. In the centre at the back, in gold, silver, and red, sat the Valdar symbol, the elongated six-pointed star.

'Not so much room as last time, I think,' said Mrs Peabody with a wry smile, pulling at the robe.

'I beg your pardon. How rude. I haven't changed dress sizes in, in, in...'

'Yes?' Said Mrs Peabody, pausing.

'In a very long time,' snapped Grand Sally.

'So, they were someone else's dresses I let out last month, then?'

'Impertinent woman, let me be. I've never been so insulted in my life, the cheek of it.' Molly appeared at the top of the stairs. She looked beautiful; her hair was clasped high on top of her head with just a couple of strands hanging past her ears. A beaded necklace set the open-necked dress off perfectly. The golden colours of the dress shimmered in the hall lights as she lifted the hem to descend the stairs. 'My word, Mrs Peabody, my granddaughter looks quite the lady.'

'She does indeed.'

'My dear, you look beautiful,' said Grand Sally, dabbing a tear from her eye. 'Absolutely beautiful.'

Mrs Peabody wrapped a black shawl around

Molly's shoulders against the cool night air. 'Now you be 'avin yourself a grand time, dearie, and don't get up to any mischief.'

'I'm sure I won't, Mrs P,' replied Molly with a chuckle.

'And you, Mrs Peabody, no mischief either,' said Grand Sally. 'Can't leave her alone for a minute,' she whispered in Molly's ear.

'Blimey, Mrs G, this suit itches somefing rotten,' said Charlie, moving uncomfortably up the hall.

'Don't be ridiculous, boy. Stand up straight and stop wriggling. It's the feel of quality, that's what it is, and please stop calling me that awful name. Sally will do fine. Right then, if we are all ready, let's be off. Has everyone taken a nail from the jar?'

'No,' said Molly and Charlie, both rolling their eyes. Molly opened the jar on the hall table and took a nail, giving one to Charlie and one to herself.

'You might be pulling faces now, but you'll thank me later,' said Grand Sally. 'Remember now, it will act as protection, but not if you go throwing yourself in harm's way.'

Charlie chatted to Harold in the front of the car

as they drove. Molly looked out the side window from the back seat, watching people going about their business. Some returning home from work, mothers getting their children in for bed, people standing outside pubs laughing and joking, policemen walking their beat, and vans delivering their goods. 'I was thinking of mum today,' she said whistfully.

'Oh yes,' replied Grand Sally.

'Nothing in particular, I was just wondering what she was up to, how she was.'

'Don't worry about your mother, darling, she's a big girl, she'll be fine. And if you think you've heard the last of her, think again; she'll appear just when you least expect it. You are her only daughter after all, she's not just going to just leave you, mark my words.'

'I know Gran, that's what I'm worried about, but I'm not going anywhere without dad.'

Harold drove in and stopped behind two other cars that were waiting at a huge set of ornate metal gates.

'So, tell me again, what this is all about, Mrs G,'

said Charlie from the front seat.

Charles, if I've told you once, I've told you a dozen times, now why don't you wait and see. If we ever get in that is. Whatever is going on, Harold?'

'I really don't know, madam.'

'Well go and find out!' Said Grand Sally impatiently.

Luckily for Harold, the car in front moved forward. Four young men in light blue uniforms and peaked hats were at the gates, checking the cars through. Harold eased the car forward and pulled down his window as he drew alongside one of the guards.

'And who do we have here, then, sir?' the guard asked, looking at a list as he spoke. Before Harold could answer, Grand Sally had pulled down her window.

'Just what is going on, young man?' she barked.

'Oh, it's you, madam,' said the guard, almost standing to attention. 'Good evening. I'm terribly sorry for the delay. We are checking all the passengers and cars as they come in, an added security measure.'

'Security? What on earth are you talking about? Let me through immediately.'

Another uniformed man appeared at the window.

'Sorry, madam, do you have your tickets? We are under the Grandmaster's orders, I'm afraid.'

'Of course, I have,' said Grand Sally, fumbling in her bag and producing some bright red cards.

'Thank you, madam,' said the uniformed man, waving at the men at the gate to let them pass.

Grand Sally wound the window up. 'Added security, checking us in, never in all my years.'

Molly looked out through the rear window, back to the gate as the last car came through. Sparks flew off the gate, and blue flashes jumped up the tall railings, as they were electrified to keep out unwelcome visitors.

Following the cars in front, Harold drove up a winding road towards flickering flames in the distance ahead. All the cars were directed by wardens to park off-road on the grass as they arrived. Ahead of them lay a huge field overlooking the forest that curled around three sides of the Great Hall of Valdar. Two white stone statues of great, muscular men, thirty feet high, stood on either side of the entrance to the field, both holding stone platters above their heads in which fires burned brightly. The field was alive with activity, people, lights, and smells. Molly gazed in wonder at it all. Harold parked the car and opened the rear door for Grand Sally. 'This looks amazing said Charlie as he stepped out onto the grass. Driven by excitement, he marched off toward the lights and smells.

'Come back, Charles, at once! You'll get lost!' bellowed Grand Sally.

'This is fantastic Gran,' said Molly, still enthralled by the great statues.

'I know, isn't it wonderful, darling, a celebration of the magic and wonder of the Valdar. Once everyone has arrived, we will be called to order by the Master of Ceremonies, Radnor Falsorth, and then in a long procession we all head down the hill over there,' she said pointing, 'to the Great Hall in the distance and Randor, sings us all in.'

'Sings?' Said Molly.

'Oh yes, you just wait, it's wonderful. Now then, where is that mischievous boy?'

'Don't worry, gran, I'll find him,' said Molly, heading off.

'Wait! I don't want you getting into any more trouble.'

'I won't, I've got protection, one of the nails from the jar, in my pocket; remember?' Called Molly back.

To her amazement, men on stilts covered in huge baggy trousers were striding through the crowds with painted faces, wearing big top hats, and juggling balls and batons. The atmosphere was electric. In the middle of the field stood a huge round stage, lit up by small burning torches around the outside. A band was playing nearby as circus acts performed their acts on a stage, as Charlie pushed his way to the front railing to watch the trapeze artists, the Flying Fabrizios. Three men and three women, all clad in bright orange, were swinging at tremendous speeds from one to another. Flying through the air, twisting and spinning, as they were lit up by the flickering torches below. The Flames of Zaradine followed the Fabrizios. Fire eaters. Charlie couldn't believe his luck. He had managed to sneak into a circus once before and hide at the back to watch, and the fire-eater was his favourite act. Now there were ten of them, right in front of him, with painted red faces. Breathing fire like dragons, they leapt about the stage in formation, juggling flaming sticks and fiery hoops, every so often shooting flames from their mouths out over the audience, to screams, gasps, and cheers.

'There you are,' said Molly, nudging Charlie from behind. 'I've been looking for you everywhere.'

'Mol, this is fantastic. Did you see the Fabrizios and the Fire-Eaters?'

'Yes, I saw it all from back there. How do they do all that?'

'Magic, that's how,' said Charlie, grinning from ear to ear. 'Come on, let's go and see what else there is.'

Once they were clear of the crowd, Charlie turned to Molly.

'Sorry if I've been a bit off lately, just that business in Banshee Bog spooked me a bit.'

'It doesn't matter, I...' Molly was cut short as two boys walked straight into Charlie, giving him a shove.

'Here, watch it!' he said angrily.

'Mind where you're going, oik,' said one of the boys.

'Yes, oik, watch out,' said the other.

Both boys had the same dark brown hair, parted on the same side, green eyes and white faces, both dressed in little blue suits. 'What's a common oik like you doing here anyway? The standards must be really low this year, James,' said one to the other.

'Yes, they'll be letting in beggars and thieves next year. You wait, John.'

'I expect the parents are a low sort. Oiks as well, no doubt,' replied John.

Charlie clenched his fists in anger.

'Now, just hang on a, there's really no need for all of this,' said Molly, getting in between them.

'You're the Chatsworth girl, aren't you?' said James with a snigger. 'We've heard of you.'

'I beg your pardon,' said Molly, 'I've never...'

'Everybody knows about you. You're the one who has a scumbag for a father,' said John.

'Another oik,' said James.

'Runs in the family,' said John, giving Molly a look of disgust.

Charlie had had enough and punched James, knocking him to the ground.

'Charlie, no!' shrieked Molly, as Charlie jumped on top of him. John jumped on Charlie 's back, and quickly all three were rolling around, kicking and punching wildly at each other. A man stepped out from the crowd and hurried toward them. Pulling them apart, Charlie jumped to his feet, ready for another go. 'Just what is going on here? Rolling around in the dirt like commoners,' barked the man.

'We were minding our own business, Father, when this oik came along and started trouble,' yelled James, nursing a throbbing eye.

Molly recognised the man as Baradium from the park, the one who wanted her grandmother thrown out of the Valdar.

'You're just a liar!' said Charlie, rushing in for another go, but the man pushed him away.

'Feisty little devil, aren't you?' He said, lowering a staff in Charlie's direction. It had a red crystal on its end, which glowed ominously.

'It is a lie. I saw them, they started it,' said Molly angrily.

'Shut up, Chatsworth,' snapped John.

'Quite please, John, I'm dealing with this,' snapped Baradium. 'Yes, you're the Chatsworth girl, Edward's daughter, the girl in the park. How interesting. Well, that explains a great deal. Here with your grandmother, are you?'

'They're with me, Baradium,' said a familiar voice from behind.

'Crystalian. Now, why am I not surprised,' sneered Baradium. 'The Grandmaster's lackey.'

'Is there a problem here?' Asked Crystalian.

'Just keep your little dog on a lead, will you? He can't go around attacking innocent people. There are homes for children like that.'

'They're coming with me now,' said Crystalian, gesturing to them both.

'Miss Chatsworth,' said Baradiaum. 'Enjoy your evening at the festival, won't you, because you and your grandmother won't be attending anymore.' Baradium turned and walked away. The twins followed, sneaking a sly grin back at Charlie.

'Honest, Crystalian, I might 'ave laid the first blow, but they were lookin' for it.'

'Those boys are horrible, and that awful man?' said Molly.

'That is Baradium, one of the Council of Twelve.'

'I know,' said Molly.

'Then you should also know, he's not a man to mess with,' replied Crystalian. 'And they are his sons, known as the Gemini twins. He is a man of great influence, and you, Charlie, don't need any more unwanted attention. Now let's find your grandmother, the march will be starting soon.'

When they found Molly's Grandmother, she was chatting to a group of people, keeping them enthralled in her usual way. 'Oh, there you are,' she said as Molly and Charlie approached with Crystalian. 'Let me introduce you both. This is Mr and Mrs Kwani. Mr Kwani is one of the Council of Twelve.' An elderly African man with spectacles, looking rather like a wise old owl, thought Molly, gave her and Charlie a big smile and shook their hands. 'And, this is Peter and Jenny Yarrowood, and their two daughters, Penny and Charlotte.' The Yarrowoods were a jolly couple, full of enthusiasm.

'Hello, Molly,' said Mrs Yarrowood. 'Your

grandmother's been telling us all about you, you're quite a talented young lady, I hear.'

'Well, I..,' said Molly, not knowing quite how to answer.

'And who's this young man?' asked Mr Yarrowood.

'This is Charles, a new addition to the family,' said Grand Sally.

Peter grabbed Charlie's hand and gave it a good squeeze and a friendly shake. 'And what sign are you, lad?'

'Uh, sign?' Burbled Charlie.

'E is a Leo,' said Mrs Kwani with a penetrating look. 'The Lion, the warrior spirit is in that boy.'

'If Mrs Kwani says you're a Leo, then that's good enough for me,' said Mr Yarrowood, 'she can see through anyone. And you, Molly, what sign are you?'

'She's a Virgo,' said Grand Sally, jumping in.'

'A leader, very intelligent, my word, we'll all have to watch our step, Mr Kwani,' said Mr Yarrowood, laughing. 'These two will be running the show, if we're not careful. And you, Sally, bearing up okay? Enquired Mr Yarrowood.'

'Do you know what they're talking about?' Whispered Charlie to Molly.

Molly rolled her eyes. 'Well, yes, and no.'

'We all know what you're going through, Molly, said Charlotte in Molly's ear. 'It happens to all of us at your age.'

'I thought I was going mad,' said Molly quietly.

'I know,' said Charlotte, 'we all think that when it starts, the Awakening can be really hard sometimes.' 'I take after my mother, as a Time Keeper, but Penny's a fantastic Telepath.'

'The sickness can be a bit much,' said Penny.

'You're not kidding,' agreed Molly.

'They call it the Awakening, but all I wanted to do was sleep,' said Charlotte.

'I felt sick a lot and my head,' said Molly, making a face. 'But since Gran gave me a potion, I've felt a lot better.'

'Aunt Flossy,' said Charlotte and Penny in unison,

'I think I take after Gran,' said Molly, moving closer to Charlotte and Penny. 'I've seen and heard a lot of...things,' she whispered.

'Don't worry, we know,' they both said together

again.

'We have two brothers here somewhere as well,' said Charlotte, looking around, 'Harry and George.'

Molly leaned closer to Charlotte. 'Who are they?' She whispered, nodding toward a woman leading a line of girls.

'They're Valdarie,' replied Charlotte. 'They're born with the gift of sorcery.'

Molly watched as the woman at their head lifted her staff, firelight catching silver runes carved along it. 'And her?' Molly asked.

'That's Seren Vael,' the girl replied. 'A Valdarie Sorceress. She teaches them to control their gift; how to listen to the light before they try to command it.

'The light?' Molly asked, frowning. 'What do you mean?'

Charlotte didn't answer straight away. Her eyes followed the Valdarie as they passed 'The light of the Valdar, it's a power within.' One of the girls in the line stumbled, and Seren Vael's staff struck the ground sharply. The line moved on. 'In the past, some Valdarie chose the wrong way,' she said, glancing back at Molly.

'I will say good evening to you all,' said Crystalian, bowing his head.

'Are you not coming on the march then?' Asked Grand Sally.

'No, I have... other things to attend to.'

As he walked off, Molly trotted after him. 'Crystalian, has Grumblewit said anything about my dad yet?'

'Not yet, Molly, he's too frightened to talk at the moment.'

Molly lowered her head in disappointment.

'Good night,' said Crystalian softly.

The sudden, shrill voice of Randor Falsorth, Master of Ceremonies, rang out across the field. 'My Lords, Ladies and Gentlemen, if you would all take your places for the march, please, we are ready to leave for the great Hall.' Everyone assembled four deep in a long line down the right-hand side of the field. Jimmy and George Yarrowood reappeared to join their family as Randor Falsorth called out again. 'As in years gone by, when we depart for the Great Hall, every other person on the outside line is required to collect a burning torch at the top of the hill.' Molly stood with Mrs Yarrowood, Penny and Charlotte, and Mr and Mrs Kwani were just in front with Grand Sally. Charlie stood with Mr Yarrowood, Harry, and George.

'Have you met the Gemini twins yet?' asked Harry.

'Yeah, I 'ave. Let's just say they weren't too friendly if you take my meaning. But one of them will be nursing a black eye tomorrow,' said Charlie quietly.

'Don't worry,' said George. 'Harry and I will sort them out if they come round again.'

'Now, now, boys, that's enough, please,' said Mrs Yarrowood.

'But Mum, come on!' Moaned George. 'They're morons, you know they are,'

'Yes, they are a bit peculiar, but you know who their father is.'

Calls for quiet came down the line, and gradually silence fell. Randor took his place at the front of the line and, filling his lungs with air, he started to sing. The procession was so long it was impossible to see from one end to the other. As Randor began his song, the procession began to hum as the line departed the field. Flaming torches six feet long were passed along the line as the procession reached the top of the hill.

Come with me now as we turn to the bow
And leave all that troubles behind,
The way of the light with no darkness in sight
As we sail with truth and in kind.
For wherever we go with our hearts high and low,
Forever with peace in our mind,
The way for us all not too big or too small,
It is always love that will bind.

With hundreds of torches lighting the way, the marching crowd resembled a serpent of fire, winding its way down into the forest. Randor was singing at the top of his voice as they entered the tree line, with hundreds of Valdar humming in harmony behind him, the torchlight turning the trees from green to gold. The Great Hall stood up ahead like a palace, spreading from left to right of a road running to its middle. Six pillars stood tall around the main entrance, stretching up to a triangular roof which loomed over marble steps ascending to its doors. The parade was still singing and humming as they trod the gravel road until Randor brought the procession to a stop. 'HALT!'

'What happens now?' whispered Molly to Mrs Yarrowood.

'First, the twelve Council members leave the line, look, there goes Mr Kwani, Grendellbar, Saren Vael, Avindor and there's Baradium.'

Molly gave him a deep scowl as he passed by.

'Then Randor says a few words, they all march in, and we charge in behind. Well, not charge, exactly, but you'll see.'

The Council of Twelve stood in single file with Grendellbar behind Randor, leading the twelve council members. Randor stepped forward and rapped three times with his staff on the great door. 'Let those within show the way to those without.' There was some clunking and creaking and the sound of metal bolts sliding, and the two doors swung open. The Council marched into a big cheer from the parade, and then everyone began moving forward, putting out their torches in buckets of water and placing them on the ground. Inside the Great Hall, it was as gigantic as it looked from the outside. Where it went and where it ended, Molly could not tell, but it was all so beautiful. The ceilings were adorned with plaster mouldings inlaid with gold, and chandeliers hung down, dressed with burning candles.

Charlotte and Penny huddled around Molly.

'Can you believe it? It's an amazing place, isn't it,' said Penny.

'Come on, let's get some food,' said Charlotte. 'I'm starved.'

Everyone funnelled down to a hall big enough to fit 10 Plumberry Road in ten times over. There, food, drink and music were waiting.

'Come on, Charlie, we'd better get a move on,' said Harry, pushing his way forward.

'Yeah, before the hyenas get all the grub,' added George, laughing.

'Mind your manners,' ordered Mrs Yarrowood, 'it's not feeding time at the zoo, you know.'

'Yes, mum,' said George and Harry, rolling their

eyes.

An hour had gone by. Molly was just finishing some trifle, while Grand Sally was on her third piece of cake. Harry and George were busy slipping red jelly into unsuspecting ladies' handbags, and Charlie was wrapping up sandwiches for later and stuffing down his tenth sausage roll, when Molly felt the hall grow almost silent. In place of the noise from the crowded hall, a lone whispering voice filled her ears. *'E...tahno ro...maie, e...tahno ro...maie,'* said the slow, seductive whisper. Molly poked a finger in her ear, wiggling it around, one then the other. But it was no use; the whispering remained. Everyone was still chatting, eating, and having a merry time; no one else was hearing the whisperer. The voice now drew her uncontrollably toward a corridor at the end of the hall. No one noticed as she slipped away through the crowd and passed into the corridor.

She wandered down the passage, the noise from the hall fading into the background. The passage opened out to a spectacular space, a colossal round hall with a domed roof. Great paintings of the Council of Twelve, past and present, stood out from the walls. Tiers of wooden seats sprang up from the ground around three-quarters of its circumference. At the front of the chamber stood a golden podium, its ornate pedestal rising to support a set of open wings. Behind it, six golden thrones sat to its left and six to its right, with one throne larger than the rest in the middle. On the wall behind the podium hung the huge golden Valdenium Star towering over everything beneath it, and in a large circle at the centre of the hall, set into the floor in coloured marble, the twelve signs of the Zodiac. Still, the whispering voice persisted. *'E...tahno ro...maie, e...tahno ro...maie.'*

'Quite an adventure you had a few nights back,' said a voice from behind.

Startled, Molly turned quickly, and the voice faded away. There stood Grendellbar. 'I heard a voice, like a whisper, was it you?'

'No, said Grendellbar with a curious frown.

'O...kay,' said Molly, feeling a tinge of embarrassment for following a voice in her head that led to nowhere. 'It was very clear, *Etahno, Romaie,* it kept saying, over and over.'

'Say that again,' said Grendellbar, wide-eyed.

'Ethano...Romaie,' replied Molly, feeling like she might have done something wrong.

'Come with me,' said Grendellbar firmly.

Walking across the vast hall, Grendellbar led the way down an adjoining corridor. Reaching the end, he paused at a set of double doors. 'The words you spoke, Etano Romanie, is an ancient language, the language of...the Seraphim.' Grendellbar pushed open the large doors. Molly gasped as she entered another large, round hall. Great white statues with great wings stood in alcoves set into the curved walls. A large granite bowl protruded from the floor in the middle of the room, and green flames flickered at the centre. Grendellbar closed the doors behind them. 'In a time long ago, no longer remembered, another language was spoken. An ancient language, not spoken by any of us, for it was not for our lips to speak. A tongue that was born when the world was young, a language, only spoken by the Seraphim.'

'Angels,' whispered Molly, as she was transported to another time by the green reflections from the fire that danced across the walls.

‘Yes,’ said Grendellbar, ‘and you heard their call.’

‘Who were they all?’ Asked Molly in wonder.

‘The Seraphim were immortals that flew across the skies on great white wings, stronger and faster than any of us and with knowledge and intellect far superior to our own. Lofiiel was their King, the greatest of all warriors, and Tien was their Queen, whose beauty surpassed all things any human had ever seen. But their one purpose, the one reason they were here, was to defeat and destroy an evil called...the Sla.’

‘I know that name, I've seen one in a dream,’ spouted Molly.

‘The Sla, an acursed creature. Once human, their evil deeds had cursed them to the very depths of the earth, only to rise once more to forever roam in this world as a Wraith. With a craving for the gift of life that they once had, they remained hidden by day in the darkest and foulest places. Roaming the land in the dead of night, jealously looking to prey on the weak and the witless. Charms were made for protection, and the anointed would recite their spells to drive them away, and for a long time, they were kept at bay. That was, until the rise of the worst Sla of all, Angoule the Red. Grendelbar pointed to a large painting on the wall depicting a scene of a great battle. 'He was named the Red for as time would prove, no blood split was enough. He claimed Lordship over all Slas, and anything foul and wicked that walked, crawled or flew upon the earth. Angoule's hate of humans and their gift of life was immeasurable. Uniting all Slas, he took all their misery, jealousy and hate of the living, and gave it order, and with it came the most terrifying army ever seen. Some fought back, and armies were led out to meet them by the bravest of men and women, but how can the living kill what is neither dead nor alive? Just as all seemed lost, they appeared. Shining and golden like the brightest stars in the night sky, the Seraphim swooped down on the Slas in their hundreds. Male and Female, ferocious warriors that knew no fear. They fought long and hard, driving Angoule and his Sla armies back from our lands, sending them back to the darkest depths from where they came. Time passed, memories faded, and Slas slipped into folklore, a fable, as something to be forgotten. But, another war was brewing, and the Seraphim themselves were to be betrayed.' As Grendellbar continued, he would point to each Seraphim statue in turn as he mentioned their name. 'Zarangoth. General of all Seraphim armies and second only to Lofiel and Tien had, in secret, taken a human wife. By Seraphim law, above all else, any personal involvement with humans was forbidden. Soon, Zarangoth's human wife Aseer was with child. But she fell ill, and although Seraphim were bestowed with gifts of healing, it was beyond his power to heal. Death was near. But Zarangoth would not give up and had the Seraphim physician, Zelique, brought to him. To save her life. Zelique cut open the belly of Aseer and delivered a half-human, half-Seraphim boy. Zarangoth's commanders, his closest allies, had also taken human wives in secret, and more children were born. Half human, half Seraphim. They were to become known as the Nephilim. Their numbers grew, too many to keep secret, and word reached Lofiel. Lofiel was so angered that he ordered Zarangoth be brought before him, and that all the children were to be found...and destroyed.'

'Destroyed!' said Molly, 'But that's terrible.'

'But Zarangoth was too quick, and had all the children hidden in secret caves in the mountains. Lofiel searched and searched for the children, but he could not find them. In the search, Zarangoth's wife was hurt and accidentally killed. Zarangoth's grief was so great and his rage so large that he gathered his own army and declared war upon Lofiel and Seraphinium itself.'

'Seraphim against Seraphim, the gates of Seraphinium were breached, and Lofiel and Zarangoth fought upon the steps. Lofiel was brought down by Zarangoth and wounded, but before Zarangoth could finish him, the great Seraphim Barakiel took up Lofiel's sword, the sword of Athlis and brought Zarangoth to his knees. Zarangoth and his commanders, Thangorn, Vognast, Razakiel, and Belegnoth, were brought before a cavernous mouth at the ends of the earth. The mouth of Hellgorium. There, they were separated, body from spirit, and banished to the dark depths below, Hellgorium. Never to be seen again, forever to be known as the

Fallen. In the unlikely event that any of them should escape, their heads were removed from their bodies and buried separately, so that they may never be able to retake them. The heads were taken, and their whereabouts would remain a secret. But a prophecy foretells that should the five skulls be discovered and brought together at one time and place, the power of Zarangoth would rise once more. And it was after this terrible war,' he continued more quietly, 'that many of the Seraphim laid down their immortality. Burdened by grief, weariness, or shame, they surrendered their eternal flame, their immortality and became known as the Halfwings, still mighty, still wise, but bound to the mortal world. 'From these Halfwings came their children: gentler, humbler, yet bearing the old gifts. These became the first of the Valdar, keepers of sight and mind, and the Valdarie, in whom the spark of true sorcery bloomed. 'So,' he said, turning back to Molly. 'The Valdar descend from the Halfwings. We are the last quiet echo of the Seraphim, the living memory of that ancient war.'

'Wow,' whispered Molly as she gazed up at the statues. 'Belegnoth. That's who Lord Skeldrin is trying to find?'

'He is?' replied Grendellbar wearily.

'And my father is helping him.' Molly rubbed her face with her palms in frustration. 'We have to find him, Grendellbar, find him and stop him before it's too late.'

'That we most definitely must,' said Grendellbar.

Grendellbar continued talking, but Molly's attention was drawn away by the green flames growing larger behind him. 'Grendellbar, should that be happening?' She said, pointing at the flames. The fire grew higher and wider. A figure began to form within the flames. Molly stepped back. Grendellbar stood in front of her as the image of Lord Skeldrin appeared in the fire.

'Good evening, Grandmaster.'

'Skeldrin,' said Grendellbar in a hoarse voice.

'It is I,' he said in a superior tone. 'I thought I would drop in on your little party, albeit just an image. I would like to have come by personally, to spice things up s bit, but I'm a little busy as you may have guessed.'

'You have been,' said Grendellbar. 'What do you

want?'

'Come, come, Grendellbar, it's been so long, no chit chat, no small talk.'

Molly looked from behind Grendellbar, her heart racing at the sight of this imposing, fiery figure of Lord Skeldrin.

'Very well,' said Grendellbar, seeing this as an opportunity. 'Belegnoth?'

'Oh yes, that fellow, he was a fiery chap as well, said Lord Skeldrin. 'What about him?'

'Don't take me for a fool, Skeldrin, you know what I mean.'

'Grendellbar, do you really expect me to tell you all my plans? Where would be the fun in that? What would you have to do all day? But what an auspicious place to be, just look at the audience,' he said, opening his arms of fire to the Seraphim statues.

Molly had not spoken to this man. He was the one person, the key to getting her father back and putting her family back together. She stepped out from behind Grendellbar. 'I want my father back,' she spouted.

Lord Skeldrin turned around. 'Molly Chatsworth, Edward's daughter,' he said with glee in his voice.

'What have you done with him?'

'I haven't done anything with him. He is not mine to give or to take, he helps me in my quest, he helps because he wants to.'

'I don't believe you. My father would never do the things you do.'

'You really don't know your father,' laughed Skeldrin.

'But I do,' said Grendellbar, stepping forward, 'and although the girl may not know him like you and I, anybody that is in your employ, has been beguiled, blackmailed, or forced into servitude.'

Skeldrin smiled agreeably, his eyes reflecting the green of the fire.

'I want him back,' yelled Molly angrily.

'Don't bother, Molly, this is what he wants, suffering and torment,' said Grendellbar, putting a comforting hand on Molly's shoulder.

'Grendellbar, you had your opportunity once and you let it go. If you get in my way now, there will be casualties. There always are in war.'

‘Well then, there's only one thing left to say,’ said Grendellbar, taking off his white cloak. ‘You'd better prepare for war!’ Grendellbar pushed Molly backwards and, with a swift, fluid twist, whipped his white cloak into a spiralling arc unfurling in a graceful twirl that swallowed the flames, smothering the fire beneath a wave of white. ‘My apologies, Molly, are you alright?’ Asked Grendellbar softly as he helped her up.

‘Yes, I’m fine,’ answered Molly with a swallow, her heart still racing.

Grendellbar retrieved the remains of his cloak from the granite bowl.

‘The flames are still there,’ said Molly, watching them flicker back to life.

‘Oh yes, they never go out,’ said Grendellbar, being careful not to reveal why. ‘You run along now, before your grandmother has a fit. I have a great deal to do,’ he said, twiddling his beard thoughtfully. ‘But Molly, not a word to anyone about this, not even your grandmother.’

‘Grendellbar, what does Etahno Romaie mean?’ Asked Molly.

Grendellbar gave a big sigh. 'That for now is a mystery, but I do know someone who might be able to help.'

CHAPTER X

—THE FOREST OF THORNS—

Hatherleigh Huges, a well-dressed man with a bold moustache, arrived in the filing halls beneath the Hall of Valdar. Hatherleigh had been assigned as the new Head of Security, in charge of *The Department of Supernatural Objects.* Anything showing paranormal, dangerous effects would come under the proviso of the *DSO.* A position he had wanted for some time. It was different, unusual, arranging security and protection for anything categorised, as out of the sphere of normality. He was a fit, well-built man who prided himself on his appearance and status, and security appealed no end, and when his chance arrived, he embraced it enthusiastically. He was accompanied by two other men, Ethan and Blaine, who were even bigger than he was, both wide and tall, at over six feet; they towered over everyone they passed. The filing halls were vast, containing records from the very beginning of the Valdar. All facts, figures, and items, filed, checked, double-checked and triple-checked were here. The head of this department was Arthur Rumley, pen in one hand and notebook in the other, ready to write down anything you said and file it away for later, at least that was the rumour. 'Ah, there you are, Hatherleigh,' said Rumley, his spectacles teetering on the end of his nose. 'You've come for the sniveler?'

'If you mean Grumblewit Arthur, then yes,' replied Hatherleigh, not caring for Rumley's turn of phrase.

'He must be important if he comes under the *DSO.* Very well, follow me. It's really not the norm this you know, jailing, interrogation, not what we do here,' grumbled Rumley as he walked. 'We file things, catalogue things, itemise, document, register, record, not lock people in filing rooms. Locking people up, we haven't done that since....'

'You offered the room,' said Hatherleigh quickly.

'Offered!' spouted Rumley. 'I don't recall offering anything.'

'Be that as it may, it was quick and convenient.'

'Yes, I know, out of the way down below and out of sight, but still, it's an imposition. Guards everywhere, checking me in and out of my own department; it's outrageous. There is another level below this for just such a thing.'

'That hasn't been used for years,' said Hatherleigh wearily. 'But more importantly, has he said anything?'

Various people came to ask questions, but to no avail. Written down, every word he said, and not a jot of it usable. Just keeps banging on about it's not his fault, we've got it all wrong. My clerks have had enough of his whining.'

'Well, we can relieve you of that,' said Ethan.

'There'll be no whining while I'm driving,' said Blaine.

Weaving their way through the filing halls and startled clerks, they reached a corridor with a low arched ceiling. Two guards stood by the entrance. Grumblewit could be heard whimpering as the guard approached the door. 'Hatherleigh, thank heavens, get me out of this dungeon,' cried Grumblewit as the door swung open.

'Pull yourself together, Grumblewit, this is a filing room, not a prison,' said Hatherleigh with an impatient sigh.

'Then why have I been locked in here? It's torture that's what it is, torture!'

'Because you have been associating with some rather questionable types lately, and there are questions that need answering.'

'It wasn't my fault Hatherleigh, you don't understand how seductive Lord Skeldrin is,' said Grumblewit hopelessly.

'What did I tell you Hatherleigh,' said Rumley, rolling his eyes.

'Watch how you roll those eyes Rumley and who at, they may get stuck up inside your head,' snarled Grumblewit. 'Write that down why don't you.'

But Rumley was already jotting it down in his notebook. 'Oh, yes, he can be quite foul-mouthed as well.'

'Thank you, Arthur, we'll take it from here,'

replied Hatherleigh.

'Come along, Smiler,' growled Blaine, gripping Grumblewit's arm. Ethan lifted Grumblewit by the other. Raising him off the chair, they led him out of the room, his legs running in midair.

'Very well,' said Rumley, putting away his little notebook, 'please don't bring him back anytime soon.'

'I'm innocent, I tell you, innocent,' cried Grumblewit as he passed through the filing halls.

Outside, Grumblewit was pushed into the rear seat of a car, Hatherleigh sat on one side of him and Ethan squashed in on the other. Blain sat in the front. Two other cars, one in front and one behind, were going to act as escorts. Blaine started the car, following the car in front down the gravel drive. 'In some way, we the Valdar, have failed you Grumblewit and somehow we must bring you back to the fold,' said Hatherleigh determinedly. 'You're going for a stay with a wholesome family, the Yarrowoods, a second chance. If they can't persuade you back around, nobody can. I don't know what Skeldrin offered you, but I hope it was worth your while. And just in case you're thinking of absconding from the Yarrowoods, Ethan and Blaine and the rest of these men in front and behind, will be staying with you.'

'They won't be enough Hatherliegh, and you're putting an innocent family in danger,' said Grumblewit, looking pitifully at the floor.

'Come now Grumblewit, don't be so glum, you should be proud of yourself.'

Grumblewit raised his head, giving Hatherliegh a puzzled look.'

'Yes, you've reached the status of a *Supernatural Object.*'

Silence reigned in the car between all four men as an hour passed, lost in their own thoughts. The rumble of the cars slowed as they all took the turning for Marshwood, home to the Yarrowoods. It was a long road, fields on one side and a forest on the other. Grumblewit began to fidget, feeling uneasy. Swinging around a sharp bend, Blaine pushed hard on the brakes, throwing everyone at the back forward. The lead car had come to an abrupt stop. 'What are you doing?' complained Ethan, as he prised himself off of the back of the seat in front.

'That's what we're doing,' said Blaine, pointing at the road. A large tree was lying across the road, making it impossible to pass. Ethan got out to talk to the other drivers, as Grumblewit began to fidget even more.

'What's the matter with you, man?' said Hatherleigh impatiently.

'This is Lord Skeldrin's work,' said Grumblewit, looking about nervously.

'Nonsense, it's just a tree that's blown down in the night.'

'There were no storms or high winds last night,' squealed Grumblewit. 'You, Valdar, are too relaxed, Hatherleigh; you don't realise the length of Lord Skeldrin's reach.'

'What do you mean by that?' said Hatherleigh curiously.

'Exactly how it sounds, he's everywhere, don't you understand he's everywhere! There is nowhere he can't go, and nothing he can't do.'

For a moment Hatherleigh felt unnerved as he looked at the fear in Grumblewit's eyes.

'You know I speak the truth Hatherleigh,' said Grumblewit desperately.

Hatherleigh pondered momentarily as his intuition began to twitch.

'Ignore him, Mr Hatherleigh, he's just a fool,' growled Blaine.

Ethan came back to the car. 'What's the matter with him?' he said, looking over the seat at Grumblewit.

'He thinks Lord Skeldrin's running around the countryside pushing down trees,' replied Hatherleigh dismissively, ignoring his own intuition.

Ethan and Blaine began to laugh.

'Yes, you laugh, go on, but something's not right, I tell you,' wailed Grumblewit.

'Portland thinks there's a turning not far back, we'll turn around and see where it takes us, we must be able to get around this somehow,' said Blaine, ignoring Grumblewit's warnings as he started the car.

At Marshwood, the Yarrowoods were awaiting their new arrivals. Penny and Charlotte were in their bedroom trying out some makeup and lipstick they had been secretly gifted from a recent visit to their aunts, while Mr Yarrowood was in the garden trying to keep Harry and George amused, with attempts to interest them in his vegetable patch. 'Now then, boys, what do you know about cabbages?'

'Da...d,' complained Harry.

'We'll turn into cabbages if we stand here much longer,' laughed George.

'You laugh, but a cabbage is quite an extraordinary thing. You know, under the right temperatures, they can last for up to six months.'

'Fascinating,' exclaimed Harry.

'So does that mean six months of cabbage?' Asked George with a worried look.

Mrs Yarrowood was busy in the kitchen, peeling potatoes to go with the evening's meal for their guests. As she peeled, she caught her finger with the knife. But she didn't flinch; instead, she froze. She stood and watched as the blood dripped into the porcelain sink, spiralling toward the plug hole. Outside, Mr Yarrowood could feel something was wrong and was drawn to the kitchen window. He ran across his veg patch back to the house and in through the back door. He saw the blood. Snatching a tea towel from the worktop, he gently wrapped it around Mrs Yarrowood's hand. She was in a trance, her head was filling with jumbled images, and she was desperately trying to make sense of them. 'Mother, what is it?' Asked Mr Yarrowood.

'The thorns, the thorns,' she replied in a whispery voice.

'Thorns?' said Mr Yarrowood.

'Thorns they keep showing me thorns, and Hatherleigh. Peter, they're in great danger!'

A look of horror came over Mr Yarrowood's face. 'The Forest of Thorns.'

Penny and Charlotte sensed something was wrong and came down from upstairs, as did Harry and George, who came in quickly from the garden.

'What is it, Dad? What's wrong?' asked Charlotte.

'It's Hatherleigh, he's in danger, and it's got something to do with the Forest of Thorns.'

'But Peter, that was put to sleep years ago, and nobody goes in there anymore,' said George.

'This is Skeldrin, remember, and if he's found a way to wake it up and he diverts them there.'

'Well, you're not going on your own, I'm coming with you,' said George.

'And so am I,' said Charlotte, 'you may need a healer.'

'So am I,' said Penny.

'We all are,' said Harry, 'The more help the better.'

'Now just hang on,' said Mrs Yarrowood, now out of her trance.

'Come on, there's no time to argue,' said Mr Yarrowood impatiently.

Portland, driving the lead car, had found the road they had seen earlier and turned off, the other cars following behind. After a short time, the road started to narrow and wind, and the light began to dim, shrouded by the tree canopy above. Minutes passed as they drove deeper into the forest, passing under a large sign that was faded and unreadable, hanging above the road, when suddenly there was a loud bang and the lead car veered off to the left, stopping with a jolt. 'O...h, now what,' groaned Blaine as he pulled up behind. Portland stepped out of the lead car to check the tyres. He found the problem on the passenger side straight away. Sticking out of the front tyre was an enormous thorn. He bent down and pulled it out, and the rest of the air hissed out through the hole. For a thorn, it was huge, the size of his little finger, and as he stood up to examine it further, he felt a sharp pain in his back. It hurt so much, he dropped to his knees. Blaine, who was watching, jumped out of the car to help. Portland fumbled behind himself to find what it was, but there was a second sharp pain, then a third. His fingers found what was stabbing him; it was more thorns. Just as Blaine reached Portland, a thorny vine slithered out through the tree line towards him. The vine quickly wound around Blaine's ankle, the thorns biting into his boot. He let out a cry as the thorns dug in. Then another swung out from the trees and wound around his waist, gripping him tightly and lifting him into the air. Another vine wound around Portland, pulling him screaming up into the canopy. Now Ethan jumped out of the car to help his friend Blaine. Eathan watched in horror as Blaine disappeared up into the trees before he could get to him, as another vine crept up behind him. It coiled around his legs and then up around his body, dragging him into the forest as he cried out in pain from the biting thorns. 'What just happened?' Said a stunned Hatherleigh.

'They're gone, don't you understand, gone,' cried Grumblewit. 'I told you, I told you, but you would not listen.'Grumblewit flung open the car door and leapt out, avoiding the first lashing vine, and ran back down the road and past the rear car, as fast as his legs would carry him. The driver in the rear car sat frozen in fear, but the vines came looking and wound around the car, crushing it like cardboard to the sound of his screams, and pulled the car away into the trees. If he could just get to the faded sign, he might be safe, thought a desperate Grumblewit as he ran. But a vine lashed out, tripping him over. As he lifted his face from the mud, a cold voice echoed through the trees.

'Grumblewit, what have you done?' said the voice of Lord Skeldrin.

'Nothing, my Lord, I have not said or done anything,' he squealed.

'Nothing?'

'No, nothing, my Lord, I swear, I swear, I told them nothing,' pleaded Grumblewit, getting on to his knees.

'But how long would it be until you did?'

'I would never betray you, never. My my Lord, please,' cried Grumblewit in desperation.

But it was no use. A thick, thorny vine came down from the tree canopy and, like a tentacle, wrapped itself around his helpless body, snatching him up and away.

The sun had lowered, and the light was fading as Hatherleigh tried hard to keep his composure. Vines slithered about the car, rocking it violently from side to side. The glass in the windows cracked and shattered, and the metal of the car groaned as it twisted. Hatherleigh braced himself for what came next. But then, the rocking suddenly stopped. The vines shrank back. Hatherleigh looked from left to right. It was hard to see through the cracked glass, but the vines seemed to be retreating. He kicked open the car door and stepped outside.

'Hatherleigh,' said a voice from behind. Hatherleigh turned to see Lord Skeldrin, vines slithering and coiling at his feet, and a Sepricorn standing at his side, with an ugly grin.

'I do not fear you,' said Hatherleigh through gritted teeth.

'Then you are a fool, Hatherleigh,' replied Lord Skeldrin, smiling. 'Your well-pressed suits and perfect moustache will do you know good now.'

'You will pay for what you have done here,' said Hatherleigh, watching the vines carefully.

'Pay, I rather think not,' said Lord Skeldrin confidently, 'you see, the odds are so stacked in my favour.'

'What do you want, Skeldrin?' demanded Hatherleigh angrily.

'Want, oh, I have taken what I wanted, you know what they say in war, never leave a man behind.'

'Grunblewit,' said Hatherleigh, nodding. 'Another you'll pay for.'

'I thought ceasing hostilities momentarily, just for a little chat with you, might be amusing. I was wrong, it isn't, I think we are done here,' said Lord Skeldrin, waving his hand dismissively. 'You'd better hurry along now, Hatherleigh, my vines are getting rather hungry for more fools.' More vines appeared, bristling with thorns, as Lord Skeldrin turned and vanished into the gloom of the forest with the Sepricorn. Hatherleigh took off at speed, back down the road. Vines lashed at him from the tree line. He kept running, as fast as he could, until a vine tripped him up, slashing his leg, but he got up quickly and limped on. Now they became more ferocious, seeing a weakness, lashing at him over and over. A hail of thorns flew from the trees, bringing him to the ground. He could see the sign hanging above the road ahead and began crawling toward it. Vines gathered about him, lashing like whips. He could feel his strength running out of him, but still, he kept going, crawling toward the sign. Then the lights appeared ahead of him. It was the Yarrowood's truck. Mr Yarrowood jumped out onto the road, and the boys leapt out from the back with axes.

'Elythrin's help us,' said Mr Yarrowood, 'It's as I feared, the trees are awake.'

'There's Hatherleigh dad,' cried George, pointing.

'Right, George, Harry, it's my job to carry him

out. It's yours to keep those vines off us. A protection spell was put on the sign years ago. Skeldrin can't have known about it, because it hasn't been broken, there are no vines past this sign.'

'Dad, be careful,' cried Charlotte.

'Right, on three, we all go in.'

'Yes, Dad,' replied George and Harry, raising their axes.

'One, two, three!' Running towards Hatherleigh, the boys swung their axes left and right, chopping and slicing as the vines lashed at them. Reaching Hatherleigh, they both chopped at the vines around him. Mr Yarrowood lifted Hatherleigh beneath his arms, dragging him as fast as he could back under the sign. Charlotte knelt by Hatherleigh, who was fading in and out of consciousness, running her hands up and down, just above his body. 'He's in a bad way, Dad, I can feel him slipping away. He'll die if we don't do something quickly.'

'Let's get home, it's his only hope.'

CHAPTER XI

— A TRIP TO ABIGNATES —

It was a Friday morning, and Molly lay on her bed thinking of Bramblewood, and with still no word from her mother, the threat of her appearing hung like a sword above her head. Just as she was imagining what she would say if she did arrive, the bedroom door burst open. 'Good morning, my princess, the Yarrowoods have been in touch. It seems you and Charles made some eager friends the other night with Penny, Charlotte, Harry and George. The whole family are going to Abignate's, and then they're stopping by the Hall of Valdar. They wondered if you would both like to go, and of course, I said yes.'

'Abignates? What's that?' asked Molly, flipping back the bed covers.

'It's a wonderful shop. It supplies the Valdar with

all manner of wonderful things.'

'U...h what things,' said Molly, yawning.

'Far, too many things to be going in to now, my dear. You wait and see.' Grand Sally pulled back the bedroom curtains, the bright light of the morning flooding the room, and then swept out again, heading for Charlie's room.

It was ten o'clock before breakfast had been eaten, and both Molly and Charlie were dressed and sitting in the living room, waiting for the Yarrowoods to arrive as Balthazar perched on Molly's shoulder.

'So where are you going?' He asked.

'Abignate's, it's a shop and...'

'I know what Abignates is. I've been there myself. All I'll say is, big toad, mind your fingers, tried to swallow me last time.'

'U...h you did say shop, not zoo?' Said Charlie.

'Yes, I did, and then we're stopping by the hall again.'

'Abignate's? I've never 'eard of that one before,' said Charlie, 'still, it'll be good to see Harry and George again. They're a good laugh, those two.'

Balthazar hopped off Molly's shoulder onto the

back of the chair, as a loud knock sounded at the front door. 'Take care, Molly Chatsworth.'

'I suppose I will,' said Molly, wondering why the raven had said it.

Mrs Peabody answered the door.

'Good morning, my dear woman, and a good morning to you, Sally,' said Mr Yarrowood, as Grand Sally arrived behind Mrs Peabody.

'Good morning, Peter,' she said, looking past him at his shabby truck. 'Really, you must get yourself some better transport, for Jenny's sake if nothing else.'

'Nonsense,' replied Mr Yarrowood. 'It's never let me down yet, and anyway, Jenny doesn't mind, do you, dear?' he said in a raised voice, waving to her in the front seat. It really was quite a sight: a big, rusty old thing with huge wheels, and it wasn't sure what colour it was trying to be, with hints of green, yellow, brown, orange, and blue. Harry, George, Charlotte, and Penny were all hanging out the back, waiting, as Molly and Charlie shot past Grand Sally, Mrs Peabody, and Mr Yarrowood and out of the door.

'Morning, Mr Yarrowood, see you, gran,' chirped

Molly.

'Yeah, morning, sir, bye, Mrs G,' said Charlie as they passed.

'Oh, goodbye then, dears,' said Grand Sally as they climbed into the back of the truck. 'Young people these days, always in such a rush.'

'They certainly are, Sally, can't keep mine still for a moment. Anyway, I'll have them back by teatime.'

Grand Sally waved from the pavement as they drove off, trying to ignore the disapproving looks from the neighbours. Mr Yarrowood chugged on for several miles, weaving through the streets of London, to hoots and shouts from alarmed oncoming drivers. 'I really don't know how you were ever allowed behind the wheel,' moaned Mrs Yarrowood.

'Are you saying I'm a bad driver?' Asked Mr Yarrowood.

'No, dear, it must be everyone else,' she replied, gripping the armrest.

'Good night at the festival, wasn't it, Charlie?' said George in the rear of the truck.

'Yeah, it was great,' agreed Charlie enthusiastically.

'Until Harry here started drooling over Sarah Silthorpe,' added George.

'Oh, shut up, George!' Snapped Harry.

Charlie laughed as Harry flushed a shade of bright red.

'What are they on about?' asked Molly.

'Girls again,' said Penny, faking a yawn.

'Did you hear?' Asked Charlotte quietly.

'Hear what?' Replied Molly.

'About Grumblewit,' whispered Penny.

'No what?' Asked Molly, eager for some good news

'It's probably being kept quiet, that's why dad had us sworn to secrecy,' said Charlotte.

'About what?'

'Lord Skeldrin got to, Grumblewit,' said Penny.

'Got to him?' Said Molly.

'He's dead,' whispered Charlotte.

'Dead!' Said Molly loudly.

'Shh,' said Charlotte, as George and Harry looked over.

'If dad finds out,' said Harry.

'He won't if you keep quiet,' said Charlotte,

nudging him with her foot.

The truck lurched to a halt, throwing everyone in the back sideways and head over heels.

'I think we've arrived,' said George on the floor.

Peregrine Lane was a bustling London Street full of busy shops. But Abignates stood out the most with its huge purple sign across the top and its name emblazoned in big gold letters. Inside, it was a treasure trove. Just like an Aladdin's cave, everything glittered and sparkled. Fountains spewed frothing water. White doves flew about in the ceiling space. Cabinets and shelves were crammed full of crystals of all shapes, sizes, and colours, statues and sculptures, herbs and potions in bottles and jars, crystal balls from small to large, and a huge, lucky toad croaked in a pool of water. Peculiar sticks smouldered on counters, giving off a smoke that smelled like flowers, and there were endless books, trinkets, lucky charms and fortune-telling cards of every description. Behind a counter, sitting on a high stool, was Mr Abignate, a very short man. He had a ring of tufty black hair around his head, and a single strip, greased across the top of a bald patch which he kept stroking to make sure it was still in place. 'Good morning, Mrs Yarrowood,' said Mr Abignate, as he saw her approaching. 'I haven't seen you for a while.'

'Good morning, Mr Abignate, I've been rather busy lately, what with all the goings on. You know how it is.'

'Yes, it's a bad business,' he said, leaning forward, looking from left to right suspiciously, and lowering his voice. 'All this business with Lord Skeldrin, you don't know who to trust anymore.'

'Well, you can trust me, Mr Abignate, I can assure you, and what business are you referring to exactly?'

'Oh, my dear Mrs Yarrowood, I didn't mean you. Don't mind me, I'm talking too much. It's all very unnerving, that's all. Knowing there is someone out there who wants to see everything in ruin. I never thought in my lifetime, I would ever see the day when...'

Mr Abignate, this is all very interesting, but I came here for some herbs, not the end of the world.'

'W...w...well, yes, of course,' stuttered Mr Abignate, 'my apologies, how can I help?'

Molly, Penny and Charlotte were trying on some crystal necklaces when they overheard two men talking in the next aisle. 'I lock my doors and windows every evening, Mr Redleaf, and I have four dogs to keep watch outside. I'm not having any of Lord Skeldrin's lot getting to me in the middle of the night.'

'Yes, I know what you mean, Mr Sneezly, I won't let my wife and children out of my sight,' said Redleaf, craning his neck to see where his wife and children were in the shop. 'Have you heard anything about that Chatsworth fellow?'

'Not since the train wreck. Vanished, not a trace can be found of him, I hear, and those at the top think we don't know,' said Sneezly quietly.

'Leaks, Mr Sneezly, leaks, there's always someone ready to gossip. There's something afoot here, mark my words,' said Redleaf quietly.

'Did you see his daughter at the festival?' Remarked Sneeezly.

'Don't tell me she was there? Said Redleaf, shaking his head. 'Strange all this Chatsworth buisness'

'There's nothing strange about it, a criminal, a traitor, that's what he is. If Chatsworth is ever found, they should lock him up and throw away the key,' said Sneezly firmly.

Molly had heard enough. She marched straight to the end of the aisle and turned into the next aisle, red-faced and angry. 'My father's not a criminal, how dare you insult him like that!'

'There you are, you see,' said Mr Sneezly. 'That's her, the daughter, the one I just mentioned.'

'I see what you mean,' said Redleaf, looking Molly up and down.

'The behaviour, it's in the family, you know, they just can't help themselves,' said Sneezly.

'Who do you think you are, saying these horrid things?' Said Molly angrily.

People in the shop were beginning to notice and gather in the aisle.

'What's going on here?' said Mr Abignate, squeezing his way through.

'What sort of shop are you running here, Abignate? Letting in this Chatsworth riff raff, it's really not on,' said Sneezly.

Now the whole shop came to a standstill.

'Chatsworths, what do you mean?'

'The girl, Abignate, she's Chatsworth's daughter,' said Sneezly.

Mr Abignate's eyes widened with a sudden realisation. 'W.. well, gentleman, u...h I really think...'

'We're not interested in what you think. What are you going to do?' Said Redleaf firmly.

'Just a minute there,' said Mr Yarrowood, pushing through to Molly. 'What's going on here?'

'Mr Yarrowood, they're insulting my father, saying he should be locked up,' replied Molly.

'Really,' replied Mr Yarrowood with a frown.

'Yarrowood, please,' said Mr Releaf, 'leave this to us, we're dealing with it.'

'I'm afraid I can't do that, gentleman. Mother!' Called Mr Yarrowood. 'Take everyone outside, would you, dear. I'll be out in a minute. And you, too, Molly, please. I'll deal with this.'

'But Mr Yarrowood, they...,

'Now, Molly, please, if you don't mind,' said Mr Yarrowood firmly.

Molly pushed through the onlookers, red-faced and angry.

'Really, Yarrowood, you should consider the company you keep,' said Redleaf. 'If the father's rotten, well...'

'Well, what, Mr Redleaf?' Asked Mr Yarrowood. 'Do you think it may rub off?'

'I'm sure we can resolve this all amicably,' said Abignate. Trying to divert his customer's attention away from the squabble. 'Nothing to see here, nothing to see.'

'Mr Abignate, I think Mr Sneezly and Mr Redleaf were wondering if you sell Expanders,' said Mr Yarrowood.

Sneezly and Redleaf looked completely confused.

'Expanders? What are you talking about, man? I don't sell anything called that,' snapped Mr Abignate.

'Are you sure?'

'Of course I'm sure, I know what I sell in my shop and what I don't.'

'Well, perhaps you should be selling them, Mr Abignate, Mind Expanders, they'd probably sell like hotcakes. Because Mr Sneezly and Mr Redleaf's minds have become rather narrow of late. A very good day to you, sir.' Mr Yarrowood turned and walked out of the shop, leaving Mr Sneezly, Mr Redleaf, and Mr Abignate speechless.

'I hope you didn't do anything stupid in there, Peter, not like the last time?' said Mrs Yarrowood.

'Don't worry, dear, nothing's broken,' he said, brushing his brown hair backwards with his hand. 'And anyway, the last time wasn't my fault.'

'Of course not, dear,' said Mrs Yarrowood sarcastically.

'Now, mother, can you get everyone back in the truck, please? I just want a quick word with Molly.'

'Come on, all of you, back in the truck,' said Mrs Yarrowood, herding them all like sheep. Molly stood on the pavement full of frustration and anger.

'Take a deep breath and let it go, Molly,' said Mr Yarrowood as he stood next to her. Molly closed her eyes and took a deep breath before the frustration and anger turned to tears. People passed by on the pavement, busy with their own troubles and cars trundled back and forth, passing motorists distracted every so often by Mr Yarrowood's multi coloured truck. 'I knew your father, or I know him, I should say,' he said, rocking slowly back and forth on his heels.

'Really?' Said Molly, her eyes springing open.

'Yes. We weren't best pals or anything, but I liked him well enough; we got on, you know. I was surprised as anyone by all of this recent business.'

'I have to find him, Mr Yarrowood, and get him back home. Stop people saying all these horrible things.'

'Don't think too harshly of those two in the shop, Molly. Everybody in there is with the Valdar, even Sneezly and Redleaf. They don't mean any real harm. They're just thoughtless, and more to the point, frightened. Lord Skeldrin has everyone on the edge of their seat at the moment. Which is just what he wants, of course. Redleaf and Sneezly need somewhere to put their fear. Your family is an easy target, somewhere to put that fear. You'll get your dad back, I'm sure,' he said, giving her a friendly pat on the shoulder, even though he wasn't sure at all. 'Now then, jump in the truck and let's be off.'

Mr Yarrowood pulled away from the curb to

hoots and yells from disgruntled drivers as they headed for the Hall of Valdar.

CHAPTER XII

— ARCHIMEDES —

The same security stood guard at the gates of the Hall of Valdar, checking everyone in and checking everyone out. Driving past the tall, imposing entrance of the Hall, Mr Yarrowood followed the road around to the rear of the building, parking the truck at the beginning of a big sprawling lawn. Long covered walkways edged the lawn, overgrown with climbing plants, leading around to more buildings on the other side of the grass.

Molly, Charlie, and the Yarrowoods stepped down out of the truck, the teenagers all assembling in a line like military cadets. 'Right, everyone, mother and I have some business to attend to, so we might be a while, so please, please, don't get up to any mischief.'

'Dad, really!' Said Harry, pretending to be offended.

'Yes, really,' affirmed Mrs Yarrowood, 'you're the eldest George, so you're in charge.'

'You mean I get the blame?'

'I always said he was a bright boy, mother,' said Mr Yarrowood, patting George on the shoulder.

'We'll be as quick as we can,' called back Mrs Yarrowood as they walked away.

'Sorry about Grumblewit,' said Charlotte, walking with Molly onto the lawn, 'I think you were hoping he might know something about your father, I mean?'

'I was, yes,' agreed Molly. 'I'm so fed up with hearing nothing but bad things about him. The sooner we can find him, the sooner we can both go home.'

The boys and Penny caught up. Harry leaned forward to add to the conversation. 'Skeldrin wouldn't have told him much,' said Harry reassuringly.

'He just used Grumblewit for information, most likely,' added George.

'From what I saw, why you wouldn't stay well clear of that fella, heaven only knows.'

'You've seen him,' exclaimed the Yarrowoods all at once.

'We were supposed to be keeping that quiet,' said Molly, rolling her eyes.

'Spill the beans then,' said Harry excitedly.

'It's only us, Mol, who's going to know,' replied Charlie, eager to tell the story.

They all huddled together, as both Molly and Charlie relayed the night at Banshee Bog.

'And then Crystalian took Grumblewit off to the hall,' said Molly, as she came to the end of the story.

'He was supposed to be coming to our house, you know,' said Charlotte.

'He was,' said Molly with surprise.

'I think the feeling was that staying with us would help him somehow. I don't know what Grendellbar and dad had planned. Maybe he would feel safe enough to say what he knew, if anything,' said Charlotte.

'You know what mums like, she can get anything out of anyone,' said Penny, laughing.

'Charlotte told me about Grumblewit Harry, but what exactly happened?' Asked Molly. Molly's eyes widened, and Charlie's mouth dropped open as Harry relayed the events at the Forest of Thorns.

'So, then we managed to get Hatherleigh out and back, home,' he said as he finished their story. 'He's here now, over in the medical wing. mum and dad are dropping by to see him, while they're here, I think.'

'Poor man,' said Molly sympathetically.

'Forests that come alive,' said Charlie, shaking his head in disbelief.

'It's on a par with demons and witches, I think,' said Harry, chuckling.

'It's not a competition,' said Charlotte, scoldingly.

The six of them wandered across the lawn, analysing both stories, for what it all meant. As they left the lawn at the other end, they walked under an arch bridging two buildings that opened to a courtyard. Other teenagers stood chatting to one another, around the edge of the courtyard, while others sat around the edge of a fountain pool in the middle of the yard, all of them trying their best to alleviate the boredom of waiting for their parents. 'Hey, look, Harry, there's Sarah Silthorpe again,' said Penny, giggling. Pennys giggling, attracting Sarah's attention. Harry's face flushed bright red as the Gemini twins walked into the courtyard from the end. A larger boy known as Thudge walked in front of them, pushing other teens out of the way, as the twins walked through.

'Hey, you lot!' Shouted John Baradium toward Molly, Charlie, and the Yarrowoods, 'This is our courtyard and I don't remember giving you permission to come into it.' Thudge gave a toothy grin, cracked his knuckles, and began thumping his palm with a closed fist.

'Look, you two, you don't own anything around here, so why don't you just run along and find Daddy?' said Charlotte.

'Quiet, stupid girl,' said John in a nasty tone, 'no one asked you. You Yarrowoods, hopeless, look at you, you should have been thrown out of this place years ago.'

'Hey, look, John,' said James with a mocking laugh, 'they have some new oik friends, the

Chatsworth girl and her oiky boyfriend.'

'Oiks attract oiks,' said John, laughing.

'You're asking for a black eye to match the other one you've got there,' said Charlie, squaring up.

'Why can't you just leave everyone alone?' Said Molly angrily.

'One more word from you and you'll be next in line for bruising, after your oiky boyfriend,' said James, sneering at Molly.

Charlie pushed up his sleeves, ready for a fight. 'Well, perhaps you would like to try?' Said George, standing side by side with Charlie.

'Thudge,' said John, gesturing to him to deal with it for them. Thudge stepped towards George and Charlie in a threatening manner.

'First lesson, oiks, why give someone a battering when someone else can do it for you,' said James with a sly wink. Thudge raised his hand ready to punch George, but as he lurched forward, with a sudden jerk, he found his arm pulled upward by an invisible force. George turned to see Penny putting her telepathic powers to work on Thudge. Her arms outstretched toward him, Thudge levitated off the ground and revolved uncontrollably in the air. Everyone burst into laughter as they watched. Thudge shrieked and squealed, waving his arms and legs wildly as he floated helplessly in the middle of the courtyard.

'Second lesson, oik,' said Harry, always bring a Telepath to a fight.

'Am I interrupting anything?' Said a loud voice from the archway. Thudge dropped to the ground with a crunch, rolling into James and John, knocking them both over like skittles, as Grendellbar entered the courtyard. 'John, James, when you've untangled yourselves from Thudge, I think you will find your father is waiting for you across the lawn, and please take Thudge with you,' said Grendellbar. A trickle of blood ran from Penny's nose. George and Charlotte moved quickly to her side, holding her up by her arms, as she buckled at the knees. 'George, Harry, Charlotte, take your sister to see Hadwin the Healer immediately, you'll find him in the main building,' said Grendellbar sternly. 'Your Telekinesis is new and undeveloped, Penny. Using it for large objects is ill-advised.'

'We'll see you guys back at the truck,' said George quietly as they passed Molly.

'Okay, see you soon,' Molly replied, looking with concern at Penny.

'Molly, Charles, I need your help with something. Come with me, please,' said Grendellbar sternly, striding off towards the other end of the courtyard.

'What does he want?' Said Charlie, looking at Molly.

Molly shrugged her shoulders.

Grendellbar led them out of the yard along a winding footpath that led to the top of a small hillside. Stone slabs cut a narrow staircase down to a big stone building near the bottom. 'If you don't mind me asking, Grendellbar, what are we doing?' asked Molly as she navigated the stone steps. Grendellbar did not answer but continued quickly on down the steps. Reaching the stone building at the bottom, Grendellbar swung open the entrance door.'

'Quickly, quickly,' he said, ushering them both in the door. Inside, they found Avindor, Crystalian, and Milee, surprised to see Molly and Charlie enter with Grendellbar. 'Thank you for coming, gentleman,' he said, closing the door firmly. 'Molly, Charles, if you would both wait here, I'll be with you in a moment.'

'I am not at all sure what we have come for,' said Avindor.

'That is as it should be, Avindor. 'There are many unwelcome ears and trust is in short supply, I think you'll agree,' replied Grendellbar, quietening his voice.

Avindor, Crystalian, and Milee noticed immediately that something was different as Grendellbar ushered them out of hearing distance of Molly and Charlie. Grendellbar, normally a calm and rational figure, now carried an urgency about him; he was agitated, and his eyes looked red and tired. 'You have heard the news regarding Grumblewit, I'm assuming?'

'Yes, Lord Skeldrin's handy work. Everyone is talking about it,' said Avindor, shaking his head, 'Ethan, Blaine, Portland all gone, Hatherleigh hanging on by a thread, I can't believe it.'

'I knew Ethan and Blaine,' said Crystalian, lowering his head. 'They were good men.'

'People are dead once again,' said Grendellbar,

looking up to the rafters as a place to project his sorrow and frustrations. Placing his hands behind his back, he began to pace slowly up and down. 'At the festival a few nights ago, Molly and I had our own encounter with Lord Skeldrin.'

'He was here?' said Avindor with surprise.

'Not in person. Somehow, he used the green Flames of Aronsirith to project an image of himself.'

'What did he want?' asked Crystalian.

'To gloat!' Answered Grendellbar bitterly.

'What did he say?' Asked Avindor.

'He warned me, warned me to stay away, or there would be casualties. And there were.'

'We cannot stay away,' said Avindor, 'he is just one man, nothing more.'

Grendellbar stopped his pacing. 'Just a man, you say,' he said as if Avindor had said something naive. 'As you know, many years ago, a young Lucious Skeldrin was a part of the Valdar, along with his father.' Avindor nodded as he recalled the past. 'Way back long ago, we also had a groundskeeper called Callahan Grange. He had a dog called Jack. Jack followed Callahan everywhere; they were inseparable. Nice little dog, friendly to everyone, and the staff adored him, all except one, Luscious Skeldrin. The dog would avoid Luscious at all costs, or he would growl and bare his teeth if they ever happened to meet. One day, Callahan's dog walked calmly in front of a car, for no explainable reason whatsoever. Callahan was inconsolable, and it wasn't long before he passed, of a broken heart. It was reported that Luscious was nearby, watching closely as the dog walked calmly into the path of an oncoming car, and was run over and killed. Lucious Skeldrin was just a teenager then.'

'So Skeldrin entered the mind of the dog and told it to walk in front of the car. Is that what you're saying?' Said Avindor.

'I most certainly am. He is now a man, and he is infinitely more powerful than he was then. His ability to bend others to his will is without question. He is evil and malicious and takes pleasure in the suffering of others. Just a man, you say, but a man that is intent on fulfilling a prophecy that will bring ruin to us all.'

Crystalian and Milee glanced fleetingly at one

another.

'Well then, we must do something before he has us all jumping in front of cars,' said Avindor.

'Precisely why we are here. There is one thing more, however.'

'More!' Said Avindor.

'My reason for being in the Chamber of Fire was that I noticed Molly leaving the festivities alone. I took it upon myself to follow her. She wandered alone into the domed hall. Once I caught up with her, she claimed she had been called. By a whispering voice that kept repeating the words, *Etahno Romaie.*'

Avindor, Crystalian, and Milee looked at each other, wondering if any of them knew what it meant.

'*Etahno Romaie* is the language of the Seraphim. I recognised the language straight away, but I didn't know what it meant. So, I went to see Professor Sloane, our expert on the Seraphim. The Professor and I searched the archives for hours. We finally found a translation. *Etahno* comes from the word *Etahnonoran,* which translated means Starlight. *Etahno* translates as Star. *Romaie* comes from the word *Romanaieden*, which means children. So *Etahno Romaie* means...'

'Starchild,' said Milee.

'Wait a minute,' said Avindor, 'I can see where you're going with this. You're jumping to conclusions.'

'Am I indeed,' replied Grendellbar enthusiastically.

'So, what does this all mean?' Asked Crystalain.

'We knew what the translation was, but not the meaning of why Molly should be hearing it. So, Professor Sloane and I continued our research, but we weren't progressing very far, until the Professor remembered a collection of scrolls written by Archimedes, kept by the Elythrin library that were due for further research. And we found something. Archimedes claimed to be visited by the Seraphim Hedronin, who imparted a wealth of science, mathematical equations and astrological movements. The works of Archimedes are our basis for what we know today, in maths, physics, astronomy, and also Seraphims. In his writings, he tells of a warning imparted by the Seraphim Hedronin. This is what he wrote.' Grendellbar took a piece of paper from his pocket and began to read.

"'It is the year 192 and Hedronin, the Light Bringer, visits me once again. I am often struck to become mute by the beauty of this magnificent winged being, but this time, the blue of the Seraphim's eyes, normally so bright and penetrating, seemed dim. A sadness lay upon his face. He is troubled. He came with a warning. A foretelling of things to come. A message for those who come after me. A message for the future. He talks of a darkness. A darkness that will rise in this world once again. It will fester and hide within the light. It will beguile, it will lie and deceive, and it will be bent on blanketing the world in shadow once more. Yet for all of these prophecies of doom, he says there is hope. A hope in the form of a child. A child sent from the stars. Raised by those who will unlikely accept their path, and their true nature. Hidden from the darkness. Hidden in plain sight. The Starchild will hear the call...'"

'There, the writing faded beyond deciphering. Gentleman, it is not just a coincidence that Virginia

Chatsworth tried to hide Molly for all these years. Hiding and smothering what she was truly meant to be. Just as it is not a coincidence that Lucious Skeldrin remained hidden behind the light of the Valdar for so many years. The two are inexorably connected. The Starchild will hear the call.' Grendellbar folded up his piece of paper. 'Molly heard the call the night of the festival, Etahno Romaie, Starchild.'

'So, the fate of us all lies upon the shoulders of that young girl,' said Avindor, looking over at Molly.

'She must not know, Avindor, the burden would be far too much for her to bear.'

'Of course,' said Avindor, nodding in agreement.

'I am asking you all now to find the Skull of Belegnoth before Lord Skeldrin. Find it and stop him before he has a chance to begin his ruin...and Molly will be going with you.'

'Grendellbar, after all you have just said,' said Avindor.

'Grandmaster, I have to agree, she would be in mortal danger,' said Crystalian, scratching his stubble.

'It is exactly because of what I have just said. In fact, I am tasking you, Crystalian, with her personal protection,' said Grendellbar, looking Crystalian straight in the eye to emphasise his point. 'This is not up for discussion. She will aid you in ways you cannot yet see. If she is as Archimedes wrote, you must take her, and I will bear the consequences.'

'Where do you suggest we start looking?' Asked Avindor.

'That comes next,' said Grendellbar.

CHAPTER XIII

— THE GATE KEEPER—

'What are they talking about over there?' Said Charlie, hitching up his trousers.

'I have no idea, but it's taking an awfully long time,' replied Molly.

'You're tellin' me, he still hasn't told us what we're doing 'ere yet.'

Although.... it might have something to do with the thing that happened the other night,' said Molly, looking over at the four men talking.

'What d'you mean?' Asked Charlie. 'What thing?'

Molly hesitated.

'I saw Lord Skeldrin again...at the festival.'

'You did what?' Exclaimed Charlie. 'Why didn't you say something?'

'Because Grendellbar asked me not to say anything to anyone.' She gave a big sigh as the burden of the secret lifted.

'Yes, but I wouldn't say I was anyone, would you?' Said Charlie, feeling irritated at not being told. 'So, what happened then?'

'There are other halls, beyond the one we were in at the festival. And there is one that is full of statues, of angels, with huge wings, and there's a fire with green flames...'

'Hang on,' said Charlie, interrupting and raising his hand. 'Angels, green flames?'

'Yes, green and Lord Skeldrin appeared in the fire.'

'Green flames and Skeldrin appeared in the fire.'

'Charlie. Are you going to keep repeating what I say?'

'Very likely, yeah,' said Charlie, shaking his head in disbelief. 'I'm still trying to get my head round what I saw Penny doing, and now you're talking about angels and green flames!'

'Molly, Charles,' said Grendellbar, making his way over.

‘We’ll continue this later,’ said Charlie, not prepared to give up until he had all the details. Molly shot him a look of impatience and rolled her eyes.

‘I’m sorry, you must be wondering what this is all about,’ said Grendellbar, arriving in front of them.

‘We were sort of wondering,’ said Molly, relieved to be rescued from Charlie's interrogation.

‘Well,’ said Grendellbar with a large intake of breath. ‘Molly, I’m going to give you the opportunity...to find your father. Find him and bring him home.’

‘You are!’ Exclaimed Molly, her eyes lighting up with excitement. ‘But how?’

‘With the help of these three men. They are the most trustworthy and loyal individuals I know, and they will be at your side every step of the way.’

‘When are we going?’ Said Molly excitedly.

‘Very soon,’ said Grendellbar, ‘In fact, now.’

‘Now!’

‘I know this is sudden, Molly, unexpected even, but time is of the essence.’

Charlie watched on, waiting for the right moment to comment.

'But what about Gran, she's not going to be happy at all.'

'You can say that again,' said Charlie, finding that moment. 'What am I going to tell her?'

'That needn't concern you, Charles,' said Grendellbar.

'That's all very fine and dandy, Mr Grendellbar, but... '

'Because you'll be going with her.'

Charlie's mouth dropped open, and not for the first time that day.

'All will become clear momentarily. Gather round, everyone, please,' said Grendellbar in a loud voice, waving to Crystalian, Milee, and Avindor.

'So, what is the plan?' Asked Avindor.

'We do not know where Lord Skeldrin is or what his next move will be, but I know of one who might. I talked with Hatherleigh as much as he was able. He said that Lord Skeldrin was not alone in the Forest of Thorns. He was accompanied by a Sepricorn. By the description he gave, the Gate Keeper.'

'The one that brought me here?' Said Molly.

'The very same,' answered Grendellbar. 'We are

going to use this Sepricorn to determine what to do next.'

'And how are we going to do that?' Asked Crystalian.

'I am going to call this Gatekeeper, with a spell, from the spell book, very adeptly obtained by your grandmother,' said Grendellbar, glancing at Molly.

'You mean the spell book she's in a lot of trouble for,' said Molly with a little frown as a reminder.

'Elithryn save us all,' said Avindor with a big exhale. 'Which means you, and by association, us, will be in the same trouble.'

'I think Lord Skeldrin and his ambitions are a far greater trouble than Baradium and the Council of twelve, don't you?' Said Grendellbar.

'And what are you going to do when it gets here?' asked Avindor.

'We are going to trap it. It has one weakness.'

'Which is?'

'It's keys. Confiscate the keys, and we're in the game. Milee, did you bring the netting and rope I asked for?'

'Yes, Gwandmaster,' answered Milee, producing a

sack.

'I will call the Sepricorn through from that bare patch of wall over there,' said Grendellbar, pointing toward it. 'Lay the netting beneath, and when the Sepricorn comes through, you and Crystalian are to trap him in it.'

'Gwandmaster, can the Sepricorn not use the keys to get out of the net?' Asked Milee.

'Yes, Milee. That is why you must remove them before he has the chance. As the Sepricorn comes through, he will have them in his hand monetarily. That is your opportunity, and the only one, I might add. So, let us prepare.' Grendellbar walked toward the bare patch of wall, removing the spell book from his pocket. Milee followed behind with the sack containing the net.

'So, what exactly is goin' on, Mol?' Asked Charlie quietly.

'Charlie, haven't you been listening at all?'

'Well, I heard a bunch of things about Sepricorn's and spells, but that means zilch to me.'

'Well, a Sepricorn is...' Molly stopped, realising how this would sound, and she didn't want to risk another one of Charlie's interrogations. 'Watch Grendellbar and wait and see.'

Milee and Crystalian laid the netting down on the ground below the bare patch of wall, placing some old wooden crates on either side to hide behind. Avindor closed the shutters on the windows, and the big stone barn grew dark. Overturning an old workbench, he called Molly and Charlie to join him behind it. The Grandmaster took a piece of chalk from his pocket and drew a symbol on the wall from the spell book as Milee and Crystalian took their places behind the crates. 'If we are all ready, then I will begin,' said Grendellbar, opening the Spell Book. Looking over his half-moon glasses, he glanced at each person in turn to satisfy himself that everyone was in place and ready to start. Standing back from the wall, he began to speak the spell from the book.

'I call the keeper of the gate,
The one who holds the key,
I call upon the only one,
Who can find the door for me,

Stop all time and help me,
Stop all night and day,
For only you will have the key,
To send me on my way.'

The Grandmaster cracked the wall three times with the bottom of his staff, and the chalk symbol on the wall began to sparkle.

'So, what happens now?' whispered Charlie, giving Molly a nudge.

'Well, there's a cloud and a tunnel, but...' Molly was interrupted by a deep thumping sound coming from the wall. Grendellbar took a few more paces backwards. A loud cracking sound sprang from the centre of the wall, and dust puffed from the joints between the stone blocks. The wall shook. Then, with a groan, the stone blocks at the centre of the wall moved forward and slid aside. Tentacles of cloud formed in the opening, reaching out along the edges of the wall. The hairs on the back of Molly's neck stood up. At the centre of the cloud, a small figure appeared, holding a set of golden keys on a large golden ring. There stood the same creature that

Molly had seen before with her grandmother, wearing the same hat on its ugly, neckless head.

'Who has called me to this place? Step up now and show your face.'

'It is I who has called you, Gatekeeper, Grandmaster of the Valdar. Step forward so I may see your face.' The Gatekeeper stepped forward, teetering on the edge of a stone block. 'NOW!' yelled Grendellbar. Milee, armed with a broom handle, knocked the keys from the Sepricorn's hand with a hard swipe. They flew through the air into the dark and out of sight. With a shriek, the Sepricorn jumped out of the cloud in a desperate attempt to retrieve them. Landing on the net, Crystalian and Milee leapt forward from behind the crates, quickly taking up the edges of the net, and they threw it over the Sepricorn. But the Sepricorn wasn't going to be captured that easily, as it kicked and gouged, finding its way out of the net, and ran quickly into the dark. Avindor, Molly, and Charlie ran out from behind the workbench.

'Where is it?' Said Avindor, shining his staff into the dark.

'I don't know,' said Crystalian, scanning the room for the creature.

'Be careful,' warned Grendellbar, 'he's here somewhere.'

A shaft of light piercing through a gap in a window shutter cut past Molly's shoulder to reveal a sprinkling of dust falling from above. Molly looked up. 'There he is,' said Molly in a loud whisper, 'up there in the roof.' The Sepricorn stood high up on a beam in the roof space.

'Trying to trick me, I think you are. Now I think you go too far, Gren...dellbar,' said the Sepricorn in his raspy, menacing voice. As they watched from below, the Sepricorn began to move. He leapt to the next beam, and the next, until he was swallowed up by the dark once again. A cold wind blew through the room as the cloud shrank backwards, the stone blocks slid back to their original position, and the gate closed.

'The Gatekeeper and the gate are linked, so unless he tells it otherwise, it will always close behind him to keep others out,' said Grendellbar. 'Now he needs his keys to get it back open.'

‘We have to get him down from there,’ said Crystalian.

‘I quite agree, but how?’ said Avindor.

‘Find his keys, find them quickly,’ said Grendellbar urgently.

‘Mol, I don’t know what this thing is, but it's not very nice,’ whispered Charlie as they stood side by side.

‘No, I am not,’ said a raspy voice from behind them. The sneaky, shrivelled creature had jumped down and stood there baring his ugly, yellow teeth. It made a sudden leap at Charlie, knocking him to the ground as it kicked and gouged in a fit of rage. As Charlie fell, he knocked Molly to the ground with him. As she rolled herself upright, her attention was drawn to a glint on the ground nearby. She scrabbled to her feet and ran to the spot. The golden keys lay sparkling on the ground in front of her, ready to be taken. Quickly, she scooped them up. But as they clunked together, they gave a sharp jingle that cut through the air, drawing the Sepricorn’s attention away from Charlie. ‘Give me them, pretty girl, give me them now, or I will snatch out your heart, and that I vow.'

'If you want them, come and get them,' said Molly as she caught sight of Milee ready with the netting. The Sepricorn let out a scream and lurched toward her. But Molly threw the keys high up in the air in front of her. The Sepricorn made a leap for the keys, but Milee threw the netting, catching him in mid-air. The net pulled him back down to the ground with a thud, and Milee bundled him up tightly. The keys dropped to the ground, and Grendellbar snatched them up, slipping them into his robe.

'Well done, Molly, Milee, quick thinking, well done everyone,' said Grendellbar.

Charlie sat up, dazed and bruised. 'Great move, Mol, but be a bit quicker next time, aye,' he said, nursing his eye.

Crystalian and Milee dragged the angry Sepricorn into a corner. Grendellbar retrieved his staff, leaning against the wall and taking it to the corner, pointed it at the Sepricorn. The crystal at the end began to glow a bright white. The Sepricorn shrank back, disturbed by its light.

'Now then, my little friend, you have been helping

a very wicked man to do some very wicked things, and you will tell me what you know.'

'I am not bound by either side and to you I do not confide,' it snarled, its eyes bulging an angry yellow.

'That's how I came with him,' whispered Molly.

'I think the bus might have been easier,' said Charlie, grimacing at the sight of him.

'What does it mean, bound by either side?' Asked Crystalian.

'It is not bound by right or wrong, good or bad,' answered Grendellbar, 'unfortunately, that includes people as well.'

'Sepricorns will work for anybody,' said Avindor, 'as long as they get paid.'

'Usually in gold,' said Grendellbar, revealing the golden keys from his robe. 'I ask you once again, Gatekeeper, what have you been doing with Lord Skeldrin?'

'Grandmaster, you ask too much. I am not within your earthly clutch. Lord Skeldrin, yes, I must confess, he wants, I do, but it's not my mess. I open doors, that's all you see, your earthly woes are not for me.'

Grendellbar dangled the keys, baiting the Sepricorn. 'Gatekeeper, you cannot leave without your keys. You are linked to these keys, you need these keys, and if you ever want them back...' The Sepricorn screeched wildly, lurching toward Grendellbar, but fell back again, repelled by the light of the staff. Grendellbar gave a big exhale. 'We can ask it questions all night, but we will never get anywhere unless we ask the right one. Maybe I was wrong to summon it,' said Grendellbar regretfully, moving away from the corner.

'I do not believe that,' said Crystalian, moving to his side. 'We did not come this far to fail.'

Everyone drew silent, trying to think of the right thing to do next.

'My keys, my keys, I will have them back, or in your head I will put a crack,' yelled the Sepricorn.

'So what is it they want exactly?' Asked Charlie.

'This Sepricorn has been helping Lord Skeldrin,' replied Molly, 'and they want to know where he's been and what he's doing. Wait a minute,' That's it, Charlie, you're a genius.'

'I am?' Said Charlie in surprise.

'Grendellbar, where was the last place Lord Skeldrin went?' Said Molly, moving alongside him.

Grendellbar thought for a few seconds.

'Of course!' Said Grendellbar sharply. 'Molly, you're a genius. The Sepricorn is not obligated to tell us what he knows, and relying on his charity to tell us is just foolish, but he is obligated to open a gate to wherever we wish. The last place he was may give you a clue to where he is going and what he is doing next.'

'A...w, I thought I was the genius,' said Charlie in a tone of disappointment.

Grendellbar walked back to the corner where the Sepricorn cowered and grumbled beneath the net. 'Gatekeeper, you will open a gate to the last place Lord Skeldrin went.'

'Yes, yes, that I can, that sounds like a perfect plan,' said the Sepricorn, sitting up eagerly.

An excitement began to build in Molly as she realised that finding her father was becoming a distinct possibility. Unravelling the net, Milee stood guard over the Sepricorn. 'Crystalian, Milee, tie a length of rope to the Sepricorn so it can't get away,' said Grendellbar, passing the keys over, the Sepricorn watching them ever more closely. 'Then let him have his keys just to open the gate, and make sure you take them back.'

'Can anyone hear that?' Said Avindor, looking up at the roof.

A tap, tap, tapping sound came from above. Grendellbar listened as more tapping sounds came from the windows.'

'Now it's over there,' said Molly, pointing at the window.

Charlie walked over to the window, peering around the shutter. A large black bird flew at the glass, then another and another. Charlie jumped back in shock as the glass began to crack. Crystalian came up behind him, slamming the shutter closed and bolting it tight. 'Crows, lots of them,' he said urgently. The roof suddenly became alive with tapping and the sound of cracking tiles, and bits of debris began to fall around them.

'Found us, found us, found us he has,' cried the Sepricorn, covering his ears.

'Who has?' Asked Milee.

'The Dark one, the dark one who sees us all, a legion has come to answer the call. The call of death, death to us all, if don't let me get through that wall,' yelled the Sepricorn.

'What is it? What's going on?' Said Molly as the flapping and tapping noise grew louder.

'Crows, hundreds of them by the sound of it,' said Crystalian, 'If they get in here, they'll rip us to shreds.'

'Yes. Lord Skeldrin knows the Sepricorn is here, and he has sent an army to get him.'

'But how?' Said Molly.

'Spies that creep, spies that crawl, spies that leap and spies that fall, listening, listening all the time, listening, listening to give him a sign,' wailed the Sepricorn.

The fury of flapping wings grew louder and louder as the crows tried to find their way into the barn.

'Get that gate open, Milee,' yelled Avindor.

The Sepricorn took the keys from Milee, drawing one from the bunch. Scampering up onto a crate, he raised the key, and like a knife through butter, the key slipped into the stone block. Turning it twice, he pulled it out. Milee took back the keys as he held the rope tight. A deep thump vibrated through the wall. The stone blocks began to rattle, dust puffed from the joints, and the stone blocks once again moved forward and slid aside. Tentacles of cloud once again gripped the wall, and a strong wind blew out from its centre. Suddenly, there was a shattering crash as tiles, wood, and debris fell from the ceiling to the floor. A hole had opened in the roof, broken out by the pecking, ripping and clawing birds. Crows began to swarm through the hole, bringing a deafening chorus of flapping and screeching. 'Come to me now,' cried Grendellbar. Gathering Molly and Charlie around him, he held his staff out before him. The crystal at its tip flared to life, pulsing with a brilliant plume of light.

Grendellbar swung the staff around and over their heads, creating a shield of light as a flock of attacking crows spiralled down toward them. The birds were repelled by the light, but more and more filled the stone barn as Grendellbar pushed Molly and Charlie back toward the swirling black gate. Crystalian fired his gun at the birds over and over with Avindor behind him, swiping at crows with his own staff, as they backed up toward the gate. They all reached the gate together. Molly and Charlie sprang up onto the crate and into the swirling cloud. Crystalian and Avindor followed behind. The barn was now swarming with attacking crows, but Grendellbar kept them repelled by the light of his staff.

'Quick, Grendellbar, get in,' cried Molly.

'No, Molly, this is not my path, you must go,' yelled Grendellbar, fending off more attacking crows.

Avindor reappeared at the mouth of the gate. 'Grandmaster,' he cried as the crows grew in numbers around him.

'Avindor, I cannot hold them back much longer. Shut the gate!'

'Tell him he has to come with us, Avindor,' cried Molly.

'Help him,' cried Charlie.

'We can't, he's protecting the gate, he can't let them in here,' yelled Crystalian, holding on to Molly, as she lurched forward toward the gate.

The blocks of the wall began sliding back into place.

'Farewell, Grendellbar, and may Elithryn be with you,' shouted Avindor.

'No!' Cried Molly, as the last block fell into place, and there was nothing left but the dark.

CHAPTER XIV

— BODY SNATCHERS —

'Open it, open it,' cried Molly desperately as she felt in the dark for some sort of handle or lever.

'We can't, we have to leave him, Molly, we have to go on, or it was all for nothing,' answered Crystalian.

Avindor lit the crystal on his staff, and the dark of the tunnel gave way. 'Look! The floor is rising,' he said in alarm as he watched the deep black of the tunnel creep and crawl over his feet, slowly moving up his shins. 'Molly, was it like this when you came through before?' He said, trying to shake his feet free of it.

'No! It's not the same,' cried Molly in horror as the deep black of the floor washed over her feet. Where were the shimmering walls and the belongings that floated through the air like before?

'Quickly, we must move, before this tunnel consumes us,' said Avindor.

'Consum us, what d'you mean consume us?' cried Charlie.

'Gatekeeper! Find the key and get us out of here, now!' yelled Crystalian. The Sepricorn had his head down, grinning from ear to ear, for he had more influence over the tunnel than they knew. Milee gave him a good shove of encouragement.

'Yes, yes, this one it be, just three turns and we will be free.' He thrust a key into the undulating tunnel wall in front of him, turning it three times, and then drew it out. A mouth to the tunnel opened up, and a crackling and rumbling ran through the walls. A dim light shone through the opening. Milee snatched back the keys and grasping the Sepricorn by the collar, jumped through the gate. Crystalian reached for Molly, pulling her with him to the other end of the tunnel, as the floor lapped over their feet, trying to hold them back. The open mouth of the tunnel groaned as they both jumped through. Avindor took hold of Charlie's jacket, as the deep black of the tunnel closed in around them both. 'Jump! He cried, reaching the end. They both jumped at the opening, tumbling through the open mouth, landing in a heap on the ground, just in time, as the tunnel closed in behind them. Charlie yelled in panic, rolling around, kicking his legs and brushing himself down to make sure there was no trace of the black of the tunnel.

'He did something,' said Molly angrily, pointing to the Sepricorn.

Tentacles from the cloud mouth withdrew, revealing a timber wall of great logs, now splintered, twisted, and bent where the tunnel entrance had broken through. Splintered wood and debris lay all around them, but as everyone watched in bewilderment, the wood and the debris jumped back to the wall, as if time itself reversed and knitted it all back together.

Crystalian took the Sepricorn by its collar and lifted it off the floor. 'I do not know what it is you just did in there, Sepricorn, but you were clearly up to something; that tunnel was trying to eat us!'

'No, no, don't blame me, I am light on foot and

soft as air, I do not stop and linger there. I always have the next key, but you push and push, you rush me, see?'

'Gatekeeper, where are we now?' asked Milee.

'I do not know, do not ask me. He did not reveal these things to me.'

'He's lying, don't ask me how, but I can feel it,' said Molly as Crystalian still held the Sepricorn dangling in the air.

'You can?' Said Charlie in puzzlement.

'Where are we?' Asked Crystalian, giving the Sepricorn a shake.

'I know exactly where we are,' said Avindor, picking up his staff from the ground. 'Welcome to the Hall of Scorpio,' he said, his arms open wide. The light from the crystal shone brightly around and upward, chasing away the dark. Crystalian dropped the Sepricorn to the floor in his own awe, as a great hall opened up before them. Molly gazed in wonder at the enormity of the huge trees that rose up as pillars along both sides of the great hall, their branches spreading out to support a great roof. 'Behold the pillars of Yggdrasil,' said Avindor. 'It is said that these trees were seedlings, taken from the great tree Yggdrasil, the Tree of Life.' A gallery circled the hall above, fashioned by ornately carved woodwork, and at the far end of the great hall, a giant stone sculpture of a scorpion.

'Carthdain is head of this house, is he not, and one of the Council of Twelve?' Said Crystalian.

'He is, and my friend.'

'And this was the last destination of Skeldrin,' said Crystalian, straining to see what was ahead.'

'So, we must find him quickly,' replied Avindor.

Molly looked back at the wall they had just come through.

'What about Grendellbar?' She asked, hoping the wall might spit him out at any moment.

'He is the Gwandmaster, he will find a way,' said Milee reassuringly, 'he always has.'

'Or will he?' Said the Sepricorn with his ugly grin.

Milee shoved him forward.

'Both of you stay close behind me,' said Crystalain to Molly and Charlie. 'I do not trust where we are,' he said, putting his finger to his lips to indicate quiet. They continued through the vastness of the hall, Molly and Charlie staring in wonder as the light from Avindor's staff cast them as giant shadows across the trunks of the great trees.

'What did you mean back there?' Said Charlie in a loud whisper, giving Molly a soft nudge. 'When you said you could feel the Sepricorn was lying?'

'It's hard to explain,' answered Molly, 'it was like a feeling in my chest when he spoke, and the feeling told my head it was wrong.'

'Well, that might come in handy in a fix, if you take my meaning,' replied Charlie, looking cautiously from left to right.

As they neared the end of the hall. Beneath the great scorpion, sat a raised throne, and on it, sat a hooded figure. 'You should not have come here, Skin Creepers,' said the figure.

'Carthadian, is that you?' Said Avindor, coming to a stop.

The figure stood up. 'This Carthadian you speak of is no more. I am the owner of this vessel now, and I am Risgrool.' it said with a gurgle and hiss. (*Risgrool in foul Sla speak means Bone Breaker.*) The hood slipped down, and a dark and distorted face with red eyes that was once Carthadian showed itself to the dim light.

'Carthadian?' Said Avindor, stepping nearer, unable to comprehend what he was seeing.

'Avindor,' said Crystalain urgently, 'that is not Carthadian anymore, step away.'

'What trickery is this?' Said Avindor with a gasp.

The dark edges of the hall came alive with the sound of hisses and nasty gurgles. Red eyes glowed brightly in the dark, and soon they were surrounded by ugly, distorted human faces with ill intent.

'What are they?' Cried Molly. 'Are they people?'

'They don't look like any people I've ever seen,' said Charlie in alarm at the grotesque faces loliping toward him.

Keep behind me,' cried Crystalain.

Avindor, Milee, and Crystalian backed up together, keeping Molly and Charlie corralled between them.

'Bind them, bind them all, and bring the wretched Skincreepers before me,' cried Risgrool. Like a swarm of hungry ants, they were set upon with hands that grappled, gripped, and pulled, snatching and scratching. Avindor's staff was torn from his hands and given as a prize to Risgrool, and in the chaos, the Sepricorn saw his chance and ripped his keys from Milee's belt, scurrying away into the darkness.

'Get off me,' screamed Molly.

Crystalian pushed and kicked them away, falling onto Molly to protect her, but the swarm was too many. With their hands bound, they were dragged forward, the hall echoing with deafening shrieks and screams as they were pushed down onto their knees before Risgrool. 'Who are you and what do you want here?' He asked with a gurgle and a snort.

'We are Valdar, and we demand you...' Answered Avindor.

'You cannot demand in my hall, Skin Creeper,' yelled Risgrool, interrupting. Nobbled hands slapped and scratched and poked at Avindor from behind. 'More Valdar,' said Risgrool, spitting on the ground. 'I like your gift, though, something to remember you by,' he said, holding the staff tightly.

'Why does he keep calling us Skin Creepers?' Asked Charlie, glancing at Molly.

'Because that's what you are,' said a screeching

voice behind with a slap and a poke.

Molly had no answer as she watched Risgrool stand up and lollop about like an ape with the staff.

'What have you done with our people?' Yelled Avindor.

'Is it not plain to see? Can you not guess? They are all here,' replied Risgrool, sweeping his arm outward at all the dozens of twisted faces. This only excited the wretches even more, and the hall filled with blood-curdling snarls and screams and snapping and screeching. 'Silence! Yelled Risgrool. 'There is one difference, of course. We have taken their skin and taken their bones and claimed them as our own. The Dark One opened the way, giving us life again, so that we may be reborn. We are Slas,' he cried, raising the staff in triumph. A chill ran down Molly's spine when she heard the name. But these were different; they weren't the same as she saw in her dream. The Slas hissed and screeched and yelled again, and their eyes glowed an even brighter red in the dark of the hall. 'Now, take them. Lock them up, lock them away, out of sight, down in the darkness. The Dark One may have use of them, and if not, we will take their skin and bones for our own!' The rough hands of the Slas took them all once more, gurgling and jaws snapping, they ran them out of the hall, down endless stairs, pushing, poking, and proding along passages, and into a room where they were shoved to the floor and locked away.

'Well, I can safely say we found out where Skeldrin has been,' said Charlie, trying to roll himself upright. 'Can we go 'ome now, please?'

'Molly, are you alright?' Said Crystalian, shuffling himself over to her.

'I'm okay,' she said, propping herself against a wall. She was feeling bruised and battered and nauseous. It had been a while since she had her last potion from her grandmother, and her current situation wasn't improving her chances of feeling any better.

'We have time now,' said Milee, studying the room.

'Time for what?' Asked Charlie.

'Time to find a way out of here,' answered Crystalian, rolling onto his knees. Getting to his feet, he listened at the door. 'I can hear movement outside, at least two are guarding the door,' he whispered.

'Well, unless we can overpower them and find a clear exit out of here, we won't be leaving any time soon,' said Avindor with a big sigh of resignation.

'You never know,' said Milee with a smile.

'You don't?' Said Charlie curiously.

'I saw a Sla in a dream once, but it didn't look like them. I was told the story about how they were all destroyed, but there was nothing said about them taking over people,' said Molly.

'That's because they couldn't,' said Avindor. 'Slas could not take a solid form or someone else's.'

'That's not what we just witnessed,' said Crystalain, moving away from the door.

'No, it is not,' said Avindor thoughtfully. 'What we just saw was a Sla that had indeed invaded a person somehow. You heard what the larger one said, that he owned this vessel now.'

'An old fella told me something similar once,' said Charlie, 'thought he was round the twist. Creep up on you when you're not lookin', snatch you when you least expect it. Beware the Body Snatchers, that's what he said, and now look, a ruddy great nest of them. Well, they better not come snatching at my door,' said Charlie, pulling his knees tightly up to his chest.

What seemed like an age passed, and the room grew cold as night drew in, when suddenly Molly spoke out as if she had no control over the words, and they had to jump out of her mouth. 'Someone is coming,' she said quickly.

'I can't hear anything,' said Crystalian, pointing his ear at the door.

"Ere come the snatchers again,' said Charlie with a grimace.

'No, someone else, a friend,' said Molly, staring at the door. There was a loud fizz, a crackling sound, and a flash of light shone under the door, some shouts and yelps, then the sound of metal clunked into the door lock, and the door flew open.

'How did you know that?' Said Charlie.

Molly shook her head because she didn't know how; she just knew. A cloaked woman stood in the doorway with a staff, its crystal at the top glowing and crackling. She removed her hood, revealing a crop of long blonde hair. 'Polousha!' Said Avindor in surprise. 'You are indeed a welcome sight. I feared you had endured the same fate as the rest.'

Two Slas lay on the floor unconscious outside in the passageway.

'We have to be quick; more of these creatures are not that far away,' said Polousha, producing a knife.

'You never know,' said Milee, winking at Charlie.

Avindor got to his feet. Taking the knife, he cut the rope from Crystalian's wrists, who, in turn, took the knife from Avindor, freeing Molly, Milee, and Charlie.

'I saw them bring you down. I've been hiding down in the lower levels for two days; luckily, they don't come down here very often,' said Polousha, looking out of the doorway to check the corridor for any stray Slas. 'Quickly, we must go. Follow me.' Polousha led them down steeper stairs, where it grew darker and wetter as they descended further into the bowels of the Hall of Scorpio.

'Where are you taking us?' Asked Crystalian.

'The Hall was built on a mountainside. There is another door to the outside down below. They haven't explored down here yet, so they don't know about it.' Descending two levels more, they made their way by the light of Polousha's staff along a twisting passage to a small metal door at the end. Crystalian pulled back two stubborn bolts holding the door. Milee helped him prise it open. The night air rushed in as they came out into an overgrown patch of woodland and a towering rockface behind them. The moonlight gave a strange silver shade to the shrubbery and trees as Milee and Crystalian shut the rusty metal door. Finding some scattered rocks that had fallen from a wall, they piled them against the door in case they were followed. 'This way, follow me,' said Polousha. Molly and Charlie trudged through the undergrowth, with Milee watching the rear and Crystalian in front, behind Avindor and Polousha. Polousha led them to a track that followed a ravine with a river below. They followed the path for a short while until it wound back up to a small clearing with good cover on all sides. 'Let's stop here for a moment,' said Polousha. Everyone knelt behind the brush and out of sight. 'Across the river down there are the stables,' said

Polousha, pointing. 'They are serviced by a bridge further down, but Slas guard it, so we can't cross. But further on is an old foot bridge, we will cross under the main bridge to that one, and then we can get to the stables and the horses.'

'Polousha,' said Avindor, gaining her attention. 'Carthdian.'

Polousha lowered her head to hide her tears. 'I was powerless to stop it. The screams...the terrible screams...I will never forget it.'

'What happened?' Asked Avindor.

'Lord Sledldrin. He has accomplished Etanu Mutara, the power to merge the dead with the living.'

'We saw,' said Charlie, 'that thing, that body snatcher that called himself Risgrool.'

'Yes,' said Polousha, 'that thing...was my husband.'

Charlie rolled his eyes and turned his head down, wishing he could swallow his foot. Molly leaned forward and took Polousha's hand, stroking it as a way to comfort. 'I'm sorry,' she said softly as she felt her sadness wash over her. They both fell together in a hug as Polousha's tears grew heavier.

Drying her eyes, Polousha gathered herself and spoke again. 'I did not see what happened before I only heard the screams, but when I came upon the balcony, he had everyone enchanted, unconscious, beneath a strange red mist. He turned to our great symbol, the scorpion, and cast a blue bolt from his cane upon it. It began to move. It turned to face him, its pincers open wide, and he gave it a command. Its tail curled over toward him, and the end of the tail opened, exposing a round black stone.'

'That's it,' said Molly, 'do you remember Banshee Bog, when we followed Lord Skeldrin and Grumblewit?

'How can we forget,' answered Charlie.

'Just before the wall fell, and the Hedrin raised the demon, Menocropolis, it said, hidden from view in a devil's tail, protected by claws that make grown men wail.'

'That's right, I remember,' said Cystalain.

'I no Carthadian knew nothing of this, or I, and even if he did, he would have sacrificed his own life rather than tell,' said Polousha. 'I don't know what power the black stone had or what power Lord

Skeldrin may have given it, but it opened a doorway for the Slas to come through and take all these poor people that lay beneath the red mist. Including my husband.'

Screeches and screams could be heard in the distance.

'They've discovered we are missing; we must move,' said Crystalian.

They picked up the track again that ran alongside the river, and coming close to the main bridge, they stopped. The Slas were out in force, led by Risgrool, all carrying weapons and burning torches. 'Find these Skin Creepers,' cried Risgrool, 'find them, beat them, bash them, break them, and bring them to me.'

One by one, they slipped under the cover of the bridge and picked up the track again on the other side. But a keen Sla spotted them moving alongside the river and raised the alarm. Blood-curdling screeches and screams filled the air as the pursuit began.

'We have been seen,' warned Crystalian.

'It is not far now, just down here,' replied

Polousha.

But two Slas jumped from above onto the path, one carrying a sword and the other an axe. The Sla with the axe swung at Polusha shattering her staff with its first blow. But Milee and Crystalian ran forward, disarming them both with swift kicks and blows and jumping upon the Slas, they threw them off the edge of the cliff face to the rocks and the river below. Then, as fast as they could, they ran to the footbridge. This bridge was made of rope and slatted timbers. 'Quick, we must get to the other side, before they realise what we're doing,' said Avindor. The bridge swayed and creaked as they stepped onto it.

'Don't look down, Molly,' said Crystalian.

'Don't worry, I'm definitely not,' replied Molly, keeping her eyes on the other side of the ravine.

As they were all halfway across the bridge, a foul voice yelled from behind. 'Polousha!' Polousha stopped, looking back through the dark. Risgrool had stepped onto the bridge with dozens of Slas behind him. 'So Polousha, you managed to escape us, I see,' he said with a gurgle.

'Do not use my name, foul beast,' yelled Polousha. 'Crystalian, give me that sword,' she said firmly.

'You cannot stop them, there are too many,' he replied, passing her the sword he had taken from the Sla.

Polousha snatched up the sword and placed it above one of the ropes holding the bridge in place.

'What is she doing?' yelled Molly.

'Run, Crystalian! Look after Molly, she's special, you know, I felt it.'

Now, Slas were heading for the main bridge to cut them off on the other side. Polusha turned around to face Risgrool once more as he lurched toward her. 'Carthadian, if there's any part of you left in there and you can hear me, we will be together again soon, my love.'

'He is gone, Skin Creeper, he cannot hear anything,' said Rigrool with a cruel laugh.

'Go back where you came from, Sla,' yelled Polousha.

'No, no, no,' screamed Molly as Polousha raised the sword.

Crystalian grabbed Molly by the waist and rushed to the end of the bridge, and as his foot touched the earth on the other side, Polousha swung the sword. Razor sharp, it sliced through the top rope easily. The bridge gave way, and Polousha, Risgrool, and all the Slas on the bridge plummeted to the raging river below.

'She's gone, she's gone!' Screamed Molly. Struggling to free herself from Crystalian's grip, she ran to the edge of the cliff, looking helplessly down into the river.

'It wasn't his fault, Molly, there was nothing he could do,' said Avindor, as he stared in shock at where the bridge had been. 'Come, kets go, let's not make her sacrifice a pointless one,' said Avindor as Milee brought three horses from the stables.

CHAPTER XV

— OUT OF THE FIRE —

A bright moon shone down upon the forest, trailed by thin clouds. All night they rode until dawn finally broke, and Crystalian brought everyone to a halt in a small clearing. 'We must rest the horses for a while, and then find some water.' Crystalain outstretched his arms to help Molly down from the horse.

'You could have done something, you could have tried harder to stop her,' she said angrily.

Crystalian bowed forward, leaning his forehead against the horse; he did not want her to see the tears welling in his eyes. Molly slid off the horse on the opposite side and walked away angry, upset and confused.

Milee managed to light a fire and kept watch as the rest all sat around it in silence, falling asleep one by one. Molly could hear the screams of Slas in her restless sleep, and the last image of Polousha falling from the bridge haunted her dreams until she awoke with a start, with a nudge from Charlie. 'Come on, sleepy, we're leaving,' he whispered.

'Come along, both of you,' said Avindor. 'We must find water, and ultimately, where we are.'

Crystalian and Milee were already mounted and waiting. Crystalian did not look any happier after his few hours of sleep as Molly approached him. 'I'm sorry for shouting at you,' she said softly, 'it wasn't your fault; I don't blame you. I've never seen someone die before, or like that.'

'It's not often someone does,' he said, putting out his hand to pull her up onto his horse.

An hour passed as they rode through the forest in search of water. Although Molly had apologised, an awkward silence remained between them. 'Why... why do you think she wouldn't try to escape with us?' she asked, breaking the silence. 'We could have cut the bridge at the other end.'

'We were asking her to leave her husband,' replied Crystalian. 'Even though he had gone, to be replaced by that...thing, her love for him still remained, and in the end, that love was stronger than her need to escape.'

'I don't think I realised how big this all was, until now. Now people are dying. Everything's happened so quickly. I tried to look at my father as something separate from all of this, no matter what I heard, but he isn't, is he?'

'No, he is not. He is as much a part of this as Lord Skeldrin.'

'We must find him, Crystalian, and stop all of this.'

'We will find him. That, I promise you.'

Charlie was sharing a horse with Milee, and he couldn't help but remember back to the artful way in which he had dispatched Bill the Butcher's men and the Slas that jumped down on them on the mountain pass.

'So where do you come from?' he asked as an ice breaker.

'I come from China, a place called Yunnan. Why, you ask?'

'I was just wondering how you know all that

fighting stuff.'

'I go to a special place as boy, to learn.'

'Sounds like school to me.'

'Yes, you right, it was school, and it is not fighting as you say.'

'Not fighting, what do you mean?'

'It taught as defence, not attack, but it also way of being and meditation.'

'Can I learn it then? It would come in very 'andy with those Slas, and a few other guys I know.'

'It takes many hours of dedication and practice, much discipline. I think you have many bad ways, many bad habits.'

'Another fing I've learnt in the last hour, Milee.'

'What?'

'I'm ruddy starvin'.'

'Ah, first bad way. Hunger for now is state of mind. Tell stomach it has eaten well and will eat well again, but for now, it must wait, and hunger will pass.'

'My stomach thinks my throat's been cut,' said Charlie as his stomach grumbled to remind him.

'You see, very bad ways. Impossible!'

Although the sky above was a deep blue and the sun was shining brightly upon the forest, the tree canopy was thick, bringing nothing but shade as they followed trail after trail. But even so, the need to find water was becoming urgent. After a while, the trail sloped downward, and the sound of moving water rushed back up. At the bottom, a small stream meandered by, and they all dismounted to take a much-needed drink. 'We must try and follow this stream as best we can, and maybe think about trapping some food before nightfall,' said Crystalian.

Charlie looked up to agree, but caught a scowl from Milee. 'Okay, okay, I know, state of mind.'

'That may have to wait,' said Avindor, 'This is Blackthorn Forest, there are many tales of this place, of people who wandered from the path and were never seen again,' he said, lowering his voice,' it is not a wise place to stray alone. It is enchanted. Do not tell the younger ones, just make sure they don't wander off.'

The company carried on following the stream, hoping for some clear high ground to appear, but it did not. The same blanket of trees and the meandering stream continued into late afternoon. 'I think we should stop,' said Crystalian at an open patch of ground. 'Let us set up camp here. I will take first watch.'

Milee lit a fire as the light grew dim, while Avindor and Crystalian quietly talked about what they had seen so far. As Molly snuggled down in front of the fire, hungry and tired, she drifted off with thoughts of her grandmother, the Yarrowoods, and ultimately, when she might get home. And as she fell to sleep, she could swear she could hear the forest whispering.

The following day, they continued, always keeping the stream in their sights as it gradually became a river.

'This is no good,' said Crystalian, bringing his horse to a halt and climbing off. 'We could wander through this forest for the rest of the week and still be lost. We need to find out where we are, and if high ground cannot come to us, we must make our own.'

'Do you know what he's talking about?' Said Charlie, looking at Molly and yawning, as they watched Crystalian picking out a tree. Finding a sufficiently high one, he began to climb it and soon disappeared into the canopy. It was a hard climb to the top, but once he reached the summit of the tree, he saw a welcome sight.

'I can see smoke from a valley to the west,' he shouted down. 'That means people.' But he heard no reply from below. 'Did you hear what I said?' However, there was still no reply. 'What on earth is going on now?' he grumbled as he climbed down. Nearing the bottom, he could see there was nobody at the foot of the tree, and the horses were gone. He slid down the trunk, jumping the last few metres. 'Hello, hello? Where are you?' he shouted. The forest was dense with foliage, and to see any distance was impossible, so he began by checking the ground for tracks. As he followed the trail, there were more hoof and footprints than there should be. Then something stopped him, a feeling and Avindor's warning about the forest. He was not alone, and before he could turn around, a blinding flash of pain erupted at the back of his head, and darkness took him.

When Crystalian awoke, his head was pounding. How long he had been unconscious, he could not tell, but the back of his head felt wet and cold from blood. 'He's awake,' said a voice from behind him. A grunted reply came from somewhere in front. Crystalian opened his eyes, but he was blindfolded, his hands were tied, and he'd been slung across the back of a horse. It was extremely uncomfortable, and he began to struggle to move himself when someone rode alongside and struck him across the back.

'You stay still,' said a man's voice.

The voice sounded strangely familiar.

Before long, the horses came to a halt. Crystalian could hear the unmistakable voice of Charlie complaining as he was pulled from the horse.

'Molly, where are you?' He shouted.

'It's alright I'm here,' she replied.

Someone shoved Crystalain forward. The ground changed from grass to canvas; he could see that much through the bottom of his blindfold as he was pushed to the floor. Charlie was still creating as he was shoved down beside him, then somebody pulled off the blindfolds. As Crystalian's eyes grew used to the light again, he could see their captors. He and his companions were inside a large tent, all on their knees and guarded by five men with guns. Before he could utter another word, another man came into the tent. Crystralian recognized him immediately. 'Gunari,' he said with surprise.

Gunari stepped forward, striking him across the face, sending him reeling backwards. 'Outcast, a traitor to your people, you do not speak to me,' he said, spitting at where Crystalian knelt.

'Stop that, leave him alone,' yelled Molly.

Gunari took her by the collar. 'I would be quiet, girl, if I were you and only speak when spoken to.'

'I think he means it, Mol,' said Charlie, sniggering nervously.

'Shut up, boy,' yelled Gunari, slapping him around the side of his head. 'I am in charge here and I do the talking.' He walked back over to Crystalian and placed his boot on his chest. 'Now then. What are you doing with an Englishman, a Chinaman, a boy and a girl, riding in this forest?'

'Gunari, listen to me carefully. I...'

Suddenly a beautiful dark-haired woman rushed

into the tent, pushing past the other men.

'I did not believe it to be true, but here you are,' she said in a voice struggling with emotion.

'Luminita!!' said Crystalian with a gasp.

'You do not speak to her,' snapped Gunari, moving his boot back onto Crystalian's chest.

'Let him go, you fool,' snapped Luminita. 'Untie all of these people at once.'

'Get out of here, woman, and know your place,' yelled Gunari, taking her by the arm.

'Let go of me,' she yelled, 'we are not married yet.'

'What is this?' snarled a loud voice. A big man with a huge stomach hanging over his trousers and an untidy cigar in the corner of his mouth filled the entrance of the tent. 'What is going on in here? You men, get outside,' he ordered. 'Gunari, you were sent to hunt for food, and unless we have become cannibals, I...' He stopped talking abruptly when he saw the man beneath Gunari's boot. 'Crystalian! Gunari, untie all of these people at once.'

'But Father...'

'Did you not hear me? I said at once!'

Gunari took out a small knife and bent down low to Crystalian. 'I will see you later,' he whispered, cutting his hands free. After releasing everyone else, he stormed from the tent.

'Zindelo, what are you going to do?' Asked Luminta.

'Hush, my child,' said Zindelo, putting a finger to Luminita's lips. 'Take these unfortunate people and show them some Romani hospitality, while Crystalian and I have a little talk. Show them we are not savages.'

'But Zindelo...'

'But, but, but, you young girls are always butting. Hush now and do as I say.'

Luminita led all but Crystalian out of the tent. Molly hesitated at the opening, concerned for what would happen to Crystalian next. 'I will be fine, Molly, you go on,' he said, getting to his feet.

'You're not going to do him any harm, are you?' said Molly, frowning at Zindelo, who let out a loud laugh.

'Do not worry, my child, I would not harm a hair on his pretty little head.'

Molly turned and stepped outside. Momentarily blinded by the sunlight, she was astonished when her eyes adjusted to the sight before her. She was in a long and wide valley teaming with people. Horse-drawn wooden caravans lined either side of the valley, all painted in wonderful bright colours, and exotic tents in blues, greens and reds stretched as far as she could see. The men were tanned and swarthy, many of them smoking pipes; the women all had long, dark hair, and many wore brightly coloured scarves around their heads, matching billowing skirts and big bangle earrings. Children were running and playing, stopping to stare at the new visitors as they came past.

'Where are we and who are these people?' asked Molly, catching up with Avindor.

'They are Romani, Crystalian's people. They live life on the road, travelling from place to place. Very secret and superstitious. As for what they are doing here, I cannot say.'

'We are here for a wedding, if you wish to know,' said Luminita. 'And yes, superstitious, is right, so mind you remember that while you are here.'

Molly ran forward to walk alongside Luminita, curious to know a few more things. 'I know your name, but you don't know mine. I'm Molly,' she said, holding out her hand.

'Yes, hello, Molly,' she replied, shaking her hand.

'I was wondering how you know Crystalian.'

'That is a long story and not for your ears, I think,' Luminta replied snappily. She stopped at a large tent. 'Now wait in here, please, all of you.'

They walked into a space with large, brightly coloured cushions laid out on the floor around the edge.

'Well, that told you, Mol,' said Charlie.

'Yes indeed,' said Avindor. 'It might be wise to watch what we say for the moment, until we know our situation better.'

Back in the other tent, Zindelo was questioning Crystalian. 'What are you doing here, and what is your purpose with these people?'

'With all due respect, Zindelo, I did not know you were here. It was Gunari who brought me to this place. And my business with my friends... well, that is my own.'

'And that is your right, but this places me in a very difficult position.'

'Then perhaps you must talk with your son.'

'I will speak to that fool of a son of mine, of that you can be certain. And you, did you know he has asked Luminita to marry him? But of course, you don't.'

Crystalian gave a big sigh as the past came flooding back.

'You are an outcast,' bellowed Zindelo, spitting out some tobacco from his cigar. 'The Romano Zakano forbids your presence here.'

'Then give me my friends and I will leave,' snapped Crystalian.

'Don't be foolish, man, your presence here has gone twice around this camp and back again. No, you will wait here. I must consult the Krisnitory and they will decide what to do with you.'

'They are here?' said Crystalian with a worried look.

'Of course, they are here, everybody is here.' Zindelo pushed his untidy cigar back into the corner of his mouth. 'My daughter is getting married.'

CHAPTER XVI

—THE GREAT VADOMA—

Molly was digging into some very welcome soup along with some crusty bread when Luminita returned to the tent. 'You, Molly, you must come with me.' Charlie, Avindor, and Milee rose to their feet. 'Oh, sit down, you foolish men, I am not going to eat her,' snapped Luminita. 'My mother Vadoma, the great and powerful Mystic, knows of this girl and wishes to speak with her. I will wait for you outside.'

'Don't suppose there's any more of that soup going, is there?' said Charlie, grinning.

Luminita shot him an irritated look and went outside.

'That would be a no, then,' said Charlie, slumping back down to the floor.

'Molly, this Vadoma very likely has a crystal ball,

which means access to the crystal network,' said Avindor, lowering his voice. 'See if you can get a message out.'

'Okay, I'll try.'

Luminita led Molly to a Vardo, a caravan, rectangular with a rounded top. Its outside was adorned with ornate carvings, painted in bright reds, blues, greens, and yellows. 'I will leave you here. My mother is inside.'

'Leave Crystalian alone!' said a sharp voice through the doorway.

Luminita flounced off, thrashing her skirt about from side to side as she walked.

'Come in, come in, I promise I will not bite you,' said the voice.

Molly climbed the yellow wooden steps apprehensively and entered the Vardo. An old woman sat at a table, a black scarf wrapped about her head and long golden earrings hanging from her ears, and at the centre of the table, there was a crystal ball.

'Come, sit beside me. You have nothing to fear,' said the old woman.

As Molly moved further down the Vardo, which smelt just like Mr Abignate's shop and had similar trinkets to her grandmother's spiritual room, the old woman smiled and stood up, holding out her hand. 'I am the great Vadoma, mystic to the Romani people. Some might say a witch, but they are without knowledge and stupid.'

'I'm Molly Chatsworth, and I'm...a Valdar,' she replied proudly.

'Well now, I am honoured to meet you, Molly Chatsworth, but I already know who you are. I had a vision of your coming and...it showed me a great many things.'

Molly watched Vadoma as she drew out a pack of cards from beneath a cloth and shuffled them.

'Come, child, sit down, and in your own words, you must tell me how you have come to be at our camp.'

Molly sat down at the table, took a deep breath, and started with Bramblewood, while Vadoma shuffled some cards and smoked a long and bendy pipe. She told the old woman everything, from her grandmother, Grendellbar, her father's disappearance, Lord Skeldrin, and the Hall of Scorpio, and their encounter with the Slas.

'What a tale you have to tell,' said Vadoma. 'I think perhaps you should use my crystal ball and contact your Grendellbar straight away.'

'So, he's alright then?' Said Molly, looking for a little extra reassurance.

'Of course. He's a Grandmaster.'

'That's what Milee said.'

'Well, he should know,' replied Vadoma with a chuckle.

'I've never actually tried it before, I just saw my grandmother do it once,' replied Molly, looking at the Crystal Ball.

'It is perfectly simple, take the ball with your hands and think of who you wish to talk to,' instructed Vadoma.

Pulling the glass ball towards her, Molly clasped it with both hands. Closing her eyes, she thought of Grendellbar. The glass ball began to glow. A few seconds passed, and Grendellbar's face appeared in the ball. 'Molly! Elithryn be praised.'

'Grendellbar, I'm so pleased to see you, I was so

worried,' said Molly excitedly, 'are you alright?'

'I'm fine, Molly, help arrived just in time. Are you alright? Tell me everything.'

'It was terrible, Grendellbar, we came out at the Hall of Scorpio. Lord Skeldrin had been there.'

Grendellbar's head bowed as Molly relayed the news about the Slas and Polousha.

'We had to run for our lives, and now...' she said, hesitating, 'we are in a Romani camp.'

'A Romani camp?'

'Yes, and I think Crystalian may be in trouble,' Molly said, looking at Vadoma.

'Trouble? Fools, all of them! Now listen to me, Molly...'

'You mind your tongue, old man; other ears are listening,' said Vadoma, leaning forward.

'And who might you be, madam?'

'I am Vadoma, the great and powerful Mystic to the Romani people.'

'Vadoma, please listen to me. There is much more at stake here than Crystalian's past, I...'

'No, you listen to me, old man. I know what is at stake here; the girl has told me everything. But

Crystalian has run from his past for too long, and now he must face it. Do you not find it strange that he just happened to end up here of all places? Is this not part of what must unfold? You know how these things work, old man.'

'I stand corrected. It does seem more than a coincidence, I must confess.'

'Then we are agreed, we let things unfold as they should?'

'For the moment, yes, but time is short. They cannot delay much longer.'

'Why? Where are they going?'

'I don't know yet, but it is not by chance that Molly should be sitting next to Vadoma, the great and powerful Mystic, wouldn't you agree?'

'Grandmaster, have you spoken to my grandmother?' asked Molly.

'I have, and of course, it did not go well. She was very angry, as indeed she has a right to be.'

'Oh no,' groaned Molly.

'It was me she was upset with, but I think she accepted my explanation in the end. Molly, let me know as soon as you can what's happening.'

'Okay, Grendellbat, I will. Goodbye then.' Molly felt lost and uneasy as his face began to diminish in the glass ball.

'It would seem your Grandmaster wishes me to look at what is yet to come, to see where this tale may go.' Vadoma took the pack of cards next to her, which she had been shuffling earlier and shuffled them again.

'Cards?' Molly said, wondering what was going to happen next.

'Yes. My special cards, Tarot cards,' Vadoma replied as she shuffled the deck. 'An ancient and mystical art. Many Gaje fear them, but that is nonsense.' Vadoma's lips tightened, and her eyebrows rose as she turned the first card. It showed a tall tower, cracked and burning, flames licking at shattered stone while tiny figures leapt from its windows. 'This is change beyond your control,' she said quietly. 'You feel as though your home and your family have been destroyed. Forces are already in motion, and no matter what you do, you cannot stop them.' Vadoma turned a second card to reveal a man clutching swords, his head turned as if he were fleeing. 'The Seven of Swords. Lies and deceit.' Vadoma hesitated, then sighed. 'I fear this would be your father, my dear. He is on a destructive path. He is lost to it. Unable to find his way back.' Molly's throat tightened. Vadoma turned the third card, which was heavier somehow. A king stared back at them, a sword upright in his grasp. 'The King of Swords,' Vadoma whispered with a shiver. 'He is...' She stopped. Her eyes locked onto the card, unblinking. Molly leaned forward just as the image began to change. The king's crown slipped and fell away, revealing slicked-back hair. His eyes darkened, turning as black as night, glaring out from a face Molly recognised all too well.

'Vadoma,' said Molly with a gasp, but Vadoma did not answer. The card tore itself free from her fingers and hovered above the table. Molly shoved herself back in the chair as the card spun faster and faster, the air humming around it. Then, with a sharp flash, it erupted into flame, collapsing into a cloud of ash and glowing cinders. Molly screamed. Vadoma gasped and broke from her trance. As the ash drifted down, she grabbed a glass of water and threw it across the table, hissing steam rising where it struck.

'Angels preserve us,' she breathed. 'Are you alright, child?'

'I'm okay,' Molly said shakily. 'What about you?'

'Saints alive... it was that man. The one you are following.' Vadoma pressed her fingers to her temple. 'When you do this kind of work, you touch another's energy, and I touched his. So much rage. So much anger. He will let nothing stand in his way. 'She shook her head, as if trying to dislodge the feeling and pressed her fingers to her temples once again, breathing slowly, as though steadying herself against an unseen force. 'There is a name,' she said at last. 'It keeps circling my thoughts. I do not wish to say it.'

Molly's stomach tightened. 'Why not?'

Vadoma's eyes flicked to the door, then to the darkened corners of the Vardo. Only when she was certain they were alone did she speak. 'Because some names have weight,' she said quietly. 'And you never know who or what may be listening.' She swallowed. 'Mor...' The word snagged in her throat. She stopped, shook her head, and tried again.

'Mor...lic.' The air seemed to thicken, the candle flames bending as if disturbed by a breath neither of them had drawn.

Molly felt it then, a cold chill crawling up her spine.

'Morlic?' she repeated, 'What is it?'

Vadoma's gaze did not leave Molly's face. 'Not what,' she said. 'But where? It is a place, perhaps best unremembered. A place...you must go. A place you will all go.' Molly pulled the last two cards from the wet tablecloth. 'Let me see those,' said Vadoma, snatching them. 'Ah, look, you see. This first card is the chariot, which means a journey. Not just a physical one, but one within yourself. You will be very different when this is all over, Molly Chatsworth.'

'Hasn't everything that's happened been enough?' Said Molly with a big sigh.

'Everything changes, my dear, but that is not always a bad thing. Now look at this last card, it shows a man looking out to sea. Yes, I see you now, going west out to sea. You will sail to this place, Morlic. Your Grandmaster was right, we have seen much on your next path.' Vadoma looked pale and drained. 'And now, I'm afraid, I need to rest. All of this has tired an old woman out. You must go back and join your friends; we will talk again.' Vadoma showed Molly to the doorway. 'Luminita?' she called out.

'Yes, Mother?' Luminita scurried from behind another Vardo.

'Take Molly back to her friends at once, and then return to me. We have things to discuss. And you, Molly Chatsworth, you are welcome at my door anytime.'

Molly followed Luminita, winding through the tents and caravans. 'Huh, look,' said Luminita, pointing, 'I see the Gaje boy has found some more food.' Charlie was sitting around a campfire, eating wild pigeon with some old men.

'Luminita, what is this word, Gaje? I keep hearing it.'

'It is our word for your people. You are a Gaje girl, like your word for us is gypsy. But we are not gypsies, we are Romani.'

Molly had heard the word gypsy before, and it

had never been used kindly. 'Hardly seems fair, everybody having names for each other. People are just people, after all, aren't they?'

'You are very perceptive, girl, and you are right,' said Luminita, shooting Molly a curious look. 'But that is not the way the world works. People persecute what they do not understand. For many generations, we Romani have been driven from wherever we settle. That is why we never stay in one place too long. But no matter, we are here now.' Luminita stopped at the tent. 'In there are your friends,'

'I am sorry for your people, Luminita. I wish I could change things for you.'

Luminita, surprised by Molly's comment, did not have a reply.

Any news?' asked Avindor, jumping up from his cushion as Molly entered the tent.

'How did it go, Molly

'Do you speak with Gwandmaster?' asked Milee.

'Yes, and yes, and more besides,' replied Molly. 'I spoke to Grendellbar and told him what's been happening. Luminta's mother, Vadoma, is a Time Keeper, and he asked Vadoma to look into what comes next, and it seems we have to go west to get a ship.'

'We are already in the southwest, and the coast is not far,' said Avindor. 'Anything else?'

'Yes, the place we're going to is called Morlic.'

'Morlic? Where in Elithryn's name is that?'

'I don't have a clue,' replied Molly.

They were interrupted by Charlie running in, red-faced and out of breath. 'I think you'd better come quick,' he panted. 'It's Crystalian, he's in big trouble.'

CHAPTER XVII

—THE STARCHILD—

Crystalian walked through a large, jeering crowd with his head down. Zindelo held his arm, and two armed men walked behind him carry a gun each. Onlookers shook angry fists, yelling as they passed by, and some even spat in Crystalian's path. Molly, Avindor, Milee, and Charlie joined the crowd, swept along with the flow. The marching crowd stopped at an open patch of ground where a canopy had been erected. Beneath it at a long table sat five elderly men, all wearing bright red top hats. The crowd, a hundred people deep, spread out around the canopy to form a circle on the grass. Zindelo led Crystalian to stand in front of the Krisnitory Judges and their disapproving scowly faces.

'Silence,' yelled Zindelo at the crowd. A hush fell.

'Gentleman, honoured Bandoliers of the Krisnitory court, you are assembled here to decide what should happen to this man. Crystalian, the heir to his father's throne, banished and disowned, named as an outcast never to return. And yet he has...' The gathered crowd grew loud and noisy once again. 'Silence!' yelled Zindelo again. 'He has now returned, and that alone has broken the Romano Zakano code, and he awaits your decision, honoured Krisnitory.'

Zindelo finished by bowing his head.

Molly and Charlie had managed to push their way to the front of the crowd. 'Hello. You are the Gaje, friends of Crystalian?' Said a young man next to them, quietly.

'Yes, we are,' replied Molly in a loud whisper. 'Who are you?'

'My name is Carlo, pleased to meet you,' he said, shaking Molly's hand. 'I am the brother of Luninita.'

'What are they going to do to him? What is this all about?'

'It's a long story,' replied Carlo.

'It normally is,' said Charlie rolling his eyes.

'But he has caused a great deal of trouble by returning. In more ways than one. It is said,' Carlo lowered his voice a little more. 'he was involved in the death of his sister.'

'Wait a minute,' said Molly. 'He was involved with the death of his...'

'Shh, keep your voice down, please,' said Carlo sharply. 'Of course not, but that did not stop his father from thinking so. And so. he was banished from his kind forever.'

'So, what's going to happen?' Asked Molly in concerned. tone

'They could decide to give him the lash, or they could decide...something much worse.'

'What?'

'Shh,' came from the people around them.

'We must wait and see,' whispered Carlo.

The Krisnitory Judges sat huddled around a large book at the centre of the table. Turning to different pages with disapproving looks, they finally closed the book, nodding with agreement. The Head Judge at the centre, the surliest of all, addressed Crystalian. 'Crystalian, you have broken the Romano Zakano

Code by being here. When you were banished, it was an alternative to anything worse. You were found many years ago to have a responsibility in the death of your sister. This is indeed a serious matter. Although you did not commit the murder, your actions were seen as instigating it.'

'Please, sir, if I may address you...'

'Quiet!' yelled the Judge. 'Do you not remember any of your customs? I think you have been with the Gaje for too long. You do not speak to this court. Someone must speak for you. Do you have such a person?'

Crystalian looked to the floor in despair as he had no one. Molly couldn't just watch this; she had to help somehow. 'I...I will speak,' she said loudly. Then suddenly, all eyes were upon her.

'Mol, what are you doin'?' Said Charlie with surprise.

'Yes, what are you doing? Asked Carlo.

'Listen, Charlie, I may not know much, but I know Crystalian wouldn't do something like they're saying, and he needs our help.'

Molly stepped out of the crowd towards

Crystalian, with Charlie following behind her. The Romani erupted, jeering and shouting and Zindelo yelled for silence again, his voice now hoarse from all the shouting.

'We will speak also,' said Avindor, pushing his way out of the crowd with Milee.

'Please, sir, may I speak?' said Molly in the politest voice she could find.

'Molly!' said Crystalian, 'please, you don't have to...'

'Shut up, man! You don't seem to have done very well up to now, so let her speak,' said Avindor, interrupting and moving to Molly's side.

'The Gaje girl wishes to say something,' said the Head Judge mockingly. The other judges chuckled and sniggered.

'Excuse me, sir, but I am not a Gaje girl, my name is Molly Chatsworth.'

The Krisnitory shuffled and muttered uncomfortably. 'Continue,' said the Head Judge sharply.

Molly took a deep breath and began. 'I have only known Crystalian for a short while, but he has saved my life more than once. He is a brave and strong man and keeps his word. I am beginning to learn that not everyone does. I don't know what happened before, but I do know Crystalian's heart is kind and honest, and that has to be worth more than anything. He wouldn't murder anyone or help. We have something really important to do, and he is helping us, so please, let him go.'

'Hear, hear, I will second that,' said Avindor loudly.

'And I,' said Milee.

'Yeah, and me, what she said, twice,' said Charlie.

The crowd muttered loudly amongst themselves as one of the Judges rifled through the Zakano book. Stopping suddenly, he pushed the big red book to the next Judge, and along the line it went, until they had all read it. The Head Judge rose to his feet and silence fell upon the crowd. 'Molly Chatsworth, you are a very brave girl, and you have spoken well. Crystalian has obviously earned your respect and friendship, and you have earned ours. You are all, it seems, loyal and true friends to him. But I am afraid it is of no matter. The Zakano Code clearly states that only Romani may speak for Romani, and you are not Romani. I am sorry, but that is our law, so if there is no one else, we will pass sentence.'

The crowd began to shout and argue, some for Crystalian, some against, until another voice broke through. 'I have someone here who will speak for this man,' said another voice. Luminita pushed through the angry crowd with her mother holding her arm. The old woman was poking at people with her cane, prodding them out of the way. Pushing out from the crowd, an angry Gunari tried to block their path.

'Luminita, Vadoma, why would you make such a fool of me?'

'Get out of our way, stupid boy,' snarled Vadoma. Gunari winced as Vadoma struck him with her cane and he moved aside.

'Leave me now, Luminita, I will be fine,' said Vadoma. Shuffling to the edge of the Krisnitory table, she turned, looking back at the crowd, scowling at them all. A sudden hush fell all around. 'What you are doing here is wrong, and it must stop now.' Turning back, she brought her cane down with a loud crack upon the Krisnitory's table, leaving a large dent in the top. The Krisnitory Judges all jumped. 'This man should not be standing here. Blamed for a death he had no part in. Banished by a grieving father and mourned by a broken-hearted mother. It is prejudice that should be on trial here, not this man. For as sure as I am that the sun will rise tomorrow, that is what killed this man's sister. Something we have all been a victim of at some point in our lives,' said Vadoma, giving the judges a hard stare.

Lots of heads nodded in the crowd. 'He has learnt his lessons and made up for any misdeeds he may have committed as a young man. If it wasn't for that son of yours, Zindelo, he would never have been here at all.'

One of the Judges stood up. 'But, Vadoma, we must...'

'Quiet!' She yelled, hitting the table with her cane again. This time, a big crack splintered through the wood, making the judges jump back in their chairs. 'You do not know who or what you are dealing with. None of you do,' she yelled at the crowd. 'This young girl here, who was prepared to face all of you, snapping like dogs, do you realise who she is?' Of course, you do not. So, I will tell you.' She pointed her cane at Molly in an almost accusatory manner. 'She...is a Starchild.'

Crystalian turned to look at Milee and Avindor. 'Oh dear,' said Avindor, putting his hand to his forehead.

'Mol, what's she talking about? Asked Charlie.

'I don't know, I don't know what that is,' said Molly, putting her hands up to her face. The crowd was in uproar and moving closer.

'Vadoma, you go too far. What proof do you have of this?' Said one of the judges, shaking his fist angrily.

'So, it is proof you want? I give you proof.' She put her hand in her pocket and shuffled towards Molly. 'Take your hands from your face, child,' she said snappily.

'Vadoma, what are you doing?' Said Molly. 'I...I...'

'I know more about you than I was telling; I saw into your soul, at my table, you are a Starchild.'

'Vadoma, I don't know what that means.'

'Not now, not today. But you will, my dear, you will,' said Vadoma, stroking Molly's face gently. 'I also know that you are a telepath, now, put out your hand and let us put an end to this nonsense.'

'I am,' said Molly, bewildered.

Vadoma took a small, clear crystal from her pocket and put it in Molly's hand. 'Now, raise and light the crystal and hurry before this crowd turns on all of us.'

'What?'

'As a Starchild, you have many abilities; the power to influence elements with your mind is one. So, light the crystal and shut these barking dogs down.'

'But how?' Cried Molly.

'Search your soul,' yelled Vadoma.

Molly's heart was racing as she looked at the baying crowd. Search her Soul? Light the crystal, but how? What did that mean? Holding out her hand, she stared hard at the crystal. Her mind raced in panic from one thought to another, but each idea was as pointless as the last. She took a deep breath to calm herself and closed her eyes. The noise around her died away. From somewhere in the back of her mind, she saw Polousha, floating out of the dark like an angel. Bathed in a shimmering white light, as beautiful as ever, she brought calm to Molly's mind. 'You can do it, Molly, just believe,' she said softly.

'But I don't know how,' said Molly in her mind.

'Tell it what you want it to do and believe,' answered Polousha.

With her eyes still closed, Molly felt the crystal resting in her palm. It was warm now, alive. All she could do was imagine it lighting up; it was all she had left. She clung to the image in her mind, wrapping it in hope and fear and everything she believed to be true.

'I believe," she whispered. "I believe.' Suddenly, the crystal began to glow. It lifted from her hand, rising slowly into the air above her, and the angry murmurs of the crowd fell away into stunned silence. A brilliant white light burst outward from the crystal, striking in every direction, and every Romani dropped to their knees in awe and fear. The crystal spun faster and faster, its radiance blinding, its hum filling the air.

Molly opened her eyes. There it was, spinning above her hand. She could feel it. Power pulsed through her fingers, through her chest, through her bones, and the warmth of the light spread through her like fire. 'Stop!' she cried. At once, the crystal's light dimmed. It fell back into her hand, heavy and spent. Molly dropped to her knees, exhausted, clutching it tightly as the world tilted. She closed her eyes. Avindor was beside her in an instant, kneeling and placing a steady arm around her shoulders.

'It's all right, Molly,' he said softly. 'Just breathe. You'll be fine.'

Vadoma's voice rang out, sharp and demanding. 'Now what have you all to say?'

But no one answered. The crowd remained frozen, staring. Molly opened her eyes again. Something had changed; she could feel it. Something felt different. Avindor stiffened beside her, his breath catching.

'What is it?' Molly asked. 'Why is everyone staring?'

Avindor didn't answer at once. He was looking at her as though he had never seen her before. 'It's your eyes, Molly,' he said quietly.

'My eyes?' She lifted a trembling hand to her face. 'What's wrong with them?'

Charlie stepped forward and knelt in front of her. 'They're blue, Mol,' he said. 'Bright blue.'

Molly gasped and covered her face with her hands. Her eyes, once brown, always brown, now gleamed a stunning cobalt blue, vivid and luminous, like light caught in glass.

'It's all right,' Crystalain said gently, helping her to her feet. 'They are... quite stunning.'

'But why are they blue?' Molly asked, her voice barely a whisper.

Vadoma raised her cane to the sky. 'It is a miracle,' she cried.

Slowly, the crowd rose, humbled and silent. Even the Krisnitory stood speechless. Zindelo stepped forward at last, coughing nervously to break the hush.

'It would seem,' he said carefully, 'that we have a very special girl among us, and that Crystalain stands at her side.' He glanced at the others. 'It is not for us to change prophecies and legends. I think you will agree?' The Krisnitory nodded, tipping their hats.

'Then,' Zindelo declared, 'as Clan Leader, and with the consent of my learned Krisnitory, I declare this trial over. This man will go free, to walk his new path.'

Again, the Krisnitory nodded. 'And there is more,' Zindelo added, a smile breaking through. 'We celebrate!' The night erupted in cheers. A wild violin burst into song, and the Romani people surged forward, lifting Molly, Crystalian, Avindor, Milee, and Charlie into the air. Someone struck up a violin, and music filled the air as they were carried away like heroes.

However, there was one person in the camp who did not celebrate, and he did not sleep so well that night. Strange voices haunted the dreams of Gunari, taunting him endlessly. 'Gunari, second son to Zindelo, second best to Crystalian, why do you wait?'

'Go away! Leave me be!' he mumbled sleepily.

'Crystalian is plotting; he will take her away from you, and everyone will laugh. How pathetic Gunari is, they will say, how weak.' Visions of Crystalian and Luminita filled Gunari's head, and rage engulfed his mind as he wandered through his dream following the sound of the whispering, tormenting voice. 'Gunari, vengeance can be yours.'

Stopping at an old tree stump, a dark, ominous figure loomed ahead of him in his dream.

'Who are you? What am I doing here?' he demanded. 'Are you a spirit? Are you death come to take me?'

'I am a friend, Gunari, one who has heard your pleas.'

'Please, what do you mean?'

'To be rid of Crystalian.'

'Who are you?' asked Gunari once more.

The tall, dark figure had a cane, and the tip began to glow blue, shedding a pale blue light on a pale white face. 'I am the one who can help you, Gunari.'

'Uhk! Why do you torment me so?' Gunari said, rubbing his eyes, trying to get a better look at whoever this was.

'It is not I that torments you, it is the return of the cuckoo that wishes to steal your nest. Do you still wish to be rid of him by any means?'

'Well, of course I do, I want him gone and out of my life. Crystalian has plagued me long enough.'

'Then you must return here tomorrow night.'

'Why?'

'Return tomorrow,' said the figure once more.'

Suddenly, Gunari was no longer in the forest; instead, he found himself back in his bed. Sitting up, shaking his head, and rubbing his face, he decided he must have had some sort of bad dream, a nightmare caused by his worries and doubts. And so, he settled back to sleep. But when he awoke in the morning, there was mud on his feet, and stretching back to the doorway of his Vardo, there were muddy footprints.

CHAPTER XVIIII

—LOVE HURTS—

Molly awoke the next morning to a horribly loud noise. Sitting up, she looked around to see where it was coming from. It was Charlie, snoring in the corner, hands clasped around his belly, that was swollen, from overindulging the night before. Molly reached for a cushion and, aiming precisely, threw it at Charlie's head. He sat up with a start.

'W..w.. what was that? What's goin' on?'

'You are,' said Molly, yawning and stretching, 'snoring, on and on.'

'Blimey, can't a lad get some kip in peace?' grumbled Charlie, turning on his side and beating his pillow back into shape.

After another stretch, Molly stood up and stepped over the cushions scattered on the floor to a wooden stand holding a porcelain bowl of water. Lean over to scoop up some water, wash her face, and she caught sight of her new blue eyes in her reflection in the water. It was hard to get used to, but they were quite stunning. Drying her face, she went outside to find the others perched on a log in front of a fire, drinking tea.

'Arise, gentleman, for the hero of the hour awakes,' said Avindor.

'Good morning,' said Crystalian and Milee together, standing up and bowing their heads.

'Please, don't, I had quite enough of that last night. I am still the same as I was.'

As they all sat back down, Zindelo walked up and joined them, coughing and spluttering as he puffed on a long, fat cigar. 'Huh, there you all are, heroes,' he said, laughing heartily. 'But heroes of what, I cannot yet say. And you, Crystalian, a prince again.' Zindelo sat down beside him. 'I knew it would turn out for the better in the end,' he said with a good slap on Crystalian's back.

'You did,' he replied with a disbelieving glance.

'Of course,' replied Zindello, with a sincerity that

wasn't as convincing as he thought it might be. 'But I could not have foreseen how. That Vadoma,' he said with a chuckle. 'And you, blue eyes! Said Zindelo, turning to Molly. 'You have quite a gift there; you possess a great power. Perhaps you could cast a spell over that idiot son of mine, aye,' he said with an embarrassed laugh.

'Please, sir, I don't cast spells. I am not a witch; I am just Molly from Bramblewood.'

'Well now, the girl certainly knows her own mind, does she not? But, just Molly from Bramble, u...h...what is it?'

'Wood!' Said everyone at once.

'My people have seen a great wonder, and they will not easily forget it, and why should they? We do not see objects float in the air and a girl's eyes turn blue, every day, that I can tell you.'

'Zindelo is right, Molly, you indeed possess a great power,' said Avindor. 'I trained for years to attain a little of what you showed us last night. Accept the honours the Romani people wish to bestow upon you, at least until we move on.'

Molly didn't want to be looked at as different or

have any honours bestowed upon her. She just wanted to find her father and go home.

'Moving on is what we must discuss, Zindelo, for we must move on quickly,' said Crystalian.

'Leave!' bellowed Zindelo, laughing loudly. 'Nobody's leaving, foolish man, at least not today. My Kizzy is getting married. No, my friend, no one goes anywhere today.' Zindelo marched off into the camp, laughing and muttering to himself. Milee looked over at Molly's troubled face.

'Gwandmaster knew of this power; he knew you are a Starchild,' he said, getting up and sitting next to her.

'He did! He didn't say anything to me, and what does it all mean?' Said Molly, frustration showing on her face.

'It is said that the soul of the Starchild was carried down by the angels themselves, as a gift to humanity. We must treasure these souls, nurture them, and guide them, for one day they will show us all the way. Another name can be a Crystal Child or an Indigo Child. But you are the next generation of us, brought to heal and to teach the world and be the guide to more, like yourselves.'

Molly cocked an eyebrow of puzzlement, not able to connect any of this with herself.

'Your abilities are rising and combining, one we saw yesterday, the power to move an object, the power over crystal. Your eyes. Halfwings came into this world with bright blue eyes, as did all Seraphim. But with great power comes the burden of responsibility and sometimes confusion. But you need not worry, we will help you carry load, sort out confusion, and when time comes, you will know what to do with your gifts.'

'He is right, Molly, it is nothing to fear,' said Avindor. 'The meaning will become plain enough as time passes.'

Molly kept herself to herself for most of the day, opting to stay in the tent to think on what she had been told. People laid offerings of food and flowers outside in honour of the Starchild. Charlie was happy to bathe in her glory and accept gifts of food from whoever wanted to give them. It was only when Molly remembered the promise she had made to herself the day before, to get in touch with her grandmother, that she thought about leaving. Taking a throw from the tent, she wrapped it around her head and shoulders, as a disguise, in the hope that no one would bother her on her way to Vadoma's Vardo. Vadoma was outside, sitting on her yellow wooden steps, smoking her long, bendy pipe. 'Back so soon, my dear? And with a silly blanket around your head.'

'I was trying to hide myself; I didn't want any more fuss.'

'Do you see anyone else with a blanket on their head? No, you are the only one. Take it off; no one is going to bother you. Be proud of yourself, especially those amazing new eyes.'

Molly pulled the blanket from her head, feeling rather silly.

'Now, tell me why you have come back to the great Vadoma.'

'I was rather hoping I might use your crystal ball again. I really should speak to my grandmother.'

'Of course, my child, you do not have to ask. It is where you left it.'

Molly climbed into the Vardo and sat at the other

end, facing the glass ball, wondering what on earth she would say first.

'Try saying hello, that is always a good start,' called Vadoma from outside.

Number 10 Plumberry Road was in uproar. Balthazar was flapping and squawking about the room as Grand Sally's crystal ball began humming loudly. All visitors to the house had been barred, and Grand Sally had asked everyone she knew to refrain from contacting her on the Crystal Network, so this could only mean one thing. Molly's face was bright and clear in the glass ball as Grand Sally rushed into the room. 'Elythrin be praised, Molly, what have I got you into? Where have you been? Where are you now? What are you doing? What's going on? What has happened to your eyes? Why are they blue?' Tell me everything and don't leave anything out. Not for the first time, Molly relayed the adventure so far, with lots of oohs and ahs and oh my words and tears fell from both of them along the way. 'I am so angry with Grendellbar. He had no right to do this. No right at all.'

'Yes, but somebody has to find dad, and besides,

I should be home soon... I think.'

'That's all very well, my dear, but I have had word, your mother is on her way. What am I supposed to say to her?'

Molly's heart lifted; finally, some interest from her mother. But as her grandmother had quite rightly pointed out, what would Grand Sally say when she arrived and discovered her only daughter was off on some wild adventure? 'I will get home as soon as I can, Grandma, but I have to find Dad first and bring him with me.'

'Don't put yourself in any more danger, Molly. Remember who he is with and call me again as soon as you know something.'

'I will gran,' said Molly as Grand Sally's face faded from the glass ball. Molly felt a terrible sinking feeling in her chest and her eyes began to water.

'There is no shame in crying,' said Vadoma from the doorway.

'Oh, Vadoma, that's all I seem to be doing. I just want everything to go back to the way it was. To wake up at home, in my own bed with my family there in the morning, is that too much to ask?'

'Of course not, it is what any girl your age would want.'

'Bramblewood, where I come from, is such a lovely place. I didn't realise how much I was going to miss it, and now I can't go back.'

'My dear, you will go back, I have seen it.'

'Really, when?'

'That I cannot say, but you will go back. I warn you, though, it will not be the same.'

'Why, what's going to happen to it?'

'Nothing. It is you who will be different, not your Bramblewood.'

Molly could not grasp this at all. No matter what happened, her love for Bramblewood would never change.

'Now let me ask you something,' said Vadoma. 'Do you have a dress for this wedding tonight?'

Molly looked at Vadoma with an eyebrow raised.

'Don't be silly...I just wanted to see your face,' said Vadoma, laughing. 'Of course, you have not. Come with me, and I will see what I can do to put a big smile on that face of yours.'

The wedding was planned for midnight beneath

the full moon, a symbol of growth and prosperity. An area in the camp had been set aside for the ceremony and lit with flaming torches as the sun set. White woodland flowers tied in bunches were strung between wooden poles around the outside; other flowers lay on the ground where the happy couple would stand. Logs in rows formed seats for the guests, and opposite the ceremonial circle, a big open-sided marquee was filled with seats and long tables covered in white cloths for the great feast to come. Mouth-watering smells came from many pots and meat roasted on fires. The clanking of jugs and bottles rang out all about the camp. The guests began to arrive, their clothing dramatically different to their normal attire. All the men were dressed in black trousers and short black jackets with white frilly shirts underneath, and all wore hats of varying shapes and sizes. A wide-coloured waistband represented their clans, and some wore flowers in their lapels. The women were a sight to behold in their beautiful dresses of yellow, red or blue, or a combination of colours. Some wore dilcos, coloured headscarves, as a sign that they were married, and others wore flowers in their hair to display that they were not. A trio of Romani men, two with guitars and one with a big red accordion, began to play soft music as everybody assembled, and it wasn't long before the ceremonial green was alive with the sound of chattering guests. Avindor, Crystalian and Milee stood on top of a fallen tree with Charlie, right at the back, out of the way. 'I wonder where Mol is, I can't see her missing this,' said Charlie.

'Hey, silly, I'm down here,' said a familiar voice.

Molly was wearing a beautiful blue dress. A touch of rouge on her cheeks and some blue earrings complemented a big smile.

'Blimey, Mol, I didn't recognise yer.'

'You look beautiful, Molly,' said Crystalian, stepping off the log and kissing her hand.

'Indeed, you do,' agreed Avindor, 'your grandmother would be proud.'

'Come on, Mol, stand up 'ere. You can see everything,' said Charlie, putting out his hand to pull her up.

It was fast approaching midnight and the moon was sitting high in the night sky. The stars lay in blankets in the night sky, sparkling like diamonds. The thud of horses' hooves came through the camp, signalling the arrival of the wedding party. First to arrive was the groom, Gyorgy, with his parents and two brothers, all as proud as peacocks as they climbed from their carriage. Slowly, they walked along the centre aisle to cheers and flower petals being thrown at their feet. Then came Zindelo's family, the big man grinning from ear to ear. Many thought that it was not his daughter's marriage that put such a big smile on his face, but the dowry he would receive from the groom's father. First to step down was Stefano, the older son of Zindelo, who then helped his mother, Lyuba, down. Zindelo followed them, lifting his daughter Kizzy down. She looked beautiful in a white lace dress; her train spread out behind her. Arm in arm, father and daughter walked the aisle to rapturous cheers and flurries of flower petals showered like snowflakes.

There was, however, one member of Zindelo's family who was conspicuous by his absence. Once again, Gunari stood by the tree stump with the dark figure he had met the night before. 'Alright, I am here, damn spirit, so what is it you want of me?' Said Gunari impatiently. The dark figure raised a cane with a blue tip that glowed, and a blue bolt of light shot out, hitting Gunari in the chest, bringing him to his knees; as the crackling light hissed and fizzled about his body. The figure stepped into the moonlight.

'I will have some respect in your tone,' said the figure standing in front of him. 'You will know who I am soon enough; what I can do for you, though, is much more important,' said the dark figure, pointing at the tree stump. Upon it sat a wicker basket with the lid tied down, and next to it a small leather pouch. 'Take that basket and place it directly in the moonlight. You will leave it for one hour, then you will return and pour the contents of the pouch into the basket.'

'And how will that help me?' Said Gunari, wincing with pain.

'Follow my instructions to the letter and your wish, no correction, our wish, will be granted.'

'I will,' replied Gunari, standing up and lowering his head in a submissive manner. He hobbled over to the stump, still feeling the effects of the fizzling blue bolt and picked up the basket and the pouch. 'And what will happen when I...' But when Gunari turned to look, no one was there. Observing the basket, he could see something was moving around inside, and he was not eager to know what. He ran from the forest to the end of the valley, where he placed the basket on a rock beneath the moonlight as instructed, then ran back to the wedding as fast as he could. The happy couple were standing amongst the flowers, and the ceremony was well underway, as he sneaked into the end of the front row.

An old man in a startlingly bright blue hat was conducting the ceremony, and the language he was speaking was not English. 'What is he saying? I can't understand a word, whispered Molly.

'It is the ancient language of my people, shared with no one else,' replied Crystalian.

The old man in the blue hat took a sharp knife from his pocket and pricked the end of Kizzy and Gyorgy's fingers, drawing blood. Taking two pieces of bread, he dabbed Gyorgy's blood on one and Kizzy's on the other. Gyorgy took the piece with

Kizzy's blood, and Kizzy took Gyorgy's. As they ate the bread, they spoke these words:

> 'My blood is your blood,
> Your blood is mine,
> Together forever,
> Until time's out of time.'

The old man pronounced them husband and wife, and everyone jumped to their feet, clapping and cheering wildly. The musicians began to play, and Gyorgy and Kizzy were lifted and carried to the marquee for the great feast. Other musicians joined the guitarists and violinists in the band. Molly was pulled up to dance by several boys, and Charlie gave in to some cheeky girls. Milee retired to bed, but Avindor stayed on to enjoy the festivities. But Crystalian found himself a quiet place behind a Vardo to smoke a pipe he had acquired. 'You have avoided speaking to me since you arrived at this camp,' said Luminita, stepping from the shadows. 'Not even a look in my direction. Did you think I would not notice?'

'And I have good reason,' said Crystalian, refusing to meet her gaze.

Luminita knelt in front of him and clasped his hand. 'I was betrothed to you years ago and I loved you then. Did you just think it would all go away?'

'Yes, I did. I thought you would move on, as I did.' He withdrew his hand and moved away. 'And now you are betrothed to another. You should not be here with me, alone like this.'

'But it did not go away,' snapped Luminita, getting up. 'As soon as I heard you were here, my heart leapt. My feelings have not changed.'

'Things are different now. I am different now. Many things have changed. I am not the boy you loved anymore, and I do not want to be.'

Luminita moved quickly to him and cupped his face in her hands. 'But I am still the same girl, and I cannot help what my heart tells me. I still love you.' Looking into his eyes, she placed her lips on his.

'Even now, at the wedding of my sister, you covet this man behind my back,' said Gunari behind them.

Luminita stepped back in surprise. 'Gunari, it is not...'

'What, it's not what it looks like? A mistake?' Crystalian stepped forward, but Gunari pulled out a knife, waving it in front of him. 'Don't come near me, either of you,' he yelled. 'Was it not enough for you to be a Prince again? Must you have another man's bride as well, your Princess? You disgust me. Both of you will pay for what you have done.' Gunari turned and ran, disappearing into the dark.

'You see, love hurts, doesn't it?' said Crystalian, glaring at Luminita.

Luminita burst into tears, turned, and ran after Gunari.

Gunari had reached the end of the valley where he had left the basket when Luminita caught up with him. 'Gunari, what are you doing?' she yelled, pulling at his arm.

'I told you, you would pay,' he snapped at her, falling to his knees. He fumbled through his pocket for the small pouch and untied the basket's lid. 'And now dark spirit, you will rid me of this cursed man.'

Chills ran through Luminita at his words. Gunari flipped the lid of the basket. 'No, Gunari!' Luminita tried to wrestle him away, but Gunari threw her off, pulling the string on the pouch and tipping a red powder into the basket. A red mist rose from the basket, forming a huge cloud. It engulfed them both as a terrible screeching came from the basket. Luminita ran, and Gunari staggered after her, coughing and choking from the cloud. Slowly, the mist cleared. Gunari looked back, rubbing his stinging eyes. He froze in fear, unable to believe what he was seeing. Standing where the basket had once been were three giant scorpions, as big as a horse. They lunged at one another with their pincers, dancing around each other, tormented and confused by their new size. One of them spotted Gunari and rushed at him with its pincers outstretched. Grabbing him by the waist, it tossed him into the air like a rag doll. A second scorpion caught him as he fell, and he was crushed and gone. Movement came from the rocks behind the scorpions. Red eyes glowed in the dark as an army of Slas emerged. The remaining Slas from the Hall of Scorpio had been summoned by Lord Skeldrin, finding their way through the forest. But Blackthorn's enchantments had served to affect them in an even darker and twisted manner, and now they were uglier and more mindless than before.

Luminita ran back to the wedding party, screaming. The music and dancing stopped. Vadoma, who knew the sound of her daughter's voice, got up from her table just as Luminita fell at her feet. 'What has happened, my child?'

'Oh, Mother, it's Gunari. He has cursed us all.'

The first scorpion came into view with the Slas, running behind, and began crashing through the camp. Men and women ran in panic, screaming and shouting inaudibly as Slas began hacking and bashing anyone and everything, setting fires with their burning torches. Other Slas came in behind the first wave axompanied by the other two scorpions, and Slas sat on their backs riding them in. Romani men came out with swords, knives, spears, guns, and anything else that resembled a weapon, taking on the Slas, dispatching them one by one. One of the scorpions scrambled up on top of a Vardo, which crumbled beneath its weight and crushed the Vardo's fleeing occupant between its giant pincers. A large group of men surrounded another scorpion, lassoing it as it lunged and swiped at them. One man managed to catch its stinging tail with his rope, and more men ran in to hold on. This only angered the beast more as it hissed and screeched, trying to wriggle free, but the Romani stood fast, tying down its pincers with their ropes. Stefano, Gunari's brother, leapt onto the creature's back with an axe. As it reared its ugly head, he plunged the axe into it. The scorpion gave out a scream, its legs collapsed beneath it, and it moved no more. A red mist rose from its body, and with a crackling and crunching sound, it shrank and shrivelled back to its original size. Crystalian and Avindor led a fight with the Slas, charging them down with horses. Turning their horses around, another scorpion came into view, but gunpowder and shot were no match for a scorpion's glistening armoured skin as they fired at it. Milee, woken from his sleep by the chaos, stood calmly by, waiting for his chance. As the scorpion's tail whipped by him, he jumped into the air, spinning as he went, and sliced through its end with an axe, chopping off its stinger. Crystalian jumped from his horse and, picking up a discarded oil lamp, he threw it at the scorpion. It smashed against its hard armour, and the oil ignited. The scorpion burst into flames. Flipping onto its back, its legs kicked wildly in the air. But as the flames leapt higher, it grew silent, and again the red mist rose from its body, and it shrivelled back to its normal size.

When the first scorpion had appeared, Charlie had wasted no time in leading Molly away to take cover beneath a Vardo far away from the chaos. 'It's those body-snatching Sla people again and giant scorpions. What was I doin' when I saw you outside that tavern that day? I've been chased by monsters ever since.'

'I don't know if it's escaped your notice, but they've been chasing me as well. Any time you want to leave, feel free.'

'Oh yeah, I'll be off then. Walk the two hundred miles or so home and then, yes, I know, I'll just drop in on old Bill, he'll be as pleased as punch to see me, no doubt. I can just see it now, come in, son, sit down, son, here's a right-hander, son, oh, and that's just before I get chopped up for his dog's dinner.'

'Well, you went to work for...'

Out of the darkness came a terrible screeching,

cutting off Molly's reply. Marching towards the Vardo, alerted by their raised voices, came the last surviving scorpion. Swiping hard with its pincers as it reached them, it smashed the Vardo apart as if it were made of matches. Molly and Charlie ducked out from beneath the wreck and ran to the next Vardo, but the scorpion was onto them. It leapt at the Vardo, smashing it with its weight. Charlie took a blow to the head from flying debris. 'Charlie,' screamed Molly. 'Charlie, you have to move now,' she cried, pulling him by his arm. But he didn't move. She had no choice now; she had to run. Scrabbling from beneath the wreckage, she was confronted by the giant scorpion. Its six eyes rolled around, focusing directly on her. It waved its tail high in the air, spreading its pincers wide. Only the wrecked Vardo now stood between them. Glancing once more at Charlie, Molly turned and ran as fast as she could toward the forest.

CHAPTER XIX

—A RELIC OF THE PAST—

The sun was rising, and a cold mist crept upon the ground as Molly sprinted through the western depths of Blackthorn Forest. On and on she ran, past gnarled and twisted trees frozen in one another's clutches, whispering their stories of ancient and long forgotten tales. Further into the gloom she ran, her pace unchanged, her gaze fixed forward. All the while, the giant beast was crashing through the undergrowth behind her. She had to stop, just to catch her breath. Her lungs ached as she sucked and blew. What about Charlie? Why wouldn't he wake up? What about the camp, the Slas? A million and one questions twirled in and out of her head, but she had no answers. She felt sick from all the running. If only she could find somewhere safe to hide. The mist was losing its battle with the hot morning sun and began melting away. Ahead, the forest floor sloped downwards, and the sound of running water echoed up from below. As she paused, the sickening screech of the horror behind caught up, its giant legs and pincers crashing and crunching through the trees. Quickly, she made for the slope and stumbled down through the undergrowth, her dress catching and ripping on every bush and bramble. The river at the bottom was icy cold, but fear pushed Molly in without hesitation. The breath rushed out of her as she hit the freezing water. Luckily, it was shallow enough to walk across, only rising to her waist. Slipping on stones on the riverbed, she pushed on, and reaching the other side, she turned, looking back. She could still hear the giant insect. Clambering up the bank, wet, muddy, and cold, she was shocked to see a small face sticking out of the trunk of a tree. Just as surprised was the face itself, vanishing as soon as it saw she had seen it. 'No wait, whoever you are, I need your help. Come back, please.'

'I cannot see you,' said a shrill voice.

'Yes, you can,' said Molly snappily.

The face reappeared, dimly. It resembled something human, and yet it was not. 'What do you want?' it asked timidly.

'There's a giant insect about to crash down that hill, and I need a place to hide. Help me, please.'

'What sort of insect is giant?' asked the face.

'It's a, well, u.. h, well, what does it matter?' She snapped impatiently. The scorpion appeared through the tree line on the other side of the river, stomping heavily into the water. 'That's what sort, quickly,' said Molly in a loud whisper.

'Oh my,' said the face looking across the water. 'Yes, yes, that way, that way.' The face directed her with its eyes towards a rough path. The path went upwards, winding its way to the top of a hill, and Molly ran up it. The scorpion would reach the other side of the river at any moment. As she came to a bend towards the top of the path, the face reappeared in another tree, moving from one to the next as she scrambled upwards. 'Quickly, quickly, take the next path,' it said, shaking a branch in the direction it wanted her to go. She could hear the menace behind, screeching at the bottom of the hill, and sprinted along the path as fast as she could. At the end of the track was a small clearing with a great hollow log wedged up against a tree. Peering inside the log, she could see that it was wet, slimy and cold, but the sound of the scorpion crashing through the undergrowth was all the encouragement she needed to crawl inside. Spitting and blowing, she tried not to scream as beetles and wood lice dropped onto her face and into her hair. Then, the tree face suddenly appeared above her in the log. 'Why is this nasty thing chasing us? It is not of this forest, where does it come from, and what does it want of us?'

'It's not chasing us, it's chasing me,' replied Molly, irritated. 'And will you please be quiet in case it hears you.' Too late. The scorpion came crashing out of the trees, running straight for the log. It clambered over and over it, backwards and forwards, around and around. Frustrated, it then began shoving the log around violently. Molly, yelling in fright, braced herself against the sides. The creature became even more frustrated as the log was too small for it to get at the prey inside. It hit it wildly with its pincers, but the log was oak, old and tough, and wouldn't give way. The giant insect took one last swipe at the log and it rolled towards a ridge. Molly was feeling sick from all the spinning, but the log stopped, its end wedged against a tree.

'I must go and find help,' said the face and disappeared.

'No, wait! Come back! Don't leave me.'

Molly, now on her front, looked towards the open end of the log as the scorpion ran at the log once more, and, clenching the log in a claw, it hurled it into the air. Spinning, tumbling, and bouncing, the log raced down the hillside. Near the bottom, the log hit a ridge of rock, and, as it bounced into the air, it gave way, breaking open and spitting Molly out into the small gorge below. She landed hard on her back and, for a moment, lay stunned and winded. The scorpion was on its way down the hill. Losing its footing on the steep slope, it too tumbled downward and bounced off the same rock, crashing into the gorge below. Stunned by the fall, it lay motionless. Molly scrambled to her feet, bruised and dazed. There wasn't time to stop; the creature lay still nearby, but it could come round at any moment. At the end of the gorge, jagged rocks stretched upward, a way to climb out. Molly got up and stumbled to the end of the gorge, and began to climb the rocks as quickly as she could, while the creature stirred quietly behind her.

Reaching the top, a patch of open ground stretched out in front of her, stopping at a small overgrown hill. Built into the hill was a tiny stone house, and sitting in its wooden door was the peculiar face from before. As she stared at the house, the scorpion rose behind her. 'HELP!' she screamed. As she went to run, the scorpion knocked her to the ground. It leaned over her. It raised its tail ready to strike. Molly's head was throbbing, and her vision was blurring. There was a sudden flash of light, a loud crackling, and then darkness.

Molly woke up with a start, feeling bruised and disoriented. She was inside the little stone house, lying on a bed of straw. The house consisted of one big room with a few alcoves for shelves, a table and chairs, and a stone chimney that went up the back wall. Candles were dotted about for light, and a big black kettle was boiling on the fire. The front door opened, and a scruffy man with long matted grey hair and a beard walked in. 'Oh, you're awake. You rest easy, young lady, while I make some tea.'

'Who are you? Where am I? And what happened to the scorpion and the face in the door?' Demanded Molly all at once.

'My, my, so many questions. The face, as you put it, that guided you here, is a Wood Nymph, and as for where the scorpion is... it has been dealt with.' The old man brought Molly a tin cup of weak tea and sat down beside her. 'No milk or sugar, I'm afraid. And now introductions, I think. My name is Zephrim, how do you do?' He said, proffering his hand to shake,

'Hello, my name is Molly,' she replied, shaking his hand. Molly's eyes were drawn to a pendant resting against his chest. It hung from a silver chain; the metal dulled with age. It was unlike anything she had seen before, two fractured wings folded around a broken circle. The silver was tarnished, darkened in the grooves, and yet something about it felt alive, quietly watching her back. Molly couldn't explain why, but the more she stared at it, the more certain she became that the pendant was not merely worn; it had meaning.

'Well then, Molly, you must tell me all about how you came to be at my door and in such an uninvited and peculiar fashion.'

'Well, my friends and I have been following...'

'So, there's more than one of you?'

'Yes, five, including me, and...'

Zephrim got up and peered through a crack in the door. 'Go on, go on, regale me with your tale.'

'Well, as I was saying, there are five of us, and we are on the trail of an evil man, Lord...'

'A lord, you say?' Said Zephrim, glancing back.

'Oh yes, and my fathers with him...'

'Your father. What's he got to do with this? And why does he follow evil lords about?'

'Well, Grendellbar thinks...'

'What was that name again?'

'Grandmaster Grendell...bar,' replied Molly hesitantly.

'No, no, no, no, no, no, no!' said Zephrim, angrily stomping on the ground. 'Muddlefy, mystify and confound him, and I suppose this evil lord is one Luscious Skeldrin?'

'Yes, but how did you know?' asked Molly, astounded.

Zephrim began pacing up and down, stamping his feet as he went, animated and furious. 'I told him no good would come of it. I warned him, I pleaded with him, but would he listen?' His ranting was brought to a halt by noises outside, and he scuttled back to the door to peer through the crack again. 'And here, it would seem, is one of your friends.' Zephrim swung open the door, and in rolled Charlie, head over heels, yelling at the top of his voice. Zephrim took a staff leaning against the wall and pinned Charlie by his chest to the floor. The staff's tip took on a fiery glow. 'I should mind my step, if I were you, lad, and whose house you are rolling into and shouting.' Molly's eyes widened as she saw the staff light up as she remembered Grendellbar and Avindor's staff.

'What 'ave you done with...' Seeing Molly on the bed, Charlie stopped shouting. Zephrim let him go and went outside. 'Here you are,' said Charlie, pleased and relieved. 'After that thing attacked us, I don't remember much, but when I woke up and saw you weren't there, I thought you were done for.'Charlie stood up, rubbing his head from knocking it on the floor. 'But then Crystalian found your tracks, and the creatures, and bits of your clothes on brambles, and 'ere we are.'

'I thought I was done for as well, but as I crossed the river, there was this face, and... oh, never mind. Anyway, I ended up here. I thought the scorpion was going to...but then it just disappeared.'

'Disappeared?'

'Yes, this man, Zephrim, he got rid of it, or so he says.'

'Sounds like witchy business to me.'

'No, I don't think he's a witch, Charlie,' said Molly thoughtfully. 'So, what's going on at the camp?'

'Two men dead and quite a fair number injured. It seems that Gunari fella is behind it all. Luminita's been wailing on about dark spirits and moon magic. Can't make head nor tail of it me-self, but there's one hell of a row goin' on, I can tell yer.' Charlie moved to the door, looking out at Zephrim. 'Who is this old fella anyway?'

'I only know his name and that he saved my life,' said Molly, getting up. 'But what's even stranger is, he knows about Lord Skeldrin. And he knows Grendellbar. In fact, he became really angry when I said his name.'

'Zephrim Kazzamah, the Grand Warlock himself. I would never have dreamed this. Are my eyes deceiving me?' Exclaimed Avindor.

'I would be immensely pleased if they were...but they are not,' replied Zephrim with a heavy sigh. 'And from what I'm hearing, you had better come in and sit down.'

Making them tea, with no milk or sugar, accompanied by some rather tasteless biscuits he had made the day before, he listened intently, not uttering a word as Avindor relayed everything in great detail. Pacing the floor, stopping at the mantelpiece to light his pipe, Zephrim mumbled. 'The world is changing; we are powerless to stop it. We sit as if teetering on the edge of a precipice, as time runs out.'

'What was that?' asked Avindor.

'Words spoken by one much wiser than any of us! Well, it seems your Grandmaster has quite a mess on his hands, so we had better help him sort it out before he brings the whole world crashing down around our ears.'

'I think that's a little unfair,' said Avindor defensively.

'Do you indeed! And what would you call fair, Avindor? Grendellbar was warned time and time again if...' Zephrim stopped suddenly and took a deep breath. 'I am sorry, Avindor. Forgive my temper, but there are events you are not aware of, and now is not the time to debate them. All of you, please wait outside for a moment while I gather my things. We have work to do.'

Outside, the questions came thick and fast.

'Who is Zephrim, Avindor? Asked Crystalian.

'And how does he know so much about the Valdar and Lord Skeldrin?' Asked Molly.

'He was before your time,' answered Avindor, glancing at Crystalian. 'A Warlock, or Valdarie, as you know them. As powerful as any I've ever seen.'

'That scruffy old man in there,' said Charlie in

disbelief.

'Yes, He was once a Grandmaster, like Grendellbar, and one of the twelve, as was Skeldrin's father.'

'Skeldrin's father?' Said Molly in surprise.

'Yes, he was one of the Twelve. After he died suddenly, there was a huge disagreement between Zephrim and Grendellbar, and Zephrim was never seen again. And that's as much as anyone knows. But what I find even stranger is how keen he is to join us.'

'What are you getting at?' asked Crystalian.

'Zephrim has taken a great deal of trouble to hide himself away from the world, here in this forest, and now he's packing to go with us without even being asked.'

'Hello,' said a shrill voice from behind them

'What is that?' cried Charlie, quickly stumbling back a few paces. A face was sticking out of a tree.

'Oh, it's him again, the one who led me here,' said Molly, drawing closer to it.

'Leave it, Mol, it might bite or somefing.'

'If my eyes do not deceive me, it is a Wood

Nymph,' said Crystalian. 'I was told of them as a boy, but only as legend and myth. Never would I have dreamt I would see one in this form.'

'Yes, a Wood Nymph I am, and I bid you welcome to my woods.'

'Your woods?' said Molly.

'Yes,' said Crystalian, bowing to the Nymph. 'There was a time when people would ask permission of trees and Nymphs to enter the forests and for safe passage.'

'Ah ha, I see you have met my young friend,' said Zephrim, stepping out of his house and closing the door behind him. 'I hope he did not startle you too much. Come along, my young fellow, we are off on a journey. A rather long one, I suspect, with no idea of when we will return... unless, of course, you want to stay here.'

'No, Master Zephrim, I would not wish to wander these woods alone again. I will willingly come with you. Maybe I will find more of my own kind.'

'Very well then, climb aboard,' said Zephrim, placing the end of his staff against the tree. The Wood Nymph slipped into the staff, its face appearing much smaller at the top. 'Come along, let's make haste.' Zephrim marched off in the direction of the river. 'Keep yourself quiet in my staff, young fellow. We are going to see some very superstitious people, and they do not need any more frights.'

The sun was high and bright in the morning sky, but the mood in the camp was sombre as the Romani made repairs to their caravans and tents. The wedding marquee that had been torn down in the attack had been roughly rehung, and beneath it lay the wounded in rows. Milee was helping by tending and nursing where he could.

'Crystalian, this is terrible,' said Molly.

'Yes...it is,' he replied as he looked around.

Out of a nearby tent came Vadoma. 'Thank the heavens,' she cried, 'you are safe, child, and you found an old Warlock for company.'

'And who might you be, madam?' asked Zephrim sternly.

'I am the Great Vadoma, Mystic to the Romani people.'

'Huh! Mystic indeed. It's a pity you did not

foresee all this, madam.'

'Hush your tongue, there's no need to be rude. You know it does not work that way. And I did see it, just not what form it would take, you foolish man.'

'But of course. I am sorry, Vadoma, it is not you I am angry with, but the sight I see before me.'

'As am I,' replied Vadoma. 'And now, all of you will come with me, please. We have made an interesting discovery in your absence.' Vadoma led them all back to her Vardo, which had been badly damaged in the attack. 'Luminita,' she said, banging her cane on the steps.

'Yes, Mother,' came a whimpering voice.

'Bring me the basket.' Vadoma stared hard at Crystalian as they waited. 'Jealousy and loneliness can drive people to do some stupid things, can they not?'

'Why do you look at me when you say that?' said Crystalian. 'I am not either.'

'No, you are not. In fact, you are a very wise man, I believe. But there was one amongst us who was not.' Luminita appeared in the doorway and handed her mother the basket without a glance at Crystalian.

'Who amongst you recognises these markings?' Vadoma said, turning the basket over to reveal a stitched marking on the side.

Avindor snatched the basket from her hand. 'This is the symbol for the Hall of Scorpio. But how did you come by this?'

'I would say it is what the scorpions were kept in before being turned into mindless monsters,' said Zephrim.

'But how could that happen?' asked Molly.

'Moonlight. They were left in it for some time, I imagine, and no doubt this was found in the open somewhere?'

'Very clever, old man of the woods. Yes, further down the valley it was found where these creatures and these Sla people ran from,' replied Vadoma, pointing.

'And a pouch of red dust came with it, no doubt?' Said Zephrim.

'Skeldrin,' said Crystalian angrily.

'Of course, those stone creatures that came to life in the graveyard,' said Molly. 'That had something to do with red dust, didn't it?'

'It most certainly did,' answered Crystalian.

'At certain times of the month, the moon is ripe for magic, and it encourages growth,' continued Zephrim. 'But unfortunately, it does not judge what it encourages. Nevertheless, it is against the very laws of nature for those creatures to become any larger than they already were. So Skeldrin adding his red dust adds the twist, but it is unlikely he would have done this himself.'

'He did not,' said Vadoma.

'Gunari,' said Crystalian. 'Like a predator, Skeldrin picks off the weakest in the herd.'

'Jealousy and loneliness will drive people to do very stupid things,' said Vadoma again, wagging her finger.' We found his remains not far from the basket, and now Zindelo is beside himself with grief and anger.'

'And the Slas, what have you done with them?' Asked Zephrim.

'We piled the bodies at the end of the valley and burnt them,' answered Vadoma, pointing to the smoke trail that rose in the distance. 'The Slas themselves were trapped in the bodies, so they could not leave. So now they will return to the foul void that they came from.'

'What were you all planning to do next?' asked Zephrim.

'If I may speak for everyone here,' said Avindor. 'Vadoma and Molly, between them, have discovered our next destination, Morlic, although none of us has a clue where it is, other than we will reach it by water.'

'I know exactly where it is,' said Zephrim with a look of unease. '*In the depths of Morlic buried deep, with deathly souls its secrets keep, for whosoever looks upon this place, death will meet them face to face.*'

Molly glanced at Charlie, swallowing hard as shivers ran up and down her spine.

'Castle Morlic stands off the coast of Scotland...at least, what's left of it does. It is hard to miss; it has an unfriendly look. Beneath it, buried deep underground, lies the Skull of Belegnoth.'

'Slowly the pieces fit together,' said Avindor. 'But how do you know about Morlic, Zephrim?'

'Because it was once my business to know of such

things,' answered Zephrim firmly.

'We should let Grendellbar know what we are up to. May we use your crystal ball, Vadoma?' asked Avindor.

'I am afraid that is not possible. During the attack, it was smashed to pieces. But do not worry, for I will find a way to get another, and I will let your Grandmaster know what is happening. I will have your horses brought to you, and two more besides. I think Zindelo will pass them up without much argument, as it was his son who brought this sorry mess upon us all. Marko, my son, can ride with you for a time and bring the horses back when you have finished.'

'I do not think it is a coincidence that we all have met at this time and place,' said Zephrim. 'Dark forces may be at work, but the forces of light push just as hard. When we are on the road and safe, I will tell you more of what I know, but until then, I will keep my silence.'

'And you left this behind when you changed for the wedding,' said Vadoma, handing Molly her nail on a piece of string.

‘Oh,’ said Molly, patting her chest, ‘I’d forgotten all about that.’

‘Do not forget it again, it is very special,’ said Vadoma.

Molly washed and changed as the horses were saddled and readied for travel.

‘Another good pickle your Grandmaster has put you in, Milee,’ said Zephrim as he waited with the horses.

‘As pleasing as it is to see you, Master Zephrim, that is not correct. Things are not black and white, not so simple. I not sorry to be here.’

Luminita stood nearby, nervously twiddling the ends of her hair through her fingers.

‘Somebody is waiting for you,’ said Marko, looking at Crystalian.

‘Why?’

‘Because she loves you, stupid man,’ said Vadoma from behind him. ‘Do you forget the loyalty of Romani women, or has all memory of those days run out of you?’

‘Nothing has run out of me, woman, but look at what has happened.’

'Huh, Gunari was an idiot, a jealous fool who would have brought trouble to himself and others, no matter what. My daughter is as much a victim here as anyone. You still have feelings for her, I see them, but you bury them deep with other troubles. Get them out for some air, man.'

'I am sorry, my friend, mother is right,' said Marko. 'But if you will not go to her, I have at least six friends who wish to be husbands, lining up to take your place. I will apologise for your absence and...'

'Alright! I will go and talk to her if it brings me some peace,' replied Crystalian. Walking over to her, Crystalian found his heart softening at Luminita's beauty and the sad look on her face.

'So, you wish to speak to me now, when you are leaving,' she said, looking at the ground.

Crystalian took her lightly by the arm and pulled her close to him. Putting his finger beneath her chin, he lifted her head and gently placed his lips on hers. 'Too long have I buried my feelings,' he said and kissed her again. 'I must leave now. I do not ask you to wait for me, but...'

'Crystalian, shh,' said Luminita, putting her finger

to his lips. 'Do what you must. For this time, I know, when you come back, you will come back to me.'

'Make haste, everyone, we have a long way to go,' called Zephrim, already mounted on his horse. 'Many things are awakening in this world besides Valdar, and they need to be put back to sleep before the ruin of us all.'

'And there's me thinkin' we'd be home by tea time,' said Charlie with a big sigh.

'Don't worry, Charlie, I'm sure tea time will come eventually,' replied Molly, laughing.

As they set off on the next adventure, Molly longed for familiar things: like her grandmother and the smell of her perfume, the big red sofas in the living room, the kitchen smells that brought such warm memories, her comfortable bed, Mrs Peabody's tea and toast, and the raven Balthazar. But a young girl's comforts would have to wait, as the quest had only just begun, and the first of many monsters had merely opened a sleepy eye.

Molly Chatsworth

will return in

The Skull of Belegnoth

www.ingramcontent.com/pod-product-compliance
Lightning Source LLC
LaVergne TN
LVHW041010150826
845672LV00001B/40

* 9 7 8 1 8 0 6 0 5 2 1 1 0 *